INSPECTOR LESTRADE:

THE BLACK TEMPLE AND OTHER STORIES

INSPECTOR LESTRADE:

THE BLACK TEMPLE AND OTHER STORIES

William Meikle

WEIRD HOUSE

TRADE PAPERBACK EDITION

TEXT © 2022 BY WILLIAM MEIKLE
COVER AND INTERIOR ART © 2022 BY WAYNE M. MILLER

EDITOR & PUBLISHER, JOE MOREY

COPY EDITING AND BOOK DESIGN BY F. J. BERGMANN

ISBN: 978-1-957121-19-2

WEIRD HOUSE PRESS
CENTRAL POINT, OR 97502
WWW.WEIRDHOUSEPRESS.COM
Join the Weird House mailing list at our website!

Acknowledgements

"The Curious Affair on the Embankment" first appeared in *THE GHOST CLUB* collection (Crystal Lake Publishing, 2017).

All other stories are original to this collection.

Grateful acknowledgement to Conan Doyle Estate Ltd. for permission to use the Sherlock Holmes characters created by the late Sir Arthur Conan Doyle.

List of Illustrations

Table of Contents

The Curious Affair
on the Embankment

Inspector Lestrade was never happy about being called upstairs to the Commissioner's office—even less so just after his breakfast when he was contentedly seated by a warm fire with a cigarette and a mug of strong tea. He tried hard to think of any mistake he could have made on recent cases that would require disciplinary action, and could think of none that might be worthy. But the constable who came for him said it sounded urgent and was 'a matter of some discretion.'

At least it doesn't sound like a bollocking.

He only took time to knock out his pipe on the grate before hurrying up through the corridors and stairwells to present himself to—not just the top man, but two Chief Inspectors and a politician; Lestrade recognized him, but at that moment could not remember his name.

The Commissioner—Lestrade always had trouble with that, for they had come up through the ranks together, and to him the man would always be 'Jonesy'—looked up as the door opened. He waved Lestrade forward to stand in front of the desk. With the other four all being seated behind it, and all facing him, Lestrade suddenly felt like he was in front of a judiciary hearing.

Maybe it is a bollocking after all.

The Commissioner took his time, shuffling papers and scraping out his pipe before looking up at Lestrade again.

"Relax, man," he said, "You're not in any bother. Not this time. We have a job for you. A delicate matter, and it's a bit hush-hush, so we do not need you running off to Baker Street for a confab with the amateurs on this one. Understood?"

Lestrade thought it circumspect to keep his reply to a simple nod—even if he wasn't in any bother, anything that required so much brass in one room smelled like trouble he did not need. His instinct was quickly confirmed as the Commissioner continued.

"Lady Elizabeth Mears has gone missing, taken by person or persons unknown from a carriage on the Victoria Embankment last night. There have been no demands, which is quite peculiar in itself for, as you know, Sir Geoffrey is one of the richest men in the country, and has the ear of the Prime Minister, so we are wondering whether this might have a political rather than a financial motive. But that is for you to find out. You will report directly to me, and speak to no one else. And this is your top priority as of right now. Anything else on your desk can wait. Understood?"

Lestrade nodded again, and this time he did have questions—many of them—but was given short shrift when he asked.

"There's no time to lose," the Commissioner said. "We have a carriage driver in custody down in the cells. You will need to speak to him first, but I will warn you, he is making little to no sense whatsoever. After that, you will most probably want to go to the Embankment to have a look round for yourself. I shall expect a report from you at two o'clock sharp. Dismissed."

No one else had spoken—they had not needed to. Lestrade could see the import of the situation in their manner and in their eyes. If the brass were that worried, then so was he.

He had just been handed a can of worms.

The man in the cell in the basement looked as unhappy as Lestrade felt. Although the room was cold and dank, he had been stripped to his underpants and shirt, and sat, hugging a mug of tea that was probably the only thing providing him any warmth. His eyes were red, as if he had been weeping, and there was a pleading whine in his tone when he spoke, like a whipped dog begging for mercy.

"Look, officer, I've bin 'ere all bleedin' night. My missus will be up to high doh by now. I've told you—I've told four of you now—what happened. The lady vanished. Where do you think I put her? She's not up my vest or down my trousers—you've checked there too. So tell me what to say so that I can get out of here. Please?"

Lestrade sat opposite the man, took out his tobacco pouch and expertly rolled two cigarettes, passing one over the table. The other man took it like a drowning man reaching for a life belt.

"Tell me. Just this one more time," Lestrade said as he lit them both up. "And if I believe you, you can go."

"That's what the last one said," the man replied. "He didn't believe me."

"Try me," Lestrade said, then shut up. He knew the look of a man who wanted to talk, and this man didn't just want to, he looked like he *needed* to.

"I picked her up from a big house at the north end of Russell Square. The note at the depot had said eight o'clock sharp, and I were there at five to the hour. She came out—a fine lady in a long black coat and hood—her head covered. I didn't see nobody else, and she told me to head for the Embankment. She said it was a round trip. I'd have a five-minute wait and then we'd be heading back. Sounded like easy money to me, so I took her down to the river—it were right foggy last night, a real pea-souper, but she knew where she wanted to go right enough. Cleo's Pin, that big ugly lump of Egyptian stone. She had me stop twenty yards upriver, said it was something she had to do alone—a promise to keep, she said. She walked into the fog ... and she never came back."

The man stopped to take a draw from his cigarette, and it was several seconds before Lestrade realized that he was done with his story. It had all come out in a rush, but it hadn't sounded rehearsed and he saw no subterfuge in the man, just a desire to get the tale told and get out of the damp cell.

"That's it? That is your whole story? Lady Mears disappeared in the fog?"

"If that was the lady's name, yes. I waited for half an hour, but there weren't nobody moving about. A Bobby—one of yours—came by on his rounds and I told him what had happened. I wish to God I'd just gone home and kept my big bloody mouth shut."

"And the lady never said a word about why she had to be at the Needle at such a strange hour?"

"Not a sausage. Just that she was keeping a promise."

"Was she carrying anything?"

"A small purse, one of them single-handed jobs. But she was a lady, and I'm a carriage driver. It's not like we were having a conversation."

Lestrade asked a few more questions but it quickly became clear that the man had told everything he knew or had seen. The Inspector took pity on him and had him freed—the brass might not like that, but an innocent man deserved better.

It was still foggy as the Inspector made his way to the scene of the crime, if there had indeed been a crime. It would not be the first time that someone had lost their footing and ended up in the river in the fog; he only hoped that the lady was not, even now, being fished out somewhere down in the Docklands. But the fact that there had been no demands—either financial or political—had Lestrade's nose twitching. A copper has a feel for the rhythm of a case, and the lack of communication told him that this was not a kidnapping. He suspected murder, but was keeping that to himself for the moment, for that wasn't anything the brass would want to hear anytime soon.

He found his way to the Needle easily enough—he'd been there the day they had the ceremony to unveil it, ten years ago now. He remembered the pomp, the bands, the great and good in their finery, and the fact that the nickname—Cleopatra's Needle—was just that. The stone was older by far than that particular lady, made for a pharaoh with a name that did not trip off the tongue quite so easily. Lestrade had walked past it many times since that ceremony and never given it a moment's thought, but now, approaching it in the fog and in the accompanying muffled silence, he felt a strange sense of trepidation. There was also another, very familiar, old copper's feeling:he felt the need to keep his wits about him—self-preservation came naturally to a policeman in this town.

He came up on the Needle slowly, watching it appear out of the fog ahead of him, looming like a mute giant over the road. There was no sign of any movement apart from the swirl of the fog itself, but that served to give the cold stone the simulation of breath, and a shiver ran up the Inspector's spine as he came within touching distance of the plinth on which it was mounted. Now that he was right up close he could see that someone had dug out the cast-iron panel on the eastern side, revealing a tin box the size of a small suitcase inside.

The box lay open, with its contents strewn around the cavity in the plinth. The material consisted of a cardboard box of hairpins, a box of cigars, several tobacco pipes, a set of imperial weights, a baby's bottle, some children's toys, a shilling razor, a hydraulic jack and some samples of the cable used in the erection, eleven photographs of young women, a small bronze model of the monument, a full set of contemporary British coinage, a rupee, and a portrait of Queen Victoria. There was also a great deal of printed material, including a written history of the transport of the monument, structural plans, a vellum copy of the inscriptions that were carved on the obelisk and a translation of the same, a number of copies of the Bible in several languages and a translation of a passage from John in many languages more, a copy of Whitaker's *Almanac,* a Bradshaw Railway Guide, a map of London, and copies of ten British daily newspapers.

Lestrade had a vague recollection that a time capsule had been concealed in the front part of the pedestal at the original ceremony. It had been intended for the capsule to be opened a hundred years ahead, in 1978, but it seemed that someone had not been prepared to wait that long.

Lestrade could not imagine what this volume of material could have to do with the disappearance of the lady, but he was also aware of the importance of not making assumptions that might later prove to have led to him missing something important. He bundled all the material back into the tin box and closed it. The box had a carrying handle affixed, and although it was almost full, none of the material had any great weight and he would be able to carry it with him back to the Yard with little effort.

He set the box aside and spent several minutes on a more rigorous search around the base of the great stone; he found nothing else of any note. If the lady had been abducted, it had been done in such a manner as to leave no trace of it whatsoever. One thing puzzled him, though, the cast-iron panel that had protected the time capsule did indeed look like it had been torn open, but it looked almost as if it had been forced outward from the inside rather than by any external action. He put that away as something to consider later, for just as he stood up, he heard—almost imagined, for it seemed little more than a whisper—a muttering, as if a conversation were going on nearby. He strained to hear—it sounded like a chorus of female voices, raised almost in shouts—but he could make out none of the words, and when he walked toward where he thought the sound originated, he lost track of it in the fog almost immediately.

He was about to head back to the obelisk when he almost walked into someone in the murk. He apologized automatically, and got a frightened squeal in reply.

"You nearly frightened the life out of me," a woman said. He was close enough to look into her face, and for a second thought that he might have walked into Lady Myers herself, for there was indeed a resemblance in the woman's features that reminded him strongly of the missing woman. But this was no lady, not if Lestrade's eye for the feminine was still working. She was dressed in an overly gaudy manner that at first suggested a working girl, but then he recognized her, realized that he knew of her. Mary Miller was her name, a singer on one of the Strand stages, and a well-known one at that, having been on the boards in a string of hit shows for the better part of this past decade.

She did not look like a seasoned performer at this juncture. She seemed confused and flustered, almost on the verge of tears. Lestrade doffed his hat and offered his assistance. His copper's nose started twitching again as soon as she answered.

"I'm looking for that bally big stone, the Egyptian thing," she said. "I know it is around here somewhere, but I'll be blowed if I can find it."

And again tears seemed close as she dabbed a handkerchief at her eyes.

"Can I ask why?" Lestrade said. "It's just that something right strange happened last night and ..."

"He took one of us, didn't he?" she said, interrupting him. "We thought it was all a big joke—of course we made the promise—it was the kind of thing you'd say just to make sure you didn't miss the chance. But we thought nothing of it. Well, you wouldn't, would you?"

Lestrade's nose had not betrayed him, there was indeed a story here, and he had just inched a bit closer to its resolution. He took Mary Miller by the arm and led her back across the street to the obelisk.

"Now, can you tell me why you are here?"

"Who wants to know?" she said, suddenly belligerent—then she spotted the hole in the plinth where the box had lain, and saw the box itself sitting where Lestrade had left it. "Who was it?" she whispered. "Who was taken first?"

Lestrade showed her his badge and her eyes went wide. Tears were close again, so Lestrade preempted them with another question.

"Mrs. Miller, I need to know. A life may be at stake."

"More than one," she replied softly. "And I fear that you are already ten years too late."

He got the story in dribs and drabs over a smoke and a cup of strong char in a tearoom across the road. The fog lifted while she told her side of the tale, but Lestrade scarcely noticed, being both astounded, and more than a little bemused, by the telling.

"There were twelve of us—a dozen young girls who wanted to better ourselves. Is that so bad? And he offered us ten good years each. Ten! You know as well as I do that we're lucky to get one or two at best in this city. So when he put out that advertisement, he got plenty of takers. I was surprised to get his card saying I'd been chosen, and I thought it was well shady—I'll tell you that for nowt—but I was down on my luck that year, and he was offering bright lights and silver. I could not turn it down, not when I needed to eat.

"We met in a room above a bar just off Covent Garden—that one with the old staircase and the fireplaces—you must know it. Twelve of us, as I said. He lined us up, took our photographs, and made us sign on the back in blood—our names, and the number ten. Next thing I know I'm in the papers, and my photograph is getting sealed inside that bloody stone, I'm getting picked to go on tour as a singer, and then I get a run of luck in the West End. I thought I did it all myself, I really did. Then, last night, he called in his promise. I got a note—two words in red the color of fresh blood: 'Needle, noon.' Somehow I did not think it would be a good idea to ignore it, so here I am and there is my tale."

It had all come out of her fast, as if she had been waiting a long time for someone to ask.

"Twelve of you, that's what you said?" Lestrade replied, and she nodded. He bent to his side, opened the tin case and got out the eleven photographs he had seen earlier. Each had a name, and the number ten, in what looked like faded brown ink on the back. He thought he already knew the answer to the next question, but he had to ask.

"Who is missing?"

Mary Miller took the photographs and rifled quickly through them before nodding.

"Elizabeth Jones should be here, Lady Muck as she is now, too good to talk to the likes of us...." She trailed off, and this time the tears did come. "It was her last night, wasn't it? He took her."

"Now that's enough of that, miss; no time for weeping, not today. What do you mean, he took her?"

"I told you, ten good years, and then he gets the rest."

"I'm not following you," Lestrade said, trying to be gentle, as the lady seemed to be on the verge of hysteria.

"Just hope you never do," she said. She looked over Lestrade's shoulder, out of the window, and all the color left her cheeks, her mouth opening in a gape that might either become a laugh or a scream.

"It's too late. He's here."

Lestrade turned toward the window, but saw only the obelisk. When he turned back toward the woman, he found he was alone at the table. She seemed to have just vanished, gone without a sound.

Just like Lady Mears.

The Inspector turned again to the window, hoping to see the woman leave the tearoom. There was nobody in the street, but there was something over by the obelisk, the faintest of vapors, like the last straggling remains of fog, even now falling into the stone, as if being sucked deep down inside.

When Lestrade finally returned to the table to put the photographs back in the tin case he found there were now only ten women there, Mary Miller's picture had gone to join that of Lady Myers.

Wherever that might be.

Lestrade had a long look up and down the Embankment when he left the tearoom, but there was no sign of the lady. He also inspected the obelisk again, but to his eyes at least it was still merely a lump of old stone. He returned to the Yard, taking the tin case with him—perhaps a closer study of its contents would indeed yield a clue that might shed a light on matters.

He had a team of constables deployed to search out Mary Miller, and put his sergeant, Clarke, in charge of a squad to track down the other ten girls in the photographs. He knew that might be an impossible task, but what he did not need right now was more well-to-do women going missing. If the press got hold of it, they would have a field day. The Ripper case was still all too fresh in the public's minds and another storm like that one would most definitely see Lestrade on the carpet, perhaps even out of a job entirely.

What with that, and the fact that he had nothing of any import to tell the Commissioner when he reported upstairs, he did indeed get the expected bollocking in response. Lestrade was not in the best of moods when he returned to his desk later in the afternoon.

Sergeant Clarke's report did not help much. Mary Miller could not be found, nor could five of the other ten women. Clarke had discovered that one of them, a June Wallis, née Graham, wife of a Scottish landowner, had gone missing in Aberdeen in suspicious circumstances after receiving a note—there was a rumor she had been seen on the night train to London, but that was as yet unsubstantiated. The only good news was that the remaining five women all lived in London, had been found, and were even now being brought into the Yard for their safekeeping. A watch had been put on the Needle in case any of the missing women should try to approach it, and the Yard had men at both Euston and King's Cross railway stations on the lookout for the missing woman from Aberdeen.

Lestrade failed to see what else he could do for the moment. He sat at his desk, had Clarke make a pot of tea, and got a pipe lit as he made a start on going through the material in the tin box.

He was thinking of Lady Mears, the first disappearance.

If I'd been at the obelisk, would I have seen her approach it? Would I have seen another puff of vapor sucked into the blasted stone, like when Mary Miller went?

He sucked angrily at his pipe as he waited for Clarke to bring the tea.

He was rapidly coming to the conclusion that the missing women were unlikely ever to be seen again.

The women started arriving in the early evening. Lestrade had Clarke deal with them, because he was still perusing the contents of the tin box in search of enlightenment. The objects were all what they appeared to be, somewhat banal indicators of life in London at the time, representations and history of the monument itself, and the news of the day. The Inspector kept returning to two items in particular; the photographs of the remaining women, and the transcription and translation of the hieroglyphs on the stone itself.

"Clarke!" he shouted, and the sergeant was at the door within seconds. "Fetch me somebody who knows this stuff." He waved the vellum representation of the carvings in the air. "And not Holmes, for pity's sake, the boss would have my guts for gaiters."

"Any suggestions, sir?" Clarke asked.

"Try the museum first, plenty of old fossils there. One of them might know something about another of their kind."

Clarke left at a run, and Lestrade went to talk to the women who had been brought in.

The five of them—Lestrade was struck by the resemblance between them all—sat around a table, drinking tea or smoking. They were silent and he saw fear in their eyes as they turned at his entrance.

"First things first, ladies," he said. "I take it you all got a note at some point recently, asking you to go to the Needle?"

His hunch had been right, all had received such a note, and the only difference in them was the time at which they had been asked to arrive. He was rather relieved to note that the first of them, a Miss Margaret Weems—a doctor at the Royal Hospital—wasn't due her appointment on the Embankment until nine that evening.

He also got more of the story than he had from Mary Miller, not a lot more, though. He tried to pin down a description of the photographer—the closest thing to a suspect he had right now and apparently the instigator of everything that followed. But apart from the fact that the man had been of slim build, and noticeably of some great age, there were few details to be had. The fact that ten years had passed, and an aged man would be now even more diminished by time—or even already be long dead— meant that, as a suspect, he was not the best material, but he was all that Lestrade had.

He was still pondering that conundrum as he went back to his office. Clarke was there with a rather portly chap in a tweed suit, who was introduced as Professor Wilkins—an expert on all things ancient Egyptian. Lestrade sent Clarke off to compile a list of photographers in the city and have men sent to each, then passed the vellum inscription to the professor.

It only took as long as the time for Lestrade to get a fresh pipe lit before the portly man exclaimed loudly.

"This is not right. This is not right at all." He waved the English translation in his left hand. "This is fine, but this ..." He waved at the vellum transcription of the glyphs. "This is all wrong. I know the glyphs on that stone intimately, and these are not those."

"So what is it then? Who would go to the trouble of transcribing a fake like that?"

"I cannot tell you who or why," the professor said. "But I know what. It is a spell, from the Book of the Dead, an incantation to provide the spell-caster with eternal life. Something to do with the making of images and the sealing of promises. All mumbo jumbo of course, but jolly fascinating all the same."

Lestrade took the vellum from the professor and was about to take another look at it, when he saw the photographs of the women laid out on his desk. There should have been ten there, but now there were only nine.

The news arrived from the Needle mere minutes later. Two constables had been on guard at the obelisk, and had stopped a woman—'a well-presented lady with a Scottish accent'—in her approach to the monument. They had only been talking for seconds when the lady disappeared, right in front of them, giving the young constables quite a turn. Nothing made much sense to Lestrade in their story, but it had a ring of truth to it. The less flustered of the two constables told of the last thing he had seen—a smoky, insubstantial figure, man-like but not a man, fading into smoke as he was sucked into the tall stone. Lestrade did not have to check the names on the remaining cards; he already knew who it must have been—the missing Aberdeen woman—no longer missing but lost, perhaps forever.

The tweedy professor had listened in puzzlement to the constables' reports and now had questions of his own, but Lestrade waved him aside.

"This spell of yours," he said. "Is there a way to counter it?"

The professor blustered. "But surely you cannot put any credence in ..."

"What I can and cannot put credence in is not of your concern. Can the spell be countered?"

"Well, you could try burning it," the professor said, then yelled out loud as Lestrade moved to do just that by taking the vellum over to the fireplace. "No, it has to be done in the presence of the caster! That is the way their magic worked. If the caster believes in it, he somehow makes it real."

"So if he believes that burning will break the spell, then all I have to do is burn it in front of him so that he can see?"

The professor shrugged. "As I said, it is all bally mumbo jumbo, but that is the theory in any case."

"It is about all I have at the moment," Lestrade said. He folded the vellum sheets and put them in his inside pocket and also put the remaining photograph there alongside it. It was time to talk to the women again; the clock on his mantel told him it was fast approaching nine o'clock.

The other four women were at the opposite end of the table from Margaret Weems, as if afraid to be too close as the time of her appointment approached. The doctor, however, was made of stern stuff. She looked Lestrade in the eye.

"Have you caught the blaggard?"

Lestrade shook his head. "We do not even know who he is, where he is, or what his motive is."

"I can tell you his motive, right enough," she replied. "He collects years. He told us as much back then in the room above the bar, ten good ones for us, then the rest for him, that was the deal, that was his promise. Well, I've had my ten, and enjoyed every minute of it. I've had a better life than most anybody I know, so if he can get good use out of what I have left in me in return, I reckon I got a good deal out of it."

Her eyes told another story—of fear and bewilderment, but she wasn't about to let it show in front of the others.

The room fell quiet. The sound of the Westminster clock chiming the hour drifted in through the open window. Margaret Weems looked up at Lestrade.

"Would you hold me? I think I should like someone to hold me."

Two of the other women smiled thinly as the doctor rose and leaned herself against Lestrade, who put his arms around her somewhat gingerly, unused as he was to public shows of affection. The lady gripped him tightly in response. He was about to protest and gently remove himself from her clutches when the air got much colder and a haze seemed to form between them and the window—a gray, smoky, haze that solidified and thickened, taking on the semblance of a thin, somewhat bent, human figure.

"It's him! It's him," one of the women at the far end of the table shrieked, and stood so fast that she overturned her chair. Margaret Weem did not look round. She had her face buried in the cloth at Lestrade's shoulder, and her grip was so tight that the Inspector was quite unable to move.

Big Ben chimed its ninth stroke. The shifting haze streamed closer to Lestrade. He turned his back so that he would be between the encroaching mist and the lady, and found that his arms were empty, her weight having lifted away leaving only its memory behind. Like Mary Miller before her, she had gone in the blink of an eye.

The gray mist, seemingly thicker now, wafted away, heading for the window.

It was only then that Lestrade remembered the vellum sheets in his pocket, but by the time he had removed them and got out his matches, the mist had already drifted off, leaving out of the window, traveling against the breeze.

Lestrade counted the remaining photographs.

Now there were eight.

"Who has the next appointment?" he asked, rather more sharply than he might have, but his dander was up, along

... eyes blazing a blue fire, a face that looked as if it had gazed into hell ...

with a developing grim determination that he would lose no more of them.

"I am at eleven," the lady furthest from him said. He looked through the photographs and found her—Charlotte Newman. Clarke had told him earlier her husband was something big at one of the city banks.

"Right; the rest of you stay here. My men will ensure your safety, although when I am done, I do not think you will have anything else to worry about."

He was aware that statement was more bravado than fact, but if it stopped the ladies fretting in his absence it would have done its job in any case.

He took Mrs. Newman by the arm and led her out of the room. He stopped by his office just long enough to collect his service revolver and the tin box with its contents, and then, accompanied by Sergeant Clarke and the two constables who had been on earlier guard duty, made his way once again down to the Embankment—and the Needle.

They arrived early, at a quarter to ten. Lestrade had the two constables and Clarke keep watch on the opposite side of the street while he went to stand at the obelisk with the lady. It was a damp night again, and thin wisps of fog drifted to and fro on the river, but they had a clear view along the whole stretch of the Embankment so they would see any new arrivals in good time.

The lady hardly spoke—seeing the Weems woman being taken had brought home to her the grim reality of her situation. Between ten and quarter past the hour she talked of their promise, of the decade that had passed too quickly, and of her good life with a good man, but as the hands of Big Ben crept ever closer to her allotted time, so she fell more and more quiet.

Lestrade passed the time smoking his pipe and periodically checking that he still had matches—and the vellum sheets—in his jacket pocket. Every so often he counted the photographs. No more had gone, so at least he could be thankful of that much.

17

The lady started to twitch around quarter to eleven, and decided that she would like to leave, and that her husband would be putting in a stern word against her treatment by the Yard. She even began to walk off until Lestrade, none too kindly, pulled her back to the Embankment wall. He might not get another chance at this, and he could not let the lady divert him from his chosen course.

And then it was too late for her to run.

Lestrade had been paying extra attention to the base of the plinth, and with good cause. At one minute to the hour, a fine mist rose in the cavity where he had found the tin box, streaming up and out until once again a thin, bent figure stood there. It was definitely more defined now.

It has been feeding.

The woman at Lestrade's side almost fell, her legs going weak. In the second that the Inspector took to keep her upright the mist had moved, surging toward them, intent on reaching the woman. Lestrade stepped in front of her and, taking out the vellum sheets, lit a match and applied it to the bottom of them.

The mist came on, gathering definition. Lestrade looked into a face that was lined with wrinkles, eyes blazing a blue fire, a face that looked as if it had gazed into hell itself.

Then the flames took hold of the vellum, so hot that Lestrade had to drop the sheets to the ground where they burned fiercely. The figure in the mist loomed high over Lestrade and the woman, tall, taller, almost as high as the top of the obelisk, the burning vellum reflecting in its eyes. The vellum kept burning—there was little left of it now but smoldering ashes. The misty figure seemed to swell again, a huge gray cloak ready to fall and envelop them.

Lestrade flinched, and for the second time that night a lady grabbed tightly at him in fear for her life.

The last of the vellum burned away. The last scrap of flame flickered, guttered, and went out. There was a single, high scream that seemed to echo the length and breadth of the Embankment. Then there was only ash on the cobbles, and a rapidly thinning fine mist that quickly dispersed in the breeze off the river and was gone.

Lestrade turned away as the woman slumped against his arm and started to weep. He gently removed himself from her clutches and counted the photographs in his pocket—eight—a steady eight. And when he took them out and turned them over, their backs were blank, and every trace of the blood signatures and numbers was gone.

He bent and gathered up the ashes of the vellum, then put them and the photographs back in the tin box. He laid it back in its place in the cavity at the base of the obelisk—a mystery for someone else to solve in ninety years' time—and pushed the cast iron covering back into place with his boot.

He stood there for a long time, watching as he smoked another pipe, but there was only the fog on the river, a weeping lady at his side, and the silent stone above.

Stage Fright

Even though *Humpty Dumpty* wasn't what you could call highbrow it proved more than ample entertainment for the full house it had attracted. Normally Inspector Lestrade would have been happy to spend an evening in the Theater Royal watching Marie Lloyd hold this audience in the palm of her hand.

But this wasn't a normal night. A friend of the Prime Minister was having some trouble in this very theater. He had asked a favor of a friend of the Commissioner, and a decidedly unfriendly team of top brass had dispatched Lestrade to Drury Lane to see what all the fuss was about. What it was about, in Lestrade's opinion, was a load of stuff and nonsense, brought on by bilious, gin-filled gentlemen getting their underwear in a twist over a spook that wouldn't be out of place in the pantomime going on below him on the stage.

That was his considered opinion after interviewing some of the aforesaid gentlemen about the aforesaid spook they claimed was haunting their box seats. They'd all told the same tale, a bit too much the same tale to Lestrade's liking for it had sounded like they'd rehearsed it between themselves beforehand. It was a tall story about a ghostly apparition that appeared in their box seats whenever they frequented this theater. There was an easy answer at hand of course, but Lestrade didn't think the brass would be best pleased if he did nothing apart from telling the gentlemen not to come to this theater.

The brass had asked him to do something, so he was doing something. Lestrade was sitting in one of those box seats, dressed in his best, most uncomfortable, stuffed shirt, unable to enjoy Marie Lloyd, and waiting for a spook he knew was never going to show. To make it worse, his four companions in the box were the same drink-addled chaps that had caused him to be here in the first place. If he had to listen to one more lewd remark about Ms. Lloyd's voluptuous charms, he'd blow his top.

The crowd roared with laughter at one of Miss Lloyd's more off-color jokes involving a chicken and an egg, then her clear high voice filled the hall in song as the audience went still and quiet in appreciation.

That was the precise moment when Lestrade began to think there might be something in the spook story after all.

The air around him went cold, like on a clear winter morning on the Embankment and he saw steam in front of his nose from his breath. The man on his right shouted out, loud enough to be heard above the music, "It's here. It's right bally here."

Then there was nothing but commotion as the inhabitants of the box all made drunken lunges for the door at the same time, resulting in a most ungentlemanly writhing heap of arms and legs on the floor. Lestrade stood, meaning to try to restore some semblance of order, but before he could utter a word his breath was taken from him as he looked up.

Something hovered above the writhing men ... he had no other word to describe it ... a thing of fine mist and shadow, a pale, wispy curl that might almost have been smoke had it not had a distinct human-shaped outline and a pair of pale, almost mirror-silver eyes that seemed to pierce Lestrade's soul.

One of the men on the floor screamed, a high, almost child-like wail of fear. Lestrade looked down, looked up again, and the pale figure was gone. He felt warm air on his face, although a trace of the cold still lingered on his 'tache when he wiped a hand across his mouth.

Down on the stage Marie Lloyd looked up, sensed that the commotion, whatever it had been, was over, and broke into another song, giving Lestrade a chance to collect his senses and finally attempt to bring the situation under control.

"Come on, gentlemen," he said. "Let's be having you up off the floor. You don't know what's been down there."

Two of them at least proved to be sober enough to look sheepish as they rose, a third had to be dragged upright and seemed ready to fall again at any moment. The fourth stayed down. When Lestrade stepped over to try to get him up he saw with a sinking heart that it was the very same friend of the Prime Minister that had gotten Lestrade here in the first place. He would not be calling in anymore favors; the blasted man was stone dead, and from the look on his face it looked like he had taken a terrible fright on the way to wherever he was going.

Lestrade realized he risked being hauled over the coals for it, but he saw no option but to take all three surviving gentlemen back to the Yard, ostensibly for further interviews, but in reality because he thought they might be safer there than anywhere else until he got to the bottom of the matter. They made his cramped office seem very busy, but frequent pots of tea and cigarettes at least had them manageable while he went to the morgue to get the verdict on the dead man.

The coroner chewed on his ever-present pipe as he stood over the body, the smell of the thick Egyptian shag doing much to dissipate the odor of death that always hung around the room.

"Well, there's enough gin in him to stop a horse," he said. "He has an inflamed liver, two stomach ulcers and lungs like black tar. But it was his heart that got him. Just packed it in and gave up after years of abuse is my take on it."

"But his face," Lestrade said. "He looks like he's bloody terrified."

"Wouldn't you be if your heart went and stopped ticking all of a sudden?"

The coroner was already moving on to another body, another slab. Lestrade knew that the poor man was never short of work.

"So, natural causes?"

"More natural than this poor bastard at least," Sharpe said, lifting a sheet and showing Lestrade a body that had at least a dozen stab wounds in the chest.

"And the expression on the face means nothing?"

"I've seen it before in heart failure cases," the coroner said and shrugged. "It happens."

Lestrade left him to it, but was feeling slightly happier as he made his way back up the stairwells to his office. If it was simply heart failure then his report to the brass could state that, in no uncertain terms, everything else about the story could be washed away as no more than the addled ramblings of gentlemen with more gin than sense. Lestrade was pretty sure he could dismiss his own sighting of the apparition as a trick of light and nerves if he was given enough beer to work on the matter.

His better mood lasted only long enough for him to get into his office, pour a mug of tea and get a cigarette lit. One of the three men, George Jennings if Lestrade had his name right, piped up.

"I can't keep it to myself any longer, chaps. We've got to come clean on this whole bally business. We've got to, or it'll be another one of us next."

"Hush, George," the more sober of the two remaining said. "We can't let ourselves get into a blue funk over a slip of a girl who was no better than she needed to be."

"What business, what girl?" Lestrade asked, and at that Jennings went red in the face. The other chap, Thomas, gave him a look that said 'shut up if you know what's good for you' and the third man, Marshall, woke from a half-slumber to inquire as to what the fuss was about.

Lestrade knew that if he was to get anywhere he'd have to talk to them separately. He chose Jennnings as the weak link in the chain and took him down the hall to the interview room. He left the door open and gave the man a cigarette, just to show it wasn't anything too official, then got down to the business of questioning.

It took awhile; some cajoling, some threatening, some appeals to a better nature that Lestrade wasn't sure the man had, but eventually he got the bones of a story, although it still wasn't making too much sense to him.

"It was Thomas' idea in the first place," Jennings said. "He'd heard about the seances from his stockbroker, heard that they were the real deal and not just the usual smoke-and-mirrors nonsense. We'd had a few beers and some gin, quite a lot of gin actually. Thomas had a hankering to ask something from his old man, who passed away last year. The rest of us thought it was all tommyrot of course, but Thomas has always had a way of getting what he wants with the rest of us, so off we trudged to Chancery Lane.

"I think we were all expecting a little old lady with a lace veil and black velvet robes, or a sultry foreign wench, but the woman, no more than a girl really, who showed us into a well appointed parlor was something of a stunner. Thomas was immediately smitten. I mean, we all were, but Thomas even more so, fawning over her like a lovestruck puppy. I do believe, given a chance, he would have whisked her off into the night right there and then, but she obviously knew what she was about, and when she seated us at the table, Thomas was placed, not by accident, on the far side from her, where she could

25

keep her eyes on him and he could keep his hands to himself.

"I must say something about those eyes of hers. At first they seemed to be light blue, like a clear summer sky, but when she dimmed the gaslight they turned silver, taking on what I thought was a faint glow. By that time she had asked us to hold hands, and when I took her right hand in my left I fair lost all thought of anything else for a time.

"Right up until that point I had stuck to my guns that this was all just a parlor trick, and if Thomas was happy to splash his money on it, I was happy to play along. From some of the things Thomas said to her, I thought he too was just having a lark. He told her she looked like Marie Lloyd for one thing; better than Marie Lloyd, he said. But the mood around the table changed dramatically when she started to speak.

"I'd been in the company of Thomas' old man many times, all the way back to when we were schoolboys, and if it wasn't him speaking out of the girl's mouth, it was someone who knew his every tic and mannerism intimately.

"'You've been drinking, boy,' the well-remembered gruff voice said. It came from the girl's lips, her cheeks, once pale, now ruddy and lined as if with years on the port, her eyes, and I swear to you this is true, brown where they had been silvery-blue.

"Thomas sat upright in his chair with a jolt as if he'd just been shot but, to his credit, regained his composure immediately.

"'Father?'

"'You were expecting someone else? Old Nick, maybe?' came the reply, followed by that same laughter-free chortle I remembered so well from my youth. I could see that Thomas was likewise impressed that this could be no other than his father speaking from the Great Beyond, especially when the old man/s voice taunted him.

"'Do you have a question for me, pup?'

"'I certainly do. It's about those diamond-mine

investments....'

Thomas didn't get a chance to finish. The old man laughed most cruelly.

"'Spent it, drank it, whored it away. You can whistle for that, lad. It's gone.'

"We were all so rapt in the girl's 'performance' I'm afraid none of us noticed that Thomas had gone quite apoplectic with rage.

"'What kind of blasted trickery is this?' he bellowed, got up out of his chair and threw himself right across the bally table, headlong into the girl, knocking both her and her chair backward under his momentum and sending the pair of them crashing to the floor.

"By the time the rest of us rose to investigate Thomas was on top of her, sitting on her chest and banging her head, hard, against the hearth of the great fireplace. I dragged him away; he was shouting obscenities, not at the girl, but at his father. I left him with Marshall and went to help the girl up.

"She would never be getting up again; her head lay at an unusual angle to the body, her neck clearly broken, and although those silver-blue eyes looked directly at me, they were focused not on me but on the Great Beyond, which she was now experiencing for herself first-hand."

Jennings stopped there, out of breath, his eyes wide, clearly both amazed and frightened by what he'd just let slip.

"Just to be clear, Mr. Jennings," Lestrade said slowly and carefully. "You have just admitted to being a witness to a murder, have you not?"

"What's that phrase?" Jennings said. "While the balance of his mind was disturbed? I can tell you Thomas was clearly disturbed."

"And what happened next? I don't remember any death like that being reported."

Jennings looked sheepish and in no mood to reply, so Lestrade pushed harder.

"Look, sir. You'll either go down as a conspirator with your friend, or you can help yourself out with the judge and tell all now. I can see you want to talk. Let it out. You'll feel all the better for it."

He'd given that speech many times to people in this very room. Some went for it, others didn't, but he knew Jennings' tongue had already been loosened, and he was proven right when the tale continued.

"Again, it was Thomas' idea," the man said. "After he recovered his senses he was most contrite, but also cold-blooded, as if at a racecourse calculating the odds. It was him that convinced us that were we to become embroiled in this affair, the scandal would end whatever standing we had in society. So, the Good Lord help us, we did indeed conspire with him. We wrapped the body in the bally curtains and under cover of night carried it away and dumped it in the Fleet sewer like an unwanted sack of potatoes. She sank away out of sight, and that was the end of it.

"Or so we thought."

Jenning's hands were shaking. Lestrade gave him something to do with them by handing him another cigarette, having to hold the man's fingers steady while lighting it for him. Jennings had tears in his eyes when he spoke again.

"We didn't speak of it again. That was nearly three months ago. It took two of those months for Thomas to get back to his normal ebullient self; I think he was expecting you chaps to turn up on his doorstep at any minute, but once it became obvious he was scot-free he came out of his shell and threw himself back into the social whirl.

"We had a riotous night out in the West End on the Friday, and on the Saturday we all piled along to the box in the Theatre Royal to see Marie Lloyd, only to find that our pale, silver-eyed girl had come with us. At first it was just another night at the shows. Thomas shouted out how much he loved Miss Lloyd and got a laugh from the crowd.

I heard a cold laugh in my left ear in reply and turned toward it. It was only her eyes that were there, only those silver eyes, but I knew who it was straight away, and it fair threw me into a funk, I don't mind telling you.

"I was out of there like a stoat after a rabbit, heading for a bucketful of gin and determined never to return. But Thomas can be most persuasive and convinced me that it was my mind working overtime, as it had in childhood when I was convinced there was someone in the bedroom closet.

"So the next Saturday there we were again, the four musketeers putting on a brave face. This time it was poor Blythe-Worthington who saw her. He said she was right there, pale eyes shining in a fine mist, right there laughing that cold laugh in his ear. It shook him up right hard. That's what prompted him to get you chaps involved, much to Thomas' chagrin.

"And now you're up to date, Inspector, for tonight was the end of it, the third time that paid for all, for Blythe Worthington at least."

Jennings looked up at Lestrade, fresh tears in his eyes. "It is the end of it, isn't it?"

Lestrade had no answer for the man, nor any for his superiors when he was called in front of them in the morning.

"So what you're telling us," the commissioner said, "is that a rich gentleman, a pillar of society, died in shock right in front of you when confronted by the ghost of a dead spiritualist, a lady whom they killed several months previously? And you expect us to believe this nonsense?"

"No, sir," Lestrade said. "I can't say as I believe it myself. But that's what they believe."

"Well I won't have it. Either they are murderers, or they are not, and we can't prove it either way without a body. Find one, and find it quickly."

Lestrade had no idea how that might be accomplished, especially if the body in question had indeed gone into the

Fleet sewer three months previously, but he knew better than to query the orders of his superiors. He left without another word, back to his office to find that the three gentlemen had been released, on the commissioner's orders, 'pending further investigation.'

He despatched a constable to fetch him something for breakfast, wrote up his notes from the night before, then, after a fortifying cup of tea, a bacon sandwich and a smoke, called for his sergeant.

"Clarkie, get your knickers on. We're going to Chancery Lane."

He gave Clarke the skeleton of the case in a carriage on the way.

"A ghost? In the Theatre Royal? Sounds a bit far-fetched to me, sir."

"And to me, Clarkie. We're not going to be able to catch a ghost. But maybe we can find a body, eh?"

On arrival in Chancery Lane they had to force the main door open to gain entry to the dead woman's apartments, but once inside they found evidence in support of Jennings' story: there were no curtains in the window in the parlor, although there was a rail, and several discarded rings on the floor and window sill. More than that, there was dried blood on the hearth, rather a lot of it. Lestrade scraped some off with the blade of his penknife and saved it in a small brown envelope he'd taken to carrying for such purposes. It was a habit he'd picked up from Sherlock Holmes, although no doubt the consulting detective would make more of it than Lestrade or the coroner in the Yard basement ever could.

Once he'd ascertained that Jennings' story held up, Lestrade undertook a study of the parlor. He was looking for the typical signs of a fraudster's trickery; hidden chambers, modified light fittings and a table built so as to be easily rocked, with a mechanism beneath it for producing raps and knocks and maybe even smoke. He was disappointed, and more than a little confused, to find nothing at all apart from a hidden bookcase filled with old books with titles like *The Secret History, The Concordances of the Red Serpent,* and *The Key of Solomon.* He saw no value in wasting any time looking at them.

He turned to his sergeant.

"The brass want a body, and we won't find one here. I doubt if we'll find one anywhere, but we'll need to put the legwork in to keep them happy. Get some lads going door to door between here and the Fleet sewer, see if anybody saw four toffs lumping a body along the road on a dark night three months ago."

"And the sewer itself?" Clarke said. Lestrade saw the trepidation in the sergeant's eyes and understood it; the Fleet sewer wasn't any place anyone would want to be near if they could avoid it.

"Not worth it, Clarkie," he said, much to the sergeant's relief. "If the body went in there and wasn't found on the riverbank soon after, it'll either be sunk, or somewhere along the Kent coast. Either way, we won't find it."

"How do we placate the commissioner then, sir?"

"I'll think of something," Lestrade replied, but in truth this case wasn't giving him anything to get a grip on.

He left Clarke to organize his men and took the carriage back to the Yard, but had scarcely enough time to get a mug of tea and a cigarette before he was called out again. His presence was needed at a house in Knightsbridge. Marshall, the gentleman who had been the most drunk the previous night, was dead.

On arriving at the scene Lestrade found George Jennings sitting on the doorstep, his head in his hands, weeping sorely. The man looked up as Lestrade approached.

"I swear to God, I did not touch him," he said. "It was her. She did it again. And I fear I might be next. You have to protect me, Inspector. You have to."

Lestrade instructed a constable to take Jennings back to the Yard.

31

"Put him in my office for the time being. Call it protective custody if the desk sergeant gets snippy about it, but nobody sees him until I get back. Understood?"

The constable nodded and took Jennings away. Lestrade watched them depart before turning back to the steps of the house. It was one of the tall, elegant townhouses in an area greatly favored by a certain kind of gentleman about town, the difference being that this one had a fresh dead body in it.

Marshall was lying, face up, in front of a rapidly cooling fire. There was an armchair on either side, each with a small drinks table, each with a glass of brandy on it. Lestrade stepped over to stand above the body and look down. The dead man's face showed the same rictus of terror as he'd seen on the other man in the morgue. The coroner might be right; it might happen in heart attack victims. But two men, both involved in the same case, both having heart attacks within hours of each other and showing the same signs of fright? That wasn't a coincidence Lestrade could afford to entertain.

On arriving back at the Yard Lestrade sent a man out to bring Thomas in. "Might as well have both of them here, just in case," he said. Then he made for his office to see what George Jennings had to say for himself this time.

The man's nerves were clearly shot. His eyes were red and moist from weeping and his hands shook so much they prevented him from even holding a cigarette. His fine head of well oiled, jet-black hair was awry and tousled where it had been combed back to within an inch of its life earlier. Tea sloshed alarmingly in the mug he held; he'd already got some down the front of his shirt, but that seemed to be the least of his worries. He talked without needing to be prompted.

"Marshall suggested a drink when we were told we could leave here earlier," he said. "And a few snifters were just what I needed at that point, so I took him up on the offer and we went round to his place. The first one went down nice and smooth, and I was halfway down the second when it happened."

He had to stop there as the memory hit him so hard that he nearly dropped the mug of tea on the desk, and when he spoke again it was hardly more than a whisper.

"It was her. She was little more than a wisp of smoke, but I will see those eyes for the rest of my born days, those silver eyes that looked into Marshall's ... and took everything he was out of him and into them. She laughed, a cold hard thing I heard as clearly as I can hear you now. Marshall gave out one short cry of terror that turned into a sigh, and then he was gone.

"Then she turned to me. I took one look into those eyes and my legs went to jelly. They gave way under me and I fell into a blessed faint. When I came back to myself again poor Marshall was already cold."

Lestrade saw the truth of it in the man's eyes, even while at the same time refusing to believe it. Was it some kind of delusion? Or was the man actually the murderer, but lost deep in some insanity that Lestrade couldn't begin to fathom? Whatever the truth of it, he resolved not to let this man out of his sight again until the case was resolved.

They were on their third mug of sweet tea and Lestrade on his third cigarette when Sergeant Clarke arrived back.

"The men are still asking around sir," he said, "but I fear we'll come up blank. No one saw anything, no one heard anything, and if they smelled anything it was just the Fleet sewer."

"About what I expected," Lestrade grunted. "What about Thomas? Has he been brought in yet?"

Clarke shook his head.

"He called our man an oik and point-blank refused your request, sir. He claims he is in no need of protection from the likes of us and is perfectly capable of looking after himself."

"And where is he now?"

Before Clarke could answer, Jennings spoke at Lestrade's back. "I know where he'll be. We have tickets for the box in the Theatre Royal. If I know Thomas, that's where you'll find him; he'll want to prove he is not afraid, that he is not guilty of any wrongdoing, and he'll do that by sitting up proud in the box for the world to see him."

Lestrade didn't bother to change for the theater, and Jennings was still wearing the shirt he'd poured tea down earlier, so they made a rather bedraggled pair among the better to do patrons heading for the upstairs boxes in Drury Lane.

Jennings had come along under duress, having at first refused point-blank to accompany Lestrade.

"I'm not safe there," he had said.

"And what makes you think you're safe here?" Lestrade replied. Jennings had no easy answer to that. After Lestrade assured him of a strong police presence in the theater he came along meekly enough, although, given that the man believed himself to be threatened by a ghost, Lestrade couldn't see how more policemen were going to be of any use to him.

It looked to be a full house again; Ms. Lloyd was the biggest draw in London at that moment, the talk of the town. They had to push their way up a crowded stairwell, and arrived in the box to find that Thomas was already there and already some way along the path to inebriation.

He saw Jennings first, managed a thin smile, then his gaze fell on Lestrade and he took on a thunderous look.

"What the blazes are you doing here? I told your man already; I have no need of your services."

Jennings preempted Lestrade's reply.

"Marshall's dead," he said baldly and with no emotion. "It was her again."

"Balderdash," Thomas replied. "There is no 'her.' You're just old women getting yourselves in a state about nothing. Come, George, have a drink with me. The show's about to start."

As if on cue, the house lights dimmed. The audience in the cheap seats cheered as the orchestra started up and the curtains swung aside to show the gaudy set of *Humpty Dumpty*. Lestrade could take no pleasure in any of it. Despite knowing that he had four officers; one of them his sergeant, out in the corridor, he felt on edge, expecting trouble at any minute.

When Ms. Lloyd herself came on stage to another rousing cheer from the audience Thomas stood and cheered along, almost knocking a half-empty bottle of gin off the balcony in the process. The singer looked up, saw the man standing there, and gave him a cheeky wave and a smile.

You'd have thought Thomas had just been transported to heaven, given his reaction.

"Did you see?" he said, sporting a grin a mile wide while pounding George Fleming on the back. "She smiled at me. And she meant it. I could see it in her eyes."

Lestrade saw that Fleming wasn't about to reply. He had his gaze fixed, not on the stage, but in the dark corner of the box to the stage side of the doorway. Something moved there, a wisp of smoky shadow, growing thicker. The color drained from Jenning's face. He moved to get out of his seat, but Thomas had him by the shoulders, still excited, like a giddy schoolboy, by Ms. Lloyd's acknowledgement of him.

Thomas was still pounding Jennings on the back when Lestrade saw the smoke shift and flow. He felt cold air on his face again. His copper's reflexes kicked in. He stood and stepped between the smoky presence and the two men. It had two silver-gray spots in it, inches apart, at the same level as his gaze, and a shiver went through him as he felt himself being appraised, and just as quickly discarded. The smoke kept coming, washing over him in a wave of cold air that felt like a winter frost that went as quickly as it had come.

He turned just in time to see it swirl and dance around Thomas before coming to rest, a coil wrapped around his

35

waist, a distinct head with piercing, silver eyes, looking directly into the man's gaze.

Lestrade distinctly heard a man's voice, older, more gruff than the two men in the box.

"You've been drinking, boy!"

The smoke shifted again; it was as if Thomas' head was engulfed in it. He squealed, a schoolboy again but this time a pained one, then it was as if his body shrank, all the air being sucked out of it and into the smoke which swelled and grew less dim, more solid.

The balcony box shook as Thomas fell back into his seat, his head rolled back at an unnatural angle, his mouth open in what would be his last, eternal scream of terror.

Silver eyes swung to fix their gaze on Jennings. The man appeared glued to his seat, his own gaze fixed on the apparition before him.

"What would you have me do?" he whispered, barely audible above the sound of laughter from the pantomime which was carrying on, oblivious to the proceedings in the box above.

The smoke curled around him, silver eyes piercing.

Jennings wailed, and, with apparent effort, turned to Lestrade. "You want a confession? Fine, we killed her, I am guilty. Please, take my confession."

"That suits me just fine," Lestrade said. "Be a good lad; come over here. We'll go down to the Yard and get it all done by the book."

Jennings nodded, and with another effort of will looked into the apparition's gaze. "I am genuinely sorry," he said. "And I will pay for it, for however long it takes before they send me to the gallows."

The silver eyes flared and, while Marie Lloyd sang a song of joy down on the stage, it swirled, danced and broke apart. The cold went as quickly as it had come and the two men were left alone with Thomas' dead body between them.

Jennings looked up at Lestrade. His eyes were red again from crying but that wasn't the only change in him.

His mop of hair was now shot through with vivid streaks of gray, like wisps of smoke.

Skulls and Skullduggery

Receiving a summons to meet Mycroft Holmes in the Diogenes Club was a matter of some note in itself; receiving it via telegram at home rather than in his office at the Yard was unprecedented. The sense of unfamiliarity was further compounded by the fact that Mycroft had sent his private carriage to deliver Lestrade to him forthwith, with hardly enough time to don a collar and tie and brush his hair. So it was with some trepidation that Inspector Lestrade descended from the carriage and strode up the steps to the main entrance of the grand old establishment that summer's evening.

He'd been here before, several times in the company of Mycroft's younger brother, but this was going to be a new experience and he could only wonder what a man with interests in all corners of the Empire might want with a lowly Inspector from Scotland Yard. He was still wondering when, having presented his card in silence to the desk clerk, he was shown into the back room that was Mycroft Holmes' personal fiefdom.

Not for the first time he was reminded of the similarities, and differences, between Mycroft and his younger sibling.

They had the same piercing gray eyes, the same still manner when listening, but where Sherlock was thin almost to the point of being angular, Mycroft was stoutly built, almost filling the confines of the armchair in which he sat, and when he waved a hand at the drinks cabinet indicating that Lestrade should help himself, it was with a languorous, almost lazy manner Lestrade had never seen in the younger man.

The other thing they had in common though was that both could be dashed infuriating. Mycroft proved to be consistent, at least, by getting to the point in a most roundabout manner.

"I don't suppose you know a great deal about the espionage business, Lestrade," he said after the inspector sat down opposite him. "But that is possibly in your favor in the matter at hand, for my problem has arisen from trusting people who know entirely too much about it. It does things to a man, this game; it affects the judgment in ways that it can be tricky to fathom. The reason I have asked you here is a matter of judgment. I need you to do something for me."

"Begging your pardon, Mr. Holmes," Lestrade interrupted, "but I'm a busy man, with several active cases on my desk and ..."

He got another lazy wave of a hand. "All dealt with. Your cases have been reassigned, and your time for the next few days is mine to command. The Commissioner knows on which side his bread is buttered, and so should you."

"But why would you want me? Surely your brother ..."

"He is off on the continent helping some mid-level dignitary with a blackmail problem. I expect it will pay him well enough to cover his lodgings for a good long time. Besides, he is not the man for this job. It is not his kind of thing. Not at all."

"And just what kind of thing might that be?"

"If you would just be quiet for a minute and cease prattling I might get a chance to tell you," Mycroft said sharply.

Lestrade knew better than to respond to that tone and sat back in his chair, sipped some of his host's admittedly very fine Scotch, and lit a cigarette.

Mycroft steepled his fingers just below the bridge of his nose, a habit he unconsciously shared with his brother, and continued. "We have been losing good men and, perhaps more importantly, losing good secrets for several months now. Our country's place in the great scheme of things is being eroded on a daily basis. The Queen cannot go on forever, and when she goes, I fear much of the Empire will start to go with her. But for now I am determined that we hold what we have. And to do that, I need to know how the secrets are getting out, for I thought—I was sure—I had all possible egress points from the country under my hand. I am loath to admit it, but it seems I was wrong.

"I had a man, one of our best, on the job. His last report indicated he may have been on to something, but he never got a chance to tell me. He turned up dead this morning, murdered most brutally."

That bald statement, coming with the same lack of emotion as the rest of it, got Lestrade's attention.

"Surely you have other men better suited to ..."

"I do not know if they can be trusted; that's the truth of the matter," Mycroft answered. "As I mentioned earlier, their judgment might be impaired, given the manner of their colleague's death. I need someone from outside the service. My brother says you are a good man. Dogged, is I believe the word that was used. I need you on the trail of this, and I need you now. Your country needs you. I need to know what that man knew, and why he died for it."

Lestrade knew which strings were being pulled as well as Mycroft did, but it was an appeal he could not turn down. He finished his drink, put his smoke out in a crystal ashtray that cost more than a month of his salary, and stood.

"I shall need to see the body."

"Of course," Mycroft said. "They are waiting for you.

41

My carriage is at your disposal for the duration. It will take you now."

Lestrade thought he might be taken to a morgue, or some discreet doctor's practice hidden from prying eyes, so he was surprised when the carriage dropped him off in Whitechapel outside an iron foundry that looked as if it had been there for a century or more.

The carriage driver indicated that he would wait around the corner, "Out of sight, out of mind, like. I'll see you come out and be over in a jiffy." Then Lestrade was left on the pavement at the closed door of the foundry, somewhat at a loss as to his next move.

It was made for him when the door opened with a shrieking creak, and a soot-blackened man swaddled in heavy overalls waved him inside to a heat that immediately had Lestrade sweating inside his heavy wool suit.

A roaring furnace dominated the far side of the shed, but the overalled man led him away from that, over to the right-hand side where a shroud-covered body lay on a long trestle. The man didn't stand on ceremony; he whipped the sheet off and motioned Lestrade forward.

Mycroft's description of the murder as brutal had, if anything, understated the ferocity of the attack. His eyes were black pits, burned out by what Lestrade's overactive imagination thought must have been a red-hot poker or something very similar. The head was almost parted from the neck, the wound flapping like an oversized mouth. Someone had stripped the man but that only brought into greater relief the smaller mouths of stab wounds that covered his torso from nipples to groin; Lestrade stopped counting at twenty, and he'd only gotten half of them. There were no defensive wounds on either hand, but in examining them Lestrade found something else, a small tattoo of a grinning skull on the man's right forearm. Lestrade was no expert, but to his eye the inking looked like it had been done very recently, perhaps in the last couple of days. It was the only thing of any note to be learned from the body.

"Is this all?" he asked. "No clothes?"

The overalled man didn't speak, but bent under the trestle and rose to hand Lestrade an overcoat. There was nothing in any of the pockets and the label on the inside lining had been ripped out; somebody didn't want this victim identified. But Lestrade knew there were overcoats, and there were expensive overcoats, and this was one of the latter. After a study of the material, the lining, and the stitchwork he believed he could make a good guess as to the tailor, or at least narrow it down to two or three, all of whom were in business not too far from where he currently stood, although they would have long since shut up for the day.

Tattoo artists, however, kept different hours to tailors of expensive overcoats, and Lestrade knew several of them who worked in this area. He at least had a place to start.

As he was leaving the foundry the overalled man, who still hadn't said a word, was wheeling the trestle, and the dead body on it, toward the open door of the roaring furnace.

"Tampering with evidence," is strictly what it should be called, but Lestrade knew what Mycroft would call it.

Tidying up loose ends.

The carriage driver was as good as his word and hove into view as soon as Lestrade reached the pavement. The man knew the first tattoo artist Lestrade named.

"Frank Garvey, Gippo Frank they calls him; he's got a back room off Brick Lane these days. Hop in, guv'nor, we'll have you there in five minutes."

They arrived at Brick Lane just as it was getting dark. The revels of the night were just beginning to get going, although judging by the raucous laughter coming from the corner pub they had pulled up outside, the locals had started early.

"Frank does his business through the back," the driver said. "It's a rough crowd in there though, guv'nor. And you'll be known."

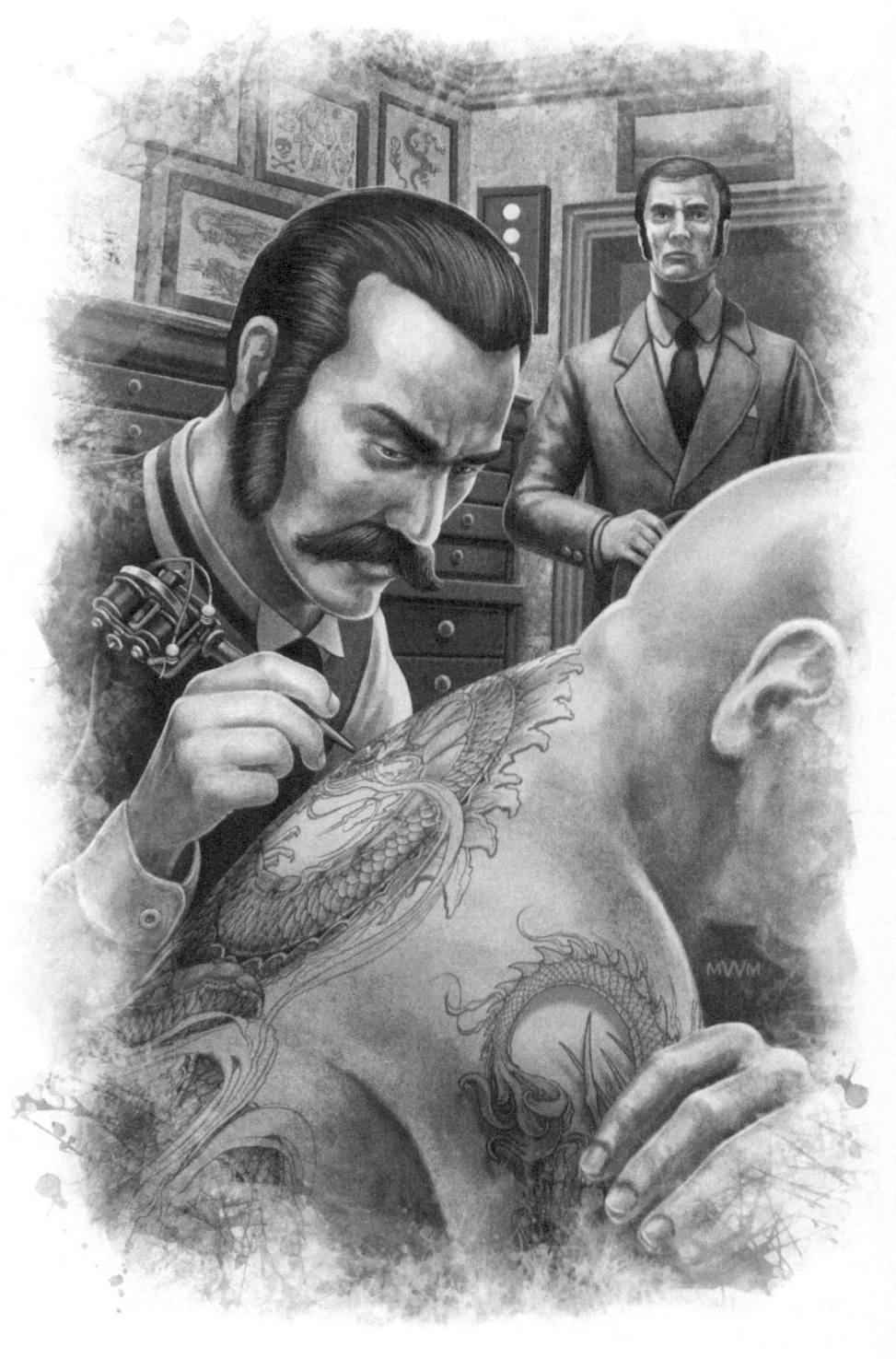

... with a gold and red and black and purple dragon coiled around him ...

Lestrade smiled grimly.

"That's why I'll be as safe as I would be in my office in the Yard," he said. "Will you wait?"

"The big man said I was to be at your disposal, day and night," the driver replied. "So I'll be here. If you could get somebody to bring me out a pint of porter, I'd be grateful, though."

The Black Bull lived up to its name; it was lit only by candlelight inside and the windows were small, and grimy with it. Patrons huddled in tight groups around small tables, and working girls lined up at the bar. Lestrade was aware that everyone present was watching him as he walked up and addressed the barman.

"I need to talk to Frank Garvey," he said.

"Who?" the barman replied, and smiled.

"The tattoo artist who works through the back," Lestrade said calmly. "And if you don't show me through to him in ten seconds, I'll have half of the coppers in London in here every night for a fortnight, so it's up to you, son."

"I don't want any trouble," the barman said.

"Neither do I, lad. That's why I'm playing nice."

The barman saw sense and showed Lestrade through the back. Before he left, Lestrade asked him to take a pint out to the carriage driver, and the barman waved away any thought of payment.

"On the house, guv'nor. A sign of good faith."

"Thanks. I've got a feeling I'm going to need it."

The barman led Lestrade into a small room only slightly better lit than the bar area. The walls were festooned with the artist's samples, and to Lestrade's admittedly untrained eye it looked like high-quality work. His gaze seemed to fall naturally on a small grinning skull, the exact same design he'd seen on the dead man's forearm.

The rest of the room was filled with Garvey and his client, a very portly Chinaman with a gold and red and black and purple dragon coiled around him, its great tail around his waist and its head filling his enormously wide

45

shoulders, a too-red tongue licking at his left ear.

"Garvey?" Lestrade said.

"Aye. Who wants to know?" a soft Irish brogue replied, although the man didn't look up from where he was putting a golden iris into a great dragon's eye.

"Lestrade, Scotland Yard."

"And what would the Yard want with a poor working lad like me?"

"I need some information. There's threepence in it for you if it's good, sixpence if it's better."

Still the man didn't look up, although he waved his free hand to indicate that Lestrade could take the seat to his left. The room smelled of ink and stale sweat along with the faint tang of blood. Lestrade lit up a cigarette before speaking.

"I'm after a man," he said, and the Irishman laughed.

"You and me both, dearie."

"No, a dead man. I believe he was in here recently; he had one of your tattoos on his forearm."

"I'm doing a dozen jobs a day here, officer. I'll need a description."

"Big lad, over six feet, black hair."

"That narrows it down to about two dozen. Anything else? Eye color?"

Lestrade saw the black, burnt holes in his mind's eye.

"They were taken," he said softly, and the Irishman whistled.

"Not dead by choice then?"

"Not by a long way. The only other thing I can tell you is that he had one of your skulls on his arm and an expensive taste in overcoats."

The Irishman laughed loudly. "If you'd said that first you could have spared us the dance. I believe I know the man you mean. Called himself John, no last name, but I get a lot of that around here so thought little of it. And yes, he got one of my wee skulls; I've had a run on them these past six months, although I can't see the attraction myself."

"When was he in?"

"Saturday afternoon, I think," the tattooist said, "although I get a bit foggy at weekends, if you know what I mean?"

Lestrade nodded. "Anything else you can tell me about him?"

"I've seen him in the bar a few times. He took a fancy to one of the girls, Siobhan. I only noticed because she's a good Irish Catholic lass and like a wee sister to me."

"And this Siobhan, where do I find her?"

"At this time of night? If she's not in the bar she'll be out on the streets somewhere, with another of them Johns. Could be anywhere. But you'll get her in the early morning tomorrow if you come back; she works in the scullery making pies."

Lestrade took his leave. The Irishman still hadn't looked up, but the big golden eye of the dragon seemed to wink at him as he left.

There was nothing more to be done that first night. He considered trying to knock up some of the tailors but didn't expect to learn any more than he knew already; one of Mycroft's men was going to be playing things close to his chest, unlikely to give anything away to someone who made his coats. A woman, however, was another matter entirely; there's many a slip between cup and lip, especially when intimacy is involved. This working girl might be just the lead he needed to find a way into the depths of the matter.

On the way out he asked the barman if she was in the bar, but got a shake of the head.

"She's out working. She'll be ..."

"... making pies in the morning. I know. I'll be back."

He went out into the night and had the carriage driver take him home to Vauxhall.

As the carriage clattered through the city Lestrade mentally reviewed his evening's work. He didn't see what else he could have done, or do, and if Mycroft wasn't

47

satisfied, well, Lestrade hadn't asked for the work, didn't need the work, so the blasted man could whistle in the wind for results somewhere else if he wanted them that badly.

Once home he had a small snifter of Scotch that was nowhere near as good as what he'd had in the Diogenes Club, said goodnight to his poor wife in the chair where she had sat in the days before the tuberculosis took her, and, feeling dissatisfied with his lot, trudged off to bed.

The carriage driver was waiting on his doorstep in the morning, and not long after the sun came up, they were once again on their way to Brick Lane.

The bar was still just as dark and, despite the earliness of the hour, still just as full of patrons, many of whom might well still have been sitting in the same seats Lestrade saw them in the previous evening. The barman stood in the same spot and jerked a thumb over his right shoulder when he saw Lestrade.

"She's in the scullery. She's expecting you. But she's not happy."

That proved to be an understatement. The black-haired woman in the scullery had her hands covered with animal fat and a face like thunder.

"Garvey tells me that he's dead?" she said without any prompting.

"Very," Lestrade answered. "I'm hoping to find out why."

"Aye? Well, get in the queue."

Lestrade waited while she washed her hands, none too rigorously, then she led him to a pair of seats beside a tall iron range and poured them both a cup of strong, sweet tea from the big black kettle that hung there. It tasted like it had been brewing for weeks, but it was just what Lestrade needed at that point. He lit them both a cigarette, then waited for her to talk. She didn't need to be asked twice.

"He was going to take me away from all this," she said,

and laughed bitterly. "It's no' the first time a man in a good coat has said it to me, but it's the first time I started to believe it, more fool me."

"He'd been coming around for a while?"

"Three months now, give or take," she said, and angrily wiped away a tear.

"And where were his digs?"

"He wouldn't tell me, said he'd take me when the time was right. At first I thought he was married, you know? But he didn't wear a ring. And these last few days he was spending a lot of time in that weird house at number fifty-four. I tried to get in there to see him a couple of times, but they have rules for the likes of me, it seems."

Information was coming at him too fast for Lestrade to keep up. He lit them both another cigarette from the butt of his old one and had her go back over something she'd mentioned.

"What weird house?"

"I told you. The one at number fifty-four."

"No, I mean, what's weird about it?"

She laughed dryly again at that. "What's not weird about it? There's always been stories about it. I've been hearing them since I got here ten years ago from the auld country. But in these past eighteen months it's been getting weirder still. Spooks and haunts is what the old folks around here say. I don't know about that, but there's been all sorts of people coming into the area, foreign gentlemen in the main. Anarchists, it's said. Bloody peculiar is what I say. All those men and only that old French bitch for a woman. What John wanted with the likes of them I'll never know."

She might not know, but Lestrade finally had the sniff of a lead.

"You said you tried to get inside?"

"Three times. Last time was just yesterday; John was supposed to take me up the West End and he never showed, so I went to find him to give him a piece of my mind. That old French bitch wouldn't let me in. She said I could see him if I had the right sigil and the right totem. I asked her what she meant by that and got a spiel about it being a rule of the house; I'd need something of his, a totem; that I could manage seeing as how I have a handkerchief he gave me. But as for the sigil? If I understood her right, she wanted me to get tattooed before I'd be allowed in, something significant to both of us. Tattooed? And me a working girl? My gentlemen don't go for that kind of thing on a girl."

"Yesterday? And she said he was there?"

"Just after eight last night. She said right off I could see him if I followed the rules."

"Sorry, lass, she was lying to you. He was dead and gone in the morning. I was round here looking for you at the same time as you were over at the house."

"Bitch."

And that was the last word she spoke before tears shook her and she turned away.

Lestrade left her to it. There was a mystery waiting for him at number fifty-four.

If he could get in.

Number fifty-four was slap-bang in the middle of a row of Georgian townhouses going rapidly to seed. As Lestrade walked up the three stone steps to the heavy wooden door he heard singing coming from inside, a gravel-voiced Frenchman by the sound of it.

"*Le dieu rêveur chante où il dort.*"

Lestrade's basic schoolboy French wasn't up to following and translating at the same time, but in any case the song cut off abruptly when he reached forward and used the heavy brass knocker to rap three times on the door. The knocks echoed around the small porch, then there was silence. For several seconds Lestrade thought he was going to be left on the doorstep, then a lock slid open on the far side of the door and it opened, only two inches or so, to show him a small, black-haired woman peering at him through the gap.

"Yes?" she said, just the one word, but enough for him to discern her accent.

His actions in response were pure gut-instinct, an old copper's hunch if you like, trusting to his gut. He rolled up a sleeve and showed her the tattoo on his forearm of a single red rose, with his wife's name, Peggy, running across it. Then he undid the top button of his shirt and drew out the locket that never left his neck, as it hadn't left hers from the day he bought it for her until the day she died.

The woman looked Lestrade up and down, then nodded. The door opened wider; she hardly looked to have the strength to shut it, being barely five foot tall and thin to the point of being angular and skeletal. She was dressed head to toe in black velvet and lace apart from a man's black waistcoat that hung loosely on her and which carried a gold fob chain slung low at her belly. When she raised a hand to motion Lestrade inside a small tattooed sparrow fluttered in the webbing between finger and thumb.

She didn't speak, just led him silently through into a long dark hallway with four doors off it and a long staircase rising up into darkness at the far end. She turned sharply to the left and motioned him through to what was obviously her room, a twelve-foot square area lushly decorated with an expensive looking Persian carpet, more velvet, black again, in tall curtain drapes that almost covered the outside wall, and artwork, portraits in the main, in heavy gilded frames, covering the walls. There was a bed in one corner, and two armchairs in front of a tall fireplace, with a drinks table between them. She motioned him to one of the armchairs that sat almost facing each other.

"You may smoke," she said, her accent clearly showing, "and please help yourself to some brandy. I am the concierge, and if you have questions, ask them now, for there might not be time or opportunity later."

Lestrade lit a cigarette and poured himself a small shot

of brandy, mostly to give him time to gather his thoughts; he had not expected to gain entry so easily, and now that he was inside he did not wish to misuse the opportunity.

"What exactly is this place?" he asked.

She smiled, and he saw the younger woman she once had been in her face.

"You know some of it already," she said, "otherwise you would not be here. There are houses like this all over the world. Most people only know of them from whispered stories over campfires; tall tales told to scare the unwary. But some, those who suffer, some know better. They are drawn to the places where what ails them can be eased."

"What ails me? Very little, if truth be told." he said, hearing the lie in his voice.

"We both know better than that, Mr. Lestrade," she said, and he almost dropped his smoke in his lap at the shock of hearing his name put so boldly.

"You can see her again, your Peggy. If you have the will, the fortitude, you can peer into another life, where the dead are not gone, where you can see that they thrive and go on, in the dreams that stuff is made of."

"My Peggy is in Heaven and far beyond my reach," he replied. He realized this conversation was not going anyplace he wanted it too, but something in his heart ached to continue it.

The woman smiled."In Heaven she may be, that is not for me to say. I am but the concierge and my job is to allocate the rooms and see that my tenants follow the rules. But believe me, Peggy is here, somewhere, if you would open your heart to the possibility."

While Lestrade was trying to make sense of the situation he'd fallen into, he realized he could hear the Frenchman singing again, distant and faint, a song heard in the wind.

"*Le dieu rêveur chante où il dort.*"

Lestrade gathered his thoughts into what he considered to be a coherent response, and came up with another question.

"Do you have many tenants?"

"Eight at any given moment," she said. "Or rather, seven as of yesterday. Room number six is currently available, if you would take it?"

Lestrade reckoned he knew who the precious tenant must have been ... Mycroft's 'John.' He could not pass up the chance to see the room where the dead man had been living.

"You said there were rules?"

"Indeed there are. Two of them you are following already; you have the sigil, and the totem. The next step is to make contact, if the room will have you. It is my place to warn you that rejection is possible, and that it might go badly for you."

"Is that what happened to the previous tenant?" he asked, and saw from her expression that he had overstepped his mark. Her smile disappeared, replaced by a blank stare.

"There is another rule of the house," she said. "A tenant's business is a tenant's business, and no other's. I am merely the concierge."

Lestrade saw he would get no more out of her without giving away the real reason for his presence, so decided to play along to get a look at the dead man's room.

"I will take number six then," he said. "Do I pay you now?"

"You will pay later," she said, somewhat ominously "if payment is required."

She said no more, and rose from her chair to signify that this part of the process was at an end. Lestrade followed her back out into the hallway. As they left the Frenchman's singing rose in volume at their back, still as if through a strong wind, but definitely coming from somewhere inside the room that Lestrade couldn't place.

"*Le dieu rêveur chante où il dort.*"

Number six was a room to the right at the top of the stairs. As they approached it someone came out of

number seven across the landing, a heavy-set chap
with a thick black beard and a bald-spot almost like a
monk's tonsure. He gave Lestrade a sharp look, then
quickly looked away, but Lestrade couldn't mistake the
recognition in the gaze.

Does everybody here know my bally business?

The concierge didn't acknowledge the other man as
he went off down the stairs but led Lestrade to the door
of number six and opened it. The room beyond was small
and nowhere near as lavish as her rooms downstairs,
containing an old iron-frame bed and a single armchair
in front of a currently cold hearth. Thin drapes covered a
window that, from the orientation of the room, must have
overlooked the rear of the property. The only other item of
note was a badly flecked mirror in an old wooden frame
over the mantlepiece.

"What do I do?" Lestrade asked.

"Wait," was all she said, then closed the door, she in
the hall and he inside the empty room.

Lestrade's first thought was to look for evidence,
anything that the dead man might have left behind. He
checked behind the mirror, down the back of the armchair
cushion, inside the pillowcases, under the mattress and
under the bed itself but found nothing there but dust and
cigarette ash.

He was about to sit in the armchair and have a smoke
when a breeze seemed to rush through the room, setting
the drapes on the window to fluttering and bringing with
it the sound, not of curtains rubbing together, but of
paper, rustling.

On investigation he found a folded set of four pages,
and it was obvious from the first that this was the dead
man's field report, the one that Mycroft had expected but
had never received. Lestrade took it back with him to the
armchair, lit up a smoke, and started to read from the
beginning. It was in a neat, legible hand, and he was soon
lost in the story it had to tell.

Monday, 21st.
Our source was right about the correct means of entry. The skull tattoo and a dead man's trinket were enough to get me inside.

The concierge is a strange old bird, full of hints and allusions and the frankly nonsensical idea that this is some kind of 'house of the dead.' If I have understood her correctly—and she was somewhat difficult to make out what with her accent and that old French cove singing at the top of his voice—I can expect to have a conversation with the man who was the owner of the ring I used to get me in. That might prove to be an interesting chat, given that I took it off his finger after I stabbed him through the heart. Still, at least he'll be at home here in his old room.

I shall get settled in for the night and tomorrow see what I can do to ingratiate myself with the other tenants.

Tuesday, 22nd
I slept badly, my dreams filled with a dead man's blood and screams that seemed to echo around me even after wakening. I broke my fast in The Black Bull. Siobhan at least was pleased to see me, although I fear my subterfuge will not please her much in the long term.

On arrival back here I made my introductions to the cove in number seven. He was most reticent at first, but I ensured that he saw my tattoo and he thawed considerably, although not enough to take me into his confidence as yet. He is definitely a player of the great game in my opinion, and of German descent unless I am very much mistaken. He is not the only one here, either. There is a quiet, studious-looking chap in room four who looks like he wouldn't say boo to a goose, but he too has a skull on his right forearm, and he is not German,

*but most definitely of Russian Jewish stock, and
I am certain that if we searched our records back
at H.Q. we shall have him listed as an anarchist
sympathizer. M's instincts have proved spot-on
again.*

*I am in a hotbed, and have my work cut out
to gain favor among them and uncover their
methods.*

Lestrade looked up from his reading. Something had
caught his eye, a shifting of the shadows in the mirror
above the mantelpiece, but it was gone as soon as he paid
attention to it. As he turned back to the papers it seemed
that someone sighed loudly, close to his left ear, but that
too had faded and gone, and the dead man's notes proved
to be more engrossing than anything else that might be
happening.

Wednesday, 23rd
I do not like this place.

*I was awakened most rudely during the night
with the whole of the bed shaking and roiling
below me such that I felt like a small boat tossed
in rough seas. It ceased as soon as I rose, but on
lighting a candle to try to find the source of the
commotion I discovered that someone had been in
the room while I slept. There was a message left
for me, a single word in German.*

"Mörder."

*I heard a creak in the hallway. Fearing that the
true nature of my visit here had been discovered
I burst out of the room ready for action and must
have looked a fearful sight, for the occupant of
number seven, obviously on his way back from
the lavatory, stepped back in shock at my sudden
appearance, then laughed.*

*"It has begun, then. Never fear, friend," he
said. "You are on a path many have trod, and*

most of us are still here to tell of it. Have courage."

By the time I had my wits about me he had already turned away and I had no opportunity to quiz him further.

When I returned to my room there was only my reflection in the mirror. No trace of any writing remained, and I was beginning to think I had merely been in the grip of a powerful dream, but a dream nonetheless.

My mood improved further in the morning when I met the German from number seven over breakfast in the Black Bull. Our encounter on the landing had obviously endeared me to him and over a pie and several pints of strong porter he became almost amicable. He has promised to show me what is required once I am 'attuned', although quite what becoming attuned requires is so far beyond my ken.

As I sit here now, the darkness growing around me, I feel apprehension grow in me. All players in the great game know this feeling, I am sure, the sense that secrets are close to being uncovered, while at the same time having to continually look over your shoulder to make sure your own secret remains safe.

The trouble is, here in this house, I find myself afraid; no, terrified, to look over my shoulder.

Thursday, 24th
I have seen it, but cannot believe it. But they do, the gray men playing their gray games here, so I must tell of what I have uncovered, although I am unsure as to its value to the service.

The German in number seven asked me this morning if I was attuned and of course, not being totally stupid, I answered 'yes.' And that simple deception was enough for him to take me fully into his confidence. We went to his room which could almost be a mirror image of mine, and he showed me two things; the tattoo on his forearm, and a pocket watch.

"This belonged to Gunter," he said as if I should know the man named. "He died six months ago. It is to him I make my reports, and he relays them to headquarters through my brother via the Berlin house, for my brother carries the chain from this very same watch."

I was starting to make connections; this was purportedly a house for speaking to the dead. And the players of the game here were using it to pass secrets, via the dead, from London to Berlin as fast as they could be spoken, with nobody in our service any the wiser. There is a wider picture too … the concierge told me there are houses like this 'all over the world.' It is such a fantastic notion I cannot bring myself to believe in it. But what if it is true? Think of the advantage in intelligence these houses might bring to anyone who can master their secret, anyone who has become 'attuned.'

I did not let any of this supposition show in my face, of course, and tried to concentrate on the man in front of me.

"How do you contact Gunter?" I asked with a straight face. I think, looking back on it, I might have made a mistake, that he knew it was something I should already be privy to. Whatever the case, he grew rather less friendly after that and asked me to leave the room, pleading a sudden convenient headache.

I have sat here through the remainder of the day, writing this up, alternating between belief and incredulity.

There is just one more thing.

Five minutes ago I looked up from my writing to see a word being drawn in ash across the face of the mirror. I knew what it would be before it

was finished, the same word as before, a single word, full of truth.
Mörder.

Lestrade turned the page over, hoping for more, but it was blank. Whatever the man's fate, he had not seen it coming. He still had the papers in his hand when a well-remembered, impossible voice spoke at his left ear.

"Put them away. Put them away now."

It was his wife's voice, his dead wife's voice, he'd have sworn it on a stack of bibles.

"Peggy?" he whispered.

The delay in obeying her was to prove costly. The door to the room was flung open and the German from number seven stood there, a knife in his hand. He motioned at the papers.

"I cannot allow you to leave with that," he said. "You should not have seen it."

"What are you going to do? Burn out my eyes?" Lestrade said calmly, and was standing from the chair even as he saw the guilty look pass across the German's face. At least now he had his murderer. He kept his eye on the knife, his voice low.

"I am an inspector from Scotland Yard," he said. "Kill me and you'll swing for it, that much I can guarantee."

"I am an officer in the German Army," the man replied haughtily. "I do my duty, whatever the cost."

He came forward, wielding the knife like a man who knew what to do with it. Lestrade backed away toward the window, thinking he might pull down a drape to use as protection.

The German laughed and kept coming. As he walked past the mirror Peggy's voice rang around the room, a single word.

"No."

The window smashed in a million pieces, the glass shredding the German's face as if he'd walked into a mincer, flaying the skin down to the bone and leaving it hanging in ragged ribbons. The man went down as if poleaxed.

He was dead by the time Lestrade got to him.

Lestrade played it by the book. He found a constable in the street who would relay a message to the Yard that they had a crime scene to work. He sent Mycroft's driver and carriage back to inform Mycroft that the job was done and that a report would be imminent, and then he took charge of the house.

The concierge was most indignant, but Lestrade was immune to her imprecations, and all too soon the place was filled with officers and the coroner's men. Statements were taken, the man identified in the papers as 'a Russian anarchist' was squirreled away for further questioning, and Lestrade smoked a series of cigarettes on the doorstep while trying to make sense of the German's last seconds of life.

It was Peggy's voice that kept coming back to him, that single, angry word that had been full of love and indignation at the same time.

Once all the furor had died down and the room cleared, Lestrade went back up to number six and stood there for the longest time in silence before saying one word.

"Peggy?"

He didn't get a reply.

That night he visited the Diogenes Club again, drank a lot of Mycroft's good Scotch and made his report. He didn't know if Mycroft believed him and he didn't care one way or the other. When he got home he spoke to Peggy in her armchair, but still got no reply. When he got to bed he wept for the first time since she had died.

Over the next few weeks his mind kept returning to the room on Brick Lane, and one Saturday morning he found himself standing on the doorstep, hand raised to knock.

He heard a carriage pull up behind him and a voice call his name. He turned to see Mycroft Holmes sitting in the carriage.

"You won't get in, I'm afraid," he said. "The house is under the control of Her Majesty's Service."

"And just what does that mean?" Lestrade asked.

"It means we shall use it for our own purposes, of course," Mycroft replied. "It has been made safe. You are not to mention it to anyone, you are not to speak of it, you are not even to think about it. You're a grown man with a brain. You know what I'm talking about."

"Unfortunately, I do," Lestrade said.

"My brother was right," Mycroft said. "You are a good man."

He put out a hand to be shaken. His cuffs went back, exposing his forearm and there, plain to be seen, was a new tattoo, Garvey's work again, a small skull whose grin followed Lestrade back to Vauxhall and his forever-empty home.

The Thing
from the Black Museum

P.C. Randall was in full flow, the attendees were rapt with his tales of infamy, debauchery and murder most foul, and Inspector Lestrade was bored to the verge of tears. He had no need to see the sad remains of more than a century of London's most heinous crimes; he saw more than enough of that on a daily basis.

Besides, the Black Museum had been set up with the intention of using its contents as training materials for young officers, and to Lestrade's mind that was the only right and proper use of it. Now here he was, babysitting, not coppers, but high-falutin' bankers in search of a cheap thrill, poring over the pasts of victims and perpetrators alike with no more emotion than if they were reading a newspaper.

Apparently the plan was to make this a regular thing, maybe even charge for admission. The thought of the great unwashed traipsing through the Yard's dirty linen appalled him. He had tried to get out of the duty, but the Commissioner had been most insistent.

"It's good for the Yard's image in the city," Lestrade's

superior had said, in a voice that also said that any argument was now over and that Lestrade had better toe the line if he knew what was good for him.

So here he was, toeing the line and trying to stifle a yawn. At least Randall was enjoying himself. He was on to the Rugeley Poisoner now and showing them Palmer's cigar case, where, it was said, he kept his strychnine pills. One of the attendees, a young, smartly dressed chap with, to Lestrade's mind at least, shifty eyes had stepped back and was perusing the boxes of exhibits that had been packed high along one side of the room's walls. He had box number twenty-three open; Lestrade only took note of it as it was the same as the street number of his house in Vauxhall.

"Here, lad, come away from there. You don't know where that stuff's been."

As the younger man closed the box and turned away Lestrade thought he saw him slip something into his jacket pocket, but he couldn't be sure, and the Commissioner might not think it good for the Yard's image in the City if they were to accuse a prominent banker of lifting a memento from the Black Museum, so he let it go.

They finally got to the end of the tour; the bankers all left, seemingly happy with the experience, and Lestrade let Randall go back to packing up the exhibits for their move to the new premises on the Embankment while he headed upstairs for a most welcome mug of tea and a smoke.

He didn't give the young banker another thought, right up to the day a week later when he was called urgently down to the cells and found the lad, his once-white shirt now blood-soaked, looking lost and bedraggled, sitting handcuffed at a table and weeping most sorely.

Lestrade's sergeant was at the cell door.

"What's the story, Clarkie?"

"Bloody murder, sir, and lot's of it. Sonny Jim here did away with a family, the Harts, over in Wapping. Husband, wife and two kiddies. Looks like he took a chisel to them

... he damn near took off the husband's head. We found him sitting, weeping on the doorstep with the bloody weapon still in his hands. We've got plenty of witnesses that saw him going in, heard the screaming, and saw him coming out. Open-and-shut case. Between you and me, sir, I think his mind is broken. He's been making no kind of sense at all."

The lad in the cell looked up, saw Lestrade, and a flicker of recognition crossed his features.

"I didn't do it!" he wailed. "Well, I did, but I didn't, if you see what I mean?"

Lestrade stepped into the cell, sat opposite the lad, rolled two cigarettes and lit them with a lucifer before passing one over. He took a deep draw on his own before speaking.

"Tell me what happened, lad," he said. "It'll go better for you if you just get it all off your chest."

"That's the thing. I remember leaving the bank to take some air at lunchtime. The next thing I know is I'm sitting on a doorstep in a street I don't recognize, with a bloody chisel in my hand. Everything in between is just a nightmare of feelings of bloody rage and fractured images of violence and mayhem. But that wasn't me. It can't have been me. Tell me it wasn't me ... please?"

"I can't tell you anything of the sort," Lestrade said and stood. "As my sergeant said, it's an open-and-shut case. You'll swing for this."

Fresh tears ran down the lad's face and Lestrade saw the confusion and no little fear there, but felt no compassion. He'd seen too many murderers trying to feign innocence to let one get to him. He had one last question though before he left, just to satisfy his curiosity.

"What was it you took from our museum that day? And don't try to deny it. I saw you."

"A handkerchief," the lad replied. "Just a silk handkerchief. It had some dried blood on it, but it was just a handkerchief. I didn't think anybody would miss it."

"P.C. Randall would probably like it back, though. Do you have it on you?"

"I did this morning," the lad replied. "Wiping my nose with it is about the last thing I remember." He patted his pockets, but came up blank. "I must have lost it, like I've lost everything else."

Lestrade left as the weeping started in earnest. Sergeant Clarke shut the door with a clang that echoed around the cells.

The case of David Wilson, banker turned homicidal maniac, was quite a sensation for almost a week in the papers but Lestrade was too busy with other crimes to pay too much attention to it. It was, however, brought back to him in sharp relief ten days later. He was called out to Wapping, and more murder; two brothers this time, George and Francis Ablass. It was a particularly brutal crime scene and, as in the Hart case, the men had their heads almost severed from their necks by a chisel. This time there was no handy suspect on the doorstep, although they did find the bloodied weapon lying in the street.

The only saving grace was that there were again plenty of witnesses more than willing to give an account of events. Lestrade walked over to where Sergeant Clarke was interviewing a portly, red-faced man with hands glistening with animal fat and wearing the leather apron of a butcher.

"Saw the whole bally thing, I did," the man said. "Ain't ever seen nothing like it outside of the abattoir, I'll tell you that for sixpence."

"And you saw who did it?"

"Saw him? Of course I did. It was John Standing, the baker from Cannon Street Road. He didn't seem quite himself though. He walked past me with a hankie to his mouth and never spoke when I gave him the time of day. Walked right over to the Ablass place, knocked on the door and, cool as you like, took out a chisel and near chopped poor George's head off when he answered.

Never even said 'Good morning.' Then he went inside and I heard a scream. Next thing I knows Standing walks out, still holding a hankie at his mouth, drops the chisel and just walks away as if he was out for a stroll."

"Nobody went after him?"

"What, and get a new mouth below the jaw for their trouble? No fear."

Lestrade had a bulletin put out for the apprehension of John Standing of Cannon Street Road. He and Clarke visited Standing's business and searched the apartment upstairs. There was nothing of note, although the baker's oven was cold, unused for at least a week, and there was a profusion of empty beer bottles strewn around the living quarters. Lestrade had Clarke leave a man on watch lest Standing be stupid enough to return, then he sent Clarke to keep an eye on the scene of the crime. He, meanwhile, headed for the Embankment. He had a coincidence on his hands.

He didn't like coincidences.

The Black Museum was in the process of being rehoused in what would eventually also be Lestrade's new working home in what was to be called New Scotland Yard, although Lestrade didn't see what was wrong with the old one. He found P.C. Randall unpacking boxes in a well-lit, airy chamber almost the size of a warehouse.

"You're missing something from box twenty-three," Lestrade said.

"Twenty-three? That's the Ratcliffe Highway box. Why would anything be missing from there?"

Something inside Lestrade lurched. Instead of clearing up a coincidence, he now had another one to add, for the Ratcliffe Highway case was one of the most infamous in the Yard's history even though it had taken place eighty years ago. It had involved two brutal multiple murders, with chisel-like implements, in Wapping.

Somebody's copying the original killings.

"Why do you say something's missing from the box, Inspector?" the P.C. asked.

Lestrade gave him the story. When he mentioned the families' names, Randall went white.

"Do you know something about this that I don't, lad?" Lestrade asked.

"Possibly. There's two things you need to know. The handkerchief that was taken belonged to John Williams, the man who, allegedly at least, committed the murders. He had it on him in his cell when he committed suicide."

"So, not a real surprise it ended up in your museum then. What's the other thing?"

"There were other suspects in the killings, and Williams was insistent all through his questioning that they were the ones we should have been looking at."

"And their names?"

"Cornelias Hart, Long Billy Ablass and Frank Mahoney."

"So someone knows the details of the original case? Are they after some kind of revenge for the perpetrator, the sins of the fathers and all that Biblical stuff?"

The P.C. looked thoughtful.

"Something on your mind, lad?"

"Another possibility, sir. But you're not going to like it."

"There's already a lot I don't like about this. Let's be having it."

"It's this place, sir. Or rather, these boxes and what's in them. I've spent a lot of time, many dark nights, alone with them, and I've felt it. It accumulates, clumps up in places, like. I've seen it shifting in the shadows."

"What are you havering about, lad?"

"Evil, sir. Pure, concentrated, evil. What if Williams was clutching that hankie when he died, and all of his fury and rage leached into it? And what if it hid here, all these years, until the young banker purloined it, let it out so to speak."

"Away and don't talk daft, lad. I can hardly go to the

Commissioner and tell him an eighty-year-old hankie did it, now can I?"

"I see that, sir," Randall replied. "But I think you should consider it."

"I'll tell you what I'll consider, son. I'll consider finding the descendants of Frank Mahoney. Whether it's a killer hankie or some conspiracy, I'd say the Mahoneys are next on the list and are going to need protection."

Back at the Yard Lestrade delegated three officers to track down the Mahoney descendants, knowing that he was sentencing them to a long day in the files at Somerset House. Sergeant Clarke returned from Wapping, having seen to the clean-up of the crime scene, with a report that John Standing was still nowhere to be found. Over tea and a smoke Lestrade told Clarke about his visit to the Black Museum, and Randall's theory. He expected skepticism and was surprised to see that Clarke was actually considering the idea.

"I had you down as a hard-headed pragmatist, Clarkie."

"Mostly, I'd agree, sir. But I had an Irish gran and she knew things before anybody should have known them, so I've always kept an open mind where such matters are concerned."

"Keep yours open for both of us then," Lestrade replied, "And I'll concentrate on the legwork."

The first part of the legwork was a visit to Newgate Prison; this new double murder, with so many similarities to the Hart case, meant that Lestrade needed to talk again to the banker, Wilson.

It was a much-chastened young man who was brought into the interview room. His well-tailored suit and shirt had been replaced by prison-issue uniform, his hair was unkempt and he had not shaved for several days. His eyes had the haunted look of a man condemned even before trial, and he took to an offered cigarette like a drowning man grasping for a lifebelt.

"Come for another look at the nutter, have we, sir?" Wilson said. "I must warn you, it has been suggested to me most forcibly by my lawyer that I say nothing at all about the killings and plead amnesia or mental funk. He says it might be the only thing that will save me from the rope."

"I would suggest, most forcibly, that your lawyer is a bloody idiot," Lestrade said, "But that is between you, your money and him. I am not here to talk about the murders, not as such. Tell me about the handkerchief. Why did you take it?"

"If truth be told, I don't rightly know. One second I was listening to your man going on about poisons, the next I was standing with the box open and my hand inside. It wasn't a thing of the head, there was little to no thought involved. It called to me, here," Wilson said, and patted at his chest over his heart, "as if it knew me."

"But it was just a handkerchief."

"Inspector, that piece of cloth wasn't 'just' anything. I carried it with me everywhere I went, as if it couldn't bear to be any distance from me. And every day that compulsion to have it close by grew stronger and stronger. I have been thinking a lot these past days; it's not as if there is much else to occupy me. My troubles really started on the steps of the bank when I took out the blasted thing. I believe I told you at our last meeting that I had blown my nose? That's not strictly accurate. What I did was cover my mouth with it ... cover my mouth and breathe in deep. And after that, all is darkness."

"And you have no idea where you lost it?"

"Somewhere in the period my lawyer doesn't even want me to think about."

Short of giving the man the third degree, which would be almost useless at this stage of proceedings, Lestrade realized he had hit a wall he wasn't going to get through. As he rose to leave he played a hunch without really thinking it through.

"Wilson? Has that always been your family name?"

"Funny you should ask that. It used to be Williams but it got changed decades ago, long before my time. Some sort of scandal that was never talked about, so I don't know the details."

Lestrade suspected that those details were something for Clarkie's 'open mind' to consider, and he determined to preoccupy himself with the legwork.

That legwork next took him to Somerset House to check on the progress on tracking down any Mahoneys. Surprisingly, the men had managed to narrow it down to no more than three families who might currently be in London, and two of the three men were already out on the beat chasing up the leads. The third man was going over the records again, making sure they hadn't missed anything. On another hunch Lestrade had him check the records for John Standing. His hunch was proved right fifteen minutes later; Standing's grandmother had been a Williams, directly related to the original suspect for the murders.

Lestrade wasn't yet able to bring himself to believe in a spirit-possessed handkerchief bent on revenge, but it did indeed seem there was a family tie that provided a link both between the old murders and the new, and also between the two cases in the present day. His hope was that if he looked hard enough, a more mundane explanation might be forthcoming. What was now obvious, though, was that either the Mahoney families or John Standing needed to be found, and quickly at that, before more bloody mayhem could ensue.

The officers returned to Somerset House just as Lestrade was leaving. There were two lines of family directly descended from Mahoney still in London. One consisted of a very old lady, Mahoney's younger sister, resident of Bedlam these past thirteen years and about as well protected as anyone could be in this city. Lestrade sent one of the men there anyway.

The other branch was a family of six currently in a

crumbling tenement on Clerkenwell Road. They hadn't found the father yet; he was an itinerant worker at Spitalfields Market and was being tracked down, but they had the mother and four young children, ages three up to eight, safely at home with two officers cluttering up their already-small room and another two outside in the street. It was a lot of men to expend on one case, and Lestrade knew the Commissioner would probably have something to say about it.

Maybe I'll tell him it's good for our image in the City.

One thing was vexing Lestrade: yes, he'd managed to track down the Mahoneys, with the help of three men and the Somerset House Records. But young Wilson and Standing had both managed to track down the other families with seemingly no help at all, as if working on some kind of instinct. That was something else Lestrade was struggling to fit into a mundane view of the matter. Maybe Holmes and Watson would be able to make sense of the web of coincidences and impossibilities of the case, but Lestrade was already on shaky ground with the Commissioner. Bringing in the 'amateurs,' no matter what their record, wasn't a luxury he could afford.

All he could do was trust the legwork.

He shared some of his concerns with Sergeant Clarke over a pie and pint in the Old Queen's Head in Clerkenwell Road. They had a seat by the window where they could see the entrance to the Mahoneys' tenement, but that did little to ease Lestrade's worrying, for he knew these old buildings to be more like warrens than dwellings, with far too many interior passages and stairwells to cover with the men he had at hand.

"If he comes, we'll have him, sir," Clarke said. "It's just one man."

"Is it just, though, Clarkie? Is it?"

This case had him on edge, had gotten to him in a way few cases had managed over the years. Child-killings had a way of doing that to any copper, even one as seasoned as Lestrade. He was determined that no more young ones would die.

Not on my watch.

"The husband? At least tell me we found him alive and well."

"All present and correct, sir. He was in a pub on Farringdon Road and he's had a skinful, but we fetched him home and he's up there with the missus and kiddies now."

They sat in the seat in the pub window, making their beer last, watching the road as night started to fall and the gaslighters did their rounds. A thin fog rolled up from the south, bringing a chill from the river, and everything took on a softer hue.

"If this gets any worse he'll be able to walk right past us and we won't know him from Adam," Clarke complained.

Lestrade didn't answer. He was watching a tall, angular man across the street, walking slowly, with a hand covering his mouth.

"Is that him?" he asked.

Clarke took a look. "Could be, sir. We've only got that butcher's description to be going on, but he fits the bill."

"Take him, then; take him now."

Clarke was quickest out into the street with Lestrade right at his heels. Clarke blew his whistle and pointed at the tall man. Lestrade saw, too late, the confused expression on the man's face. He had something in his hand, but it wasn't a handkerchief; he'd been cupping his hand against the breeze to light his pipe. And as Lestrade got closer he saw that this chap was too old by far to be Standing, by twenty years and more.

"It's not him," he shouted, but by then Clarke and two other officers were already converging on the man. The entrance to the tenement wasn't being covered and when Lestrade looked that way he saw a tall thin figure, almost lost in the fog, head up the close.

"Clarkie, he got past us. He's inside," he shouted, and headed for the entrance at a run.

Screams came down from above before he was halfway up the flight of stairs.

The Mahoney apartment was off the second landing. One of their young officers sat in the doorway, legs splayed, a pool of blood spreading between them, a second mouth gaping, white-lipped at his neck where Standing's chisel had sawn into it. His dead eyes stared accusingly at Lestrade as he passed.

A second officer slumped in the hallway, face as white as a sheet, both hands cupped at his belly where his guts were trying to escape.

"Get a doctor, right now," Lestrade shouted, hoping that someone would obey the command for he had no time to waste. Fresh screams rose from the end of the hallway, high and wailing, and a man bellowed.

"You leave my bloody kids alone. I'm warning you."

Lestrade was first into the main living area, with Clarke right at his back. The family, all six of them, were backed up against a big iron range with the husband trying, unsuccessfully, to get them all behind his back. They'd gone as far as they could for the range was lit and the heat from it must be almost unbearable for them already. John Standing was in the center of the room, a bloodied chisel dripping in his right hand, his left clutching a white handkerchief to his mouth.

Lestrade was still almost six feet away when Standing lunged forward, wielding the chisel like a short sword. Mahoney tried to bat it away with his left hand and got a deep cut across his palm for the trouble. He cursed, long and loud, the drink still in his system talking for him, and came forward, fists swinging. Standing swiveled on his right foot with all the grace of a ballet dancer and brought the chisel up and around in a backhand slice that opened up Mahoney's neck like a hot knife through butter.

The Irishman hardly knew what had killed him. His momentum kept him going forward and he slumped at

Standing's waist. The time it took Standing to shift the big man's weight aside gave Lestrade enough time to reach him. Standing was already heading for Mrs. Mahoney when the inspector leapt on his back, both arms around him trying to pin his arms to his side. Lestrade's weight caused the man to stagger and when Clarke came in low in a rugby tackle from behind all three of them fell in a tangled heap on the floor.

The fall turned Standing over, squirming beneath Lestrade. The inspector looked into a snarling, spitting face and realized that the man was trying his damndest to bring the handkerchief in his left hand back up to his mouth. Lestrade had to make an instant decision, to go for the chisel, or go for the handkerchief. His head said one thing, his gut said the other, and he went with the instinct he'd learned to trust. He made a dive for the hankie. The chisel came up, heading under his chin. Clarke got there first, grabbing the blade and hauling it away an instant before it could plunge into Lestrade's skin.

Lestrade's fingers closed on the handkerchief's material and he tugged, hard, hearing a rip. Standing screamed as if he had taken a wound. Lestrade kept tugging, felt the material come out of the man's grip and into his and a second later he had it all.

Standing went limp beneath him. Lestrade was looking into his face and saw nothing there now but fear and confusion, the same look he had seen on young Wilson when he'd first met him.

The handkerchief seemed to squirm in his grasp, as if attempting to escape. Clarke spoke from off to his left.

"I've got him sir. You can stand away."

It felt like he had a small fluttering bird in his hand. As he stood his gaze fell on Mrs. Mahoney and the children who were all bent over the dead man. He felt a sudden flash of pure rage and anger that went as quickly as it had come, then he walked calmly over to the range, used a poker to open the stove door, and threw the handkerchief in.

75

He heard a wail in his head, a man, screaming, then the door shut with a clang.

"Shouldn't that have gone back to the museum, sir?" Clarke said.

"Most definitely not," Lestrade replied.

A Day At The Circus

The traveling circus was in town, a most grand affair all the way from the south of France, its third stop on what would be a triumphant grand tour of Europe's capitals. It was the talk of polite and not so polite society, the daily business of the city forgotten for a time with the arrival of this exciting new thing in their midst. A long caravan of wagons and trailers had been snaking its way through Kent toward London for the past week and excitement had been mounting with each passing day. Now it was finally here. The whole eastern half of Hyde Park was given over to big tents, small tents, stalls and hawkers, clowns and acrobats, horse riders, exotic animals, fortune tellers, barely clothed dancers, freak shows and as many different ways of parting people from their money as could be thought of, a riot of noise and color that threatened to steal the heart of the city.

It was a fine cloudless day in early September and the citizens of London were out in their thousands to soak up the atmosphere and allow some of the color and atmosphere to rub off on them. It appeared to be working, for there was an air of jollity seldom to be found in the city this late in the summer. Inspector Lestrade watched over it with a jaundiced eye. He did not share in that sense of good-nature and frivolity. For him the circus meant just one thing ... a massive headache that had begun before the first tent went up and, he knew from past experience, would not fade until the last tent came down and they were all packed off safely back across the Channel. It wasn't the color, or even the noise he objected to; it was the associated villainy.

Pickpockets the force could handle, given enough manpower to throw at the problem, but the tents had brought with them a horde of enterprising thieves, muggers, opium dealers and more black-eyed villains than you shake a stick at, all ready to skim off whatever takings they could from the old city's populace. The police forces were stretched so thin as to be almost useless in the more populated areas of the park and all they could do was hope to keep crime down at a level that could be managed.

"I don't want your lads going in mob-handed and breaking heads," the commissioner had said just that morning. "The people of London intend to have fun, so let's allow them some small pleasure in it while we can."

The hope that matters could be left to take their own course was dashed almost before the day got going. Lestrade was among a crowd watching a strong-man bend an iron bar in his hands when he heard the distinctive peep of a copper's whistle, then another, coming from the small village of carts and wagons to the north side of the field where the traveling circus had made their encampment. He had to push his way through a crowd who seemed intent on treating the copper's whistle like a call to arms and were surging as one in the direction of the ever more frantic sound.

Lestrade arrived at the spot to find his sergeant bent over a body while three other beat coppers tried their best to keep the growing, baying, crowd at bay.

"What have we got, Clarkie?"

"A bad one, sir. Something's been at him."

The man who lay spreadeagled in almost the center of a bare patch between four wagons was barely clothed to Lesrtrade's eyes, wearing only a tight pair of briefs over some kind of silk stockings, and a small sleeveless vest that barely covered the graying hair on his chest. That was all secondary to the fact that he'd been ripped open from crotch to sternum, pink guts strewn around the torso, glistening like raw sausages. A pool of blood below him was already soaking into the summer-dried soil below. The evisceration did not look to be the killing blow; to Lestrade's eye the fatal wound must have been the large hole under his chin where his throat had been torn out. His head lay in a secondary pool of blood.

Lestrade wasn't allowed any further investigation. Somebody grabbed hard at his shoulder, pulling him upright, and he was turned around to face a tall, thin chap with a long black coat and the most ridiculous curved-upward mustache that Lestrade had ever seen. He wore face powder that made him look as pale as a cadaver, the only color the bright red lips and the piercing blue of his eyes. Lestrde saw that the man was preparing for an outburst, and preempted it with one of his own.

"And who the blazes are you, sir?" Lestrade said, letting some of his anger and frustration show, enough that the man took a slight step back and visibly calmed himself before answering in a measured tone.

"I am Pierre Monetre," the man said. His French accent was almost as ridiculous as his mustache and Lestrade doubted very much that either were real. "I am the creator, owner and ringmaster of this circus. I demand to know what has happened here. I was promised a discreet police presence."

Lestrade took a step to one side to allow the man a look at the body.

"Discretion is my middle name, sir. I presume this is one of yours, given the get-up?"

The man's bluster vanished as quickly as what little color there was drained from his face and set his lips gray.

"Dear God, it's Thibeaux, my trapeze master. I am ruined."

"Not as much as he is, sir." Lestrade took the man's arm and turned him aside, forcing him to look away from the body; he needed some things done, and he needed them done quickly, and Providence had brought him just the right man for the job.

"First things first. I need you to take inventory of your animals," Lestrade said. "I've seen those big cats you have in the cages by the big tent, and now you've seen the body. Was it one of them, do you think? Could they do this to a man? Or perhaps that dancing bear you have?"

Monetre was still trying to catch a glimpse of the body over Lestrade's shoulder.

"One of our beasts? Impossible." he said.

"Having seen the state of the body, I doubt that very much, sir, but in any case we cannot rule it out on your say-so alone. You must get your animals checked. If there's one missing and running free around this park, we're all in big trouble and you can forget any pretense at discretion. But if none of your beasts are missing, I will need to talk to the animal handlers, for it is not beyond the bounds of possibility that a beast may have been trained for such an attack and is even now back in its cage chewing on a tasty reward for its work. One way or the other, I need you to check. And I need you to check right now."

"But Thibeaux ..."

"Is not going anywhere. Please, sir ... the animals? Or shall I endeavor to become indiscreet? I can have fifty more coppers here in five minutes if you'd prefer?"

Monetre took a last look at the body, pursed his lips and nodded before turning quickly on his heel and heading off, pushing his way angrily through the crowd that was now four or five deep in a circle around the corpse.

Lestrade watched go, realizing that it hadn't taken him long to make an enemy of the man, although his gut told him that Monetre was the kind to have more of them than friends. He put it to the back of his mind; he had work to do.

"Right,' Lestrade said, turning back to the body, "Clarkie, get this mob cleared. We need space to work here."

Clearing the mob proved easier said than done. Clarke and the coppers had to use some rather less-than-gentle persuasion. But finally, some ten minutes later, the police were left, almost alone, in the space between the wagons. All that remained of the crowd were two people; a much older woman in a long cloak and hood that concealed her features and a younger woman, little older than a child, who had been weeping profusely and wasn't quite finished with it yet, her head pressed tight to the old one's shoulder.

"Who do we have here, Clarkie?" Lestrade asked.

"The dead man's mother and his daughter, sir."

Lestrade knew just by looking at them that interviewing them right now wasn't going to yield much of anything; the young one was too distraught, and the old one looked more like a block of old wood, and just about as ready as one to speak.

"Make sure they don't go anywhere. I'll need to talk to them. But first get this body shifted to our morgue and get the coroner to give it the once-over, see if we can get a clue as to what kind of beast might have made this mess."

"Yes, sir. Where will I find you?"

"Probably with that circus-master chap. I'm going to try to get this place shut down. He's not going to like it."

Lestrade got directions from a roustabout and two minutes later stood on the steps of the largest, most ornate wagon in the caravan. He had plenty of time to admire the intricate carvings and gaudily painted woodwork, as the occupant took his time answering Lestrade's knock. He found out why when he climbed up into the cabin; his heart sank to see the Police Commissioner sitting there alongside the man he had come to see, both men looking comfortable with a cigar and a glass of brandy. The circus master obviously knew which wheels to oil and had wasted no time in getting to it.

"I know what you are going to say, Lestrade," the commissioner said, preempting any discussion, "and the answer is no. If we close this place down, we'll have a riot on our hands. Too many tickets for the show tonight have been sold already, too many people are looking forward to it. On the grounds of public safety alone, I agree with Monsieur Monetre here. The show must go on."

Lestrade knew better than to even start to argue; once a decision like that is made, it's a copper's job to abide by it, if he wants to stay a copper. So he bit his lip, and shifted to his second line of attack. He addressed Monetre.

"Did you see your people about the animals?"

"Certainly," the circus master said. He looked like the cat who had got the cream. Lestrade still suspected he had more enemies than friends, but when just one of those friends was the Police Commissioner, one was enough. "They are all exactly where they are supposed to be, and none have been out of their pens or cages all day."

"And you trust your handler?"

"I should. He's my brother."

Lestrade was about to push harder when the commissioner spoke again.

"You heard the man, Lestrade," he said. "It is my belief you should be looking for a wild dog of some kind. Best get to it before it does any more damage, eh? There's a good chap."

And with that Lestrade was dismissed. Biting back a sharp remark that would only earn him a suspension, at best, he left them to their brandy and made his way back to the crime scene. He'd been in a bad enough mood at the start of the day; now he was about ready to blow his top.

Clarke had the body in the back of one of the force's wagons and was just sending it off to the morgue when Lestrade returned. There was no sign of the two women he'd seen earlier.

"What have you done with the family?" Lestrade said. Clarke must have taken appraisal of the inspector's mood, for he kept his voice low and calm when replying. He pointed to the left-hand wagon.

"They're in there, sir. The young one wouldn't settle, so I let the old lady take her away for a cup of tea, or maybe something a bit stronger. Any joy with that Monetre fellow?"

"No joy at all," Lestrade said. "But I didn't get my jotters either, so let's look on the bright side. I don't suppose you've dug up any witnesses?"

"No one heard or saw a thing, sir, at least that's what they say. They're a close-knit bunch these circus folk."

"As bad as the bloody Masons. Let's go and hear what the womenfolk have to say; maybe they'll be more forthcoming."

The wagon Clarke pointed out was far less salubrious than that of Monetre, but what it lacked in style it made up for in comfort, being almost totally lined inside in a wide variety of colorful carpets, rugs, drapes and assorted wall hangings. The old lady beckoned Lestrade forward when he stepped up to the wagon's rear entrance and ushered him inside.

The younger woman was asleep on a long bed that took up most of that side of the interior. The old lady put a finger to her lips and led Lestrade through and out the far end to sit up on the driving seat over the front axle. The horses had been unhooked and were grazing a few yards further north. She motioned for him to sit by her side and surprised him by producing an ornate silver hip flask from the folds of her clothes.

"Better than the maneater's brandy, that I can guarantee," she said, and cackled. She had let her hood slip backward to reveal that she was even older than

Lestrade had imagined; her leathery skin was etched in
a profusion of fine lines but when she smiled her eyes
sparkled and showed the girl she had been. She passed
him the hip-flask and Lestrade took a sip, then another;
he didn't know what Monetre's brandy was like, hadn't
been offered any, but this stuff was smooth and warm
and made his insides glow. He handed it back before he
was tempted to take more.

"I am sorry about your boy," he said.

"I'm not," she replied baldly and took a long swig from
the flask before continuing. "He got what he deserved; he
was a brute of a man."

Her accent wasn't French but had Lestrade baffled;
there were bits that might be Germanic, bits that might
be Italian, and other places where she sounded almost
Far-Eastern. He understood her well enough though. And
she seemed in the mood for talk, so he rolled a cigarette,
then another when she took the first from him. He lit
them both up from a lucifer and let her speak.

"He never treated her like a daughter, at least not since
she was a babe; she was more in the line of his servant,
and he didn't take kindly to her developing a mind of her
own. On your way out, have a look at her arms," she said.
"There are bruises there going back years. All his doing.
I won't waste a wink of sleep on him. He got what was
coming to him, and about time too."

"The girl has found herself a protector, is that what
you're telling me?"

"A protector? Yes, that is a fine word for it. It has not
been with her long, but you have deduced the truth of it.
There is a story, should you wish to hear it?"

"Is it pertinent?"

"You will need to be the judge of that."

Before he could reply she passed him the hip flask
again, and while he took another sip of the nectar she
began to speak, in the sing-song manner of a practiced
storyteller.

"The circus has always been on the road, I am a daughter of the circus; not always this one, but always on the road. But there are roads, and there are roads; some are dark, some are light. We had only been in your country for a day, coming up through Kent from the Channel, when I knew that the road we were on was even darker than most and I resolved to keep a close eye on matters, for I knew things were coming to a head for the girl. It wasn't anything a man would notice, but I had been a girl myself once, and knew the signs; the turn of the head, the flash of the eyes, the swing of the hips. The lass was in love, and that did not bode well for her.

"We made camp for the night in a field bounded by an ancient woodland, one full of stories and ancient presences. I felt the old ones' eyes watching my little Verka. Other eyes followed her too, and we all saw Janos, a boy who wanted to be a man, take my Verka, a girl who wanted to be a woman, into the woods that night.

"But their young love was to be disturbed, for Gorges, my son, also had eyes that saw too much. He saw them, I saw him, and all four of us made our way into the woods one after the other after the others. I hurried along at the rear, fearful as to what the man might do to the boy, and when Verka screamed somewhere in the night ahead of me I ran faster still, black branches whipping at my face, tangled roots trying to trip me at every step, with no thought other than for the safety of the girl.

"I came to them in a clearing. Gorges had Verka by the arms and was shaking the girl so violently that I thought her head might come loose from her neck. The lad was on the ground below a large oak. He had blood in his hair from a wound that I guess happened when Gorges threw him into the tree. Gorges was ranting at Verka, Verka was screaming, and Janos was shouting into the dark night of the woods, pleading for someone, something, anything to help him, raving about offering up his soul if that was what was needed in payment for aid.

"I arrived just in time to see help come.

85

... growing more solid as moonlight and starlight gave it form ...

"Something moved in the darkness under the canopy; I heard it before I saw it, a low growl and a sniff, testing the air. Janos was looking directly at it when a great black hound, shaggy-coated and almost bearlike in heft and girth, came loping out of the shadows, growing more solid as moonlight and starlight gave it form until it stood there, looming over Janos, staring into his soul with eyes as red as hot coals. Janos did not speak, the dog did not make a sound, yet it seemed that an understanding passed between them at that moment. Janos rose to his feet, reached out a hand. I cannot rightly say what happened for a cloud covered the moon in the same instant, but it was as if a black cape swirled around the boy, fluttering like a dove. When the cloud moved on and the moon returned the black dog was gone, but when the lad looked across the clearing at Gorges I saw the same red glow again, deep in the sockets of his eyes.

"Janos took a step forward, his gaze fixed on Gorges and Verka. A low growl escaped him, a sound I have never heard before from a human throat

"Gorges let out a yelp I had not heard the like of, not since he was a boy. He let go of Verka and ran past me, heading for the caravan; I do not think he even registered my presence in his haste to be somewhere, anywhere else. Verka stumbled, nearly fell, and Janos was at her side immediately. When his eyes looked into hers they were once again those of the boy, leaving me wondering if I had truly seen what I thought I had seen.

"I heard Gorges tramping around in the dark somewhere behind me, unheeding of noise in his flight. As for me, I stayed just long enough to ensure that it was a lad who embraced my Verka and not a great dog, then I too took my leave, leaving young love to matters of young love."

She took a long slug from the hip flask, and Lestrade realized that the tale was done. It had left him with more questions than answers.

"The lad, Janos, killed Gorges today? Is that what you are telling me?"

"No, you misunderstand me. I am saying the lad did not kill Gorges. Something else did."

Lestrade almost laughed. "A dark spirit of the trees? Black Shuck come out of the old tales and into the modern world? I am not one to be taken in so readily, madam."

"And yet you took the time to listen. That is all I asked for, and my story is done. What happens next is up to you."

With that she got down off the seat and clambered back into the cabin of the wagon, her swift and easy movements belying her age. Lestrade followed behind somewhat more slowly. He paused as he passed the sleeping girl to note that her arms were mottled with the traces of many old bruises; then he was almost pushed out the back end into the afternoon sunshine.

He turned to address the old lady before she could shut the door on him. "I will need to talk to both of them,' he said.

"Yes, you will," she replied, and then a solid door slammed shut in his face.

At least the lad was not hard to find. If Janos had committed a brutal murder only an hour or so previously he showed no sign of it having affected him in any way. Lestrade found him in a small tent to the rear of the main one, sitting in front of a large mirror, applying a clown's make-up.

"Janos?" Lestrade asked, almost sure that he had been sent to the wrong youth, for the lad was open-faced and clear-eyed, almost cheerful in fact.

"Yes, I am Janos. What can I do for you, sir?"

This one's accent was definitely Eastern European; Lestrade had him pegged for Polish.

"I need to talk about what happened today with Gorges Thibeaux."

"I was not there."

Lestrade heard no deception in his voice and the lad held his gaze as he spoke.

"But you do not deny that you were not on friendly terms with the man?"

"He did not like me seeing Verka, that is true. But I did not kill him. How could I? He was a big strong man, and as you can see I am but a slip of a boy."

Looking at the slim stature of the lad and having seen the brutality of the attack and the strength it must have taken, Lestrade could see his point

Lestrade decided to play a hunch, see if he could disturb this puzzling calm demeanor.

"And what about that night in the woods in Kent?"

A cloud seemed to pass across the lad's gaze.

"Verka told you about that?"

"Not Verka, no."

"The grandmother then? Did she also tell you what they did to Verka when she got back to her wagon that night? Did she tell you how Gorges shared his only daughter around the trapeze troupe? Did she tell you what they did to her, taking turns to ravish her?"

The lad's calmness had gone and there was now a fierce rage in him; Lestrade was now looking at someone he could believe to be a killer.

The lad stood suddenly, knocking his chair over. "I did not kill him," he said, almost shouting now. "But I wish to God I had."

Lestrade put out a hand, meaning to try to calm the lad. Janos swiveled on his heel, looking Lestrade in the eye. Deep down, seemingly sunk in his eye sockets, red coals flared as if stoked by bellows.

The lad growled, a rumble from somewhere deep in his chest, and bared teeth that suddenly looked too big for his mouth.

The sight so discombobulated Lestrade that he stepped back. The lad took advantage of that, pushed past and was away out of the tent before Lestrade recovered.

Lestrade followed to the tent opening and looked out. The youth was already lost in the crowd.

The remainder of the afternoon and early evening was to prove frustrating for Lestrade. Despite having men out all over the site they could find no trace of the youth. Monetre proved to be no help at all, declaring himself too busy with preparing for the big show to be bothering with 'the love lives of minor members of the traveling contingent.'

The coroner's report did not help Lestrade's mood any. The verdict was 'an attack by a large member of the Canis family' which might be factually correct but was totally useless in the current situation.

An attempt to change tack also got him nowhere; he returned to the old woman's caravan hoping to question the younger one.

The old lady let him in.

"Are ye back for more brandy so soon, Inspector?" she said.

Lestrade pushed her aside and looked to the bed. The girl was still there but now she wasn't just asleep, she appeared to be under the influence of an unknown sedative, in a slumber so sound he doubted she would be awakened by anything short of a bomb going off in her ear.

"I told you I needed to talk to her," Lestrade said.

The old woman was unrepentant. "She needs some rest. We all do. Have ye nothing better to do with your time? Do ye not have a murderer to catch?"

"I might have him by now if you'd only tell me the truth," he said, but she was already ushering him back to the door with a determination and strength that belied her age.

Lestrade got the caravan door closed in his face again for his trouble.

By the time night fell and even larger crowds gathered for the show in the big tent, Lestrade was in a foul mood indeed. He went this way and that among the stalls with the flow of the crowd, always with an eye open for sight of the missing youth.

The great and good were out in force: he spotted the commissioner again, with his wife this time and deep in rapt conversation with Monetre; he also spotted half a dozen members of parliament, three famous cricketers and the whole cast of one of the current West End stage hits. There was also the usual bevy of accompanying hangers-on and reporters and ordinary people hoping that some of the glamor might rub off on them. And everywhere you looked the circus people were raking in money from selling baubles, running three-card tricks, telling fortunes or showing off more flesh than was decent … that last always being extremely popular.

Just before seven o'clock, Monetre, having finally finished glad-handing the commissioner, moved to the entrance of the big tent and began the job of filling it up with paying customers.

"Come one, come all; welcome to the greatest show on Earth."

Lestrade tuned him out, immune to the man's silver-tongued pitch. He had no intention of shelling out good money just for the privilege of doing his job, so made his way round the back to the cluster of smaller tents where the performers were getting themselves ready for the show. He returned to the place he'd seen the youth earlier, hoping to catch him there again, but the clowns there preparing their faces were all heavier-set older men.

He passed on through to the next tent and found himself among the trapeze artists. One might have thought that this part of the show might have been canceled out of respect for the dead man, but the scantily clad men here were all joking and laughing and seemed none the worse off for their loss.

"Do you not have any common decency?" Lestrade asked, louder than he might have liked. All he got in return was a succession of sullen gazes before they turned away from him and were soon once again laughing and joking.

Slightly disgusted with their attitude, Lestrade left them to it and headed for the main tent, intending to get into the show through the back entrance, and woe betide anyone who got in his way.

It wasn't any of the circus people who stopped him; it was his sergeant, and Lestrade knew immediately by the look on Clarke's face that it was trouble he didn't need.

"We've got another one, sir. Same as before. Just a bit fresher, if you catch my drift."

"Where?" Lestrade asked, envisaging the panic that might ensue if the crowd in the big tent was to see the results of the bloody mayhem.

"Luckily it's in a dark spot, between two of those wagons," Clarke said

"Any idea who it is?"

"We got a positive identification from one of the roustabouts. It's another of them acrobat lads. Close friend of Thibeaux is what he said."

Lestrade was already moving, heading for the tents, not to see the body but to corner the trapeze troupe. He had too many questions now; it was high time he got some straight answers.

The tent was empty; the acrobats had already moved into the main arena. Lestrade headed there at a run, Clarke at his heels. A young woman in a blowsy chiffon dress tried to block their way at the entrance.

"Scotland Yard, official business," Lestrade barked. "Get out of my way or I'll have you arrested."

She got out of the way, and Lestrade arrived in the main arena just in time to see three men shimmy expertly up hanging ropes, climbing into the high reaches of the great tent's dome.

"We need to get them down from there," he said. "I've got a bad feeling about this."

"Surely there won't be any trouble in here, with all these people watching, sir?" Clarke said at his back. Lestrade was about to answer, then saw that the trouble was already here. The clowns were cavorting on the floor of the arena, parodying the stylistic moves of the acrobats above.

All, that is, except one of them. His face was mostly pure white, only red around the mouth and eyes, and Lestrade recognized him more from his build than anything else, but it was definitely the lad, Janos. He was staring upward at the acrobats, a murderous look in his eyes.

The audience's eyes were either on the acrobats or the tumbling clowns in the ring; Lestrade might have been the only person watching Janos, the only one to see his red-rimmed eyes flare even redder, to see the wispy curl of gray-black mist oozing out of him, rising up and away to the top of the dome. He saw a flickering shadow that appeared tp be moving on all fours traversing the rigging that held the tent up, heading directly for the three acrobats.

The crowd oohed and aahed as two of the acrobats caught the other after he had tumbled twice above only empty air and a long drop.

The screaming began seconds later.

Lestrade had been trying to watch closely but all he saw was shifting shadows, a black mist quickly tinged red. One of the acrobats screamed and tumbled, no one to catch him this time, head over heels, a double roll before he hit the floor of the ring with a sickening thud.

The screaming did not stop; something up there was ripping through the two men and their pain echoed around a suddenly silent crowd. The tension broke when a second man fell tumbling, a mass of bloody pulp, to land in a bloody splash near his companion.

That was the cue for pandemonium. The crowd broke from their seats in a panic and in seconds a crushing, struggling, rolling maul was gathered around the main exit. Others tried to crawl under the tent flaps only to be borne down by the weight of canvas while some of the smarter ones headed past Lestrade, making for the rear entrance.

While all this mayhem was going on around him, the youth stood near the edge of the main circle, staring upward at the top of the dome. The last of the acrobats was still up there but he was clearly already dead, the white bones of his ribs showing where they'd been splayed open to show his innards. The black mist coalesced, two eyes blazed red, then it floated down, softly, like fine rain, landing on the youth and, as if he had breathed it in, being taken inside until there was nothing to see of it but a flicker of red in his eyes. Seconds later that too was gone, leaving only a confused lad, the two policemen and three dead acrobats under the dome of the tent.

It took all night for Lestrade to get the situation under control but at least the commissioner couldn't haul him over the coals for the fiasco; the deaths had been seen by everyone—and understood by no one. One thing was clear: the youth, Janos had been on the ground the whole time so could not be held responsible in any way. The commissioner even went as far as to order Lestrade to steer clear of that line of inquiry. Lestrade expected that Monetre was behind that decision, but wherever it came from it was fine by him.

He tried to track down the old lady and the granddaughter, but was unable to find either of them, nor anyone willing to even acknowledge their existence.

The last Lestrade saw of them was as the circus broke up. The tents came down, the wagons were loaded and they all began to trundle away south in a long caravan. The old lady's wagon came past where Lestrade stood. They were near the end of the line. She sat up holding the reins, geeing the horses on. The two young lovers sat next to her, huddled close. Janos had an arm around the girl's shoulders and a smile on his face.

As for Lestrade, he would only be happy when he knew that the circus had left London and was on its way back across the channel.

He had a long look in the lad's eyes as the wagon passed him.

He saw only love in them.

An Encounter in the Morgue

When Sergeant Clarke told Lestrade that his presence was expected in the morgue, the last person the inspector expected to see crouched over a body on the slab was Doctor John Watson, but there he was, studying the corpse and deep in conversation with the coroner.

The coroner looked up at Lestrade's approach.

"I've asked John to come in and have a look at this," Carruthers said. "I needed a second opinion before talking to you."

As he approached the slab Lestrade saw it was an elderly gray-haired woman with fine features, good teeth, and skin, on her face at least, that looked to have been well looked after; this was no streetwalker, that was certain.

"Suspicious death?" he asked.

"Very," Watson replied. He came over to shake Lestrade's hand, then led him to the body. "Look for yourself."

As Lestrade moved closer to the body the gaslight above flickered wildly as if a strong breeze had blown through, then stilled and grew back to a regular flame. The Y-shaped incision on the woman's torso had already been made and her skin peeled back. Her ribs were cracked open at the sternum and splayed back to expose the heart and lungs. Lestrade immediately saw the doctors' problem; he himself was no expert, but even he knew that internal organs should not look as if they had been burned from the inside out.

"What could do that?" he asked.

"That's what we were just considering," Watson replied. "Some kind of strong acid is our best guess. There's evidence of burning in her gullet too, but none in her mouth or on her tongue. I'd say someone put a tube down her throat then slowly poured the acid in. Carruthers and I are in agreement: she was alive when it was done to her. She wouldn't have stayed that way for long, but the short time she had would have been excruciating in the extreme."

"Where was she found?"

"That's the damnable thing, Lestrade," Carruthers said. "She was here on the slab when I came in this morning and nobody seems to know who brought her in. Or who she is for that matter."

"Someone on the night shift perhaps?"

"If it was, there's no entry on the desk sergeant's log, no paperwork of any kind. And for another thing ... I'm sure I locked the door when I left last night, and it was still locked when I came in this morning. The desk sergeant has the other key, and he says no one asked for it all night.

"Well she didn't walk in under her own steam," Lestrade said. "Leave it to me. I'll get to the bottom of it."

When Lestrade left the morgue Watson was bent over the dead woman, looking most intently at something in her mouth, Lestrade left them to it; he had a mystery to solve.

He thought it must purely be an administrative error, some slackness from an inexperienced copper perhaps.

But after a couple of hours of questioning the desk sergeant, the janitorial staff, and even having Clarke rustle up some of the night shift, he was none the wiser as to how the body had arrived where it did. He was not in the best of moods when a knock came on his office door and he looked up to see Watson there.

"I thought you were long gone, Watson," he said. "A mystery woman and a suspicious death? Right up Holmes' street, I would have thought."

Watson shook his head. "Holmes is not in the city at the moment and I have no desire to interfere with the Yard's business."

"I don't see why not? It's not like it's ever stopped you before."

Watson had the good grace to look sheepish. Lestrade waved him into the office and they lit up smokes before Watson spoke.

"I may have a clue as to the identity of the victim," he said.

Lestrade waved for him to continue.

"You may have seen me examining the woman's teeth," Watson said. "Her dental work is of the highest quality. A good dentist is an artist, in a way. And like every artist, his work can be distinguished as readily as if he has left a signature there."

"You have been around Holmes too long, doctor," Lestrade said.

"Perhaps so, Lestrade. But I have also learned that his methods work more often than not. And in this case, they have worked a treat."

"You found her dentist?"

Watson smiled. "Found him, talked to him, got the woman's name and address," he said.

"What was that about not interfering in the Yard's business?"

"I prefer to call it professional curiosity," Watson replied.

"I'm sure you do. Well, out with it, man, who was she?"

"Mrs. Margaret Courtby, widow. Husband was something big in the city, died two years ago. The house is on a terrace in Belgravia."

"And you've been to the house I suppose?"

"No. I thought I might accompany you there, if you'll allow me?"

"Just don't tell the commissioner."

The house was a handsome two-story affair in the middle of a crescent, but unlike the others none of the drapes had been pulled open to allow in the sun. The front door was closed, but not locked, and when Lestrade and Watson ventured inside there was no sign of any servants, which was unusual in itself.

There was also no sign of any disturbance in the downstairs parlor nor in the kitchen and servants' quarters at the rear of the property, but they found their crime scene in a library on the first floor.

Lestrade surmised that this must have been the dead husband's study at one time; there was a masculine look to the decor, all dark wood and leather that wouldn't have been out of place in a gentleman's club. What was out of place were many of the books, which were tumbled on the floor instead of being on the shelves. The object of the obvious search was clear to see; a heavy safe, lying open, that was mounted into the wall behind one of the bookcases. Inside was a velvet-covered case lying open, the silk bed indented where jewelry had once lain.

Watson pointed out the jeweler's shop name, embossed in the upper lid of the case. "We can find out what was stolen from them," he said.

Lestrade nodded grimly. "And now we know why it was acid that was used," he said.

"We do?"

"Yes. It's not only Holmes who has his methods. Look at this lock; it's been eaten away. Professional lads pour acid into the keyholes and five minutes later Bob's your uncle. The widow must have disturbed them on the job."

"It still doesn't tell us how the body got into the morgue, though, does it?"

"One step at a time, doctor. We don't all work in intuitive leaps like you're used to. First thing is to find out where the servants have gone to and why they're not here. Then we'll chase the jewelers, find out what's been stolen. After that we can start tracking the stolen item through the underworld. Lists and method. That's the job."

As it turned out, Lestrade never got a chance to start on his list. They had just emerged back out into the street when Sergeant Clarke arrived in a carriage.

"You're needed back at the Yard, sir. There's a bit of a flap in the morgue."

"What kind of flap?"

"I can't rightly explain it, sir," Clarke replied. "Best if you see it for yourself."

"I'd better be off then. Clarkie, see if you can find out what happened to the house's servants. They're nowhere to be found."

"I'll take the jeweler's if that's all right by you, old chap?" Watson said. "It might save some time."

Lestrade nodded, and seconds later had climbed up into the carriage and was clattering away back to the Yard.

They arrived at the morgue to find the coroner, Carruthers and three young constables standing in the hall outside the door. One of the constables looked about ready to turn tail and flee if you said 'boo' to him.

"All right then, let's be having it. What's going on here?" Lestrade said.

"It's your corpse, Lestrade," Carruthers said. "If it is a corpse."

"Of course it's a bloody corpse," Lestrade said. "You've got her opened up ready to be gutted like a fish."

"That's what I thought too," Carruthers replied. "But she doesn't seem to agree with us."

"What in blazes does that mean?"

99

Carruthers didn't reply, merely stood to one side and motioned toward the door, indicating that Lestrade should see for himself.

"I don't have time for this nonsense," Lestrade said, stepped forward, opened the door, and found out that maybe he'd better make time.

She was sitting up, legs hanging over the side of the trestle, the flaps of skin of the Y incision hanging open. Above her the gas lantern flared and flickered as if in a breeze. She looked dead ... but dead people don't stroke at their neck with both hands, as if searching for something that wasn't there. She showed no sign of taking any notice of Lestrade's presence. Lestrade stood, dumbfounded, watching her for a minute before turning back out into the hallway. He closed the door quietly at behind him.

"That's not possible," he said, more to himself than to the others.

"That's what I said." Carruthers replied. "What are you going to do about it?"

"Me? It's your morgue."

"And your case."

"I'm open to suggestions."

"Take her down to the furnace and burn her?" the young, green at the gills constable said.

"Might not be a bad idea, lad," Lestrade said. "But I don't think the Commissioner would take too kindly to us losing a murder victim."

"So what's to be done?" Carruthers said. "I've got a caseload of my own, you know?"

"Set up in the cold store for now," Lestrade said. "Leave her in there to do her thing until we know more."

"And when might that be?"

Lestrade had no answer for that.

He escaped to the relative sanity of his office and a much-needed cigarette. Watson arrived again as he was lighting up. Lestrade sent him downstairs rather than try to explain the situation, and when Watson returned Lestrade had a cigarette and a cup of strong tea waiting for him.

"I've never seen anything like it," Lestrade said.

"I have," Watson said softly in a tone that startled Lestrade as the doctor continued. "We were in Afghanistan, pinned down by rebel forces in the hills and in a dashed tight spot. I was standing beside Jock Brown when he took two bullets in the forehead, right between the eyes. I was spattered with bits of his skull and brain tissue so I knew immediately he was a goner. But Jock wouldn't stand for being killed. He climbed up out of our hiding spot, half his head gone, raised his bayonet into charging position, and ran straight at the rebel position, bullets flying around him, Jock screaming like a banshee.

"The rebels fled as soon as they got a good look at him. We advanced, and I found Jock sitting under a tree having a smoke, what was left of his brains showing through a hole in his skull I could have put both my fists in. He looked up at me, smiled and said 'Hello, John. Good day for it.'

"And then he decided he'd let himself die."

Lestrade saw the truth of it in Watson's eyes which had slowly brimmed with tears as he spoke.

"And you think what we have here is the same kind of thing? Her will controlling her body? What could she be hanging on for?"

"I think I might have an answer for that too," Watson said. "I went round to that jeweler's shop, and got a story from him. It seems the lady's husband bought her a very grand diamond necklace for their thirtieth wedding anniversary ... and two days later he was dead, his heart having given out."

"And you think that's what's holding her here?"

Watson nodded. "I had another thought too, but you're not going to like it."

"'There's already a lot about this I don't like, so let's be having it."

"It came to me when I saw her sitting there, stroking at her neck. She's lost her link to her husband. And she's brought herself to the place where she might find someone to help her get it back. You said earlier she didn't walk here under her own steam? I think that's exactly what she did."

Watson had got a good description of the necklace from the jeweler. Rather than the pair of them sitting, brooding, and thinking about the not-quite-dead woman in the morgue, Lestrade took the doctor along on a tour of pawnbrokers and known fences. He already had a team, led by Sergeant Clarke, who had drawn a blank on the servants' whereabouts, going round the more probable suspects. Lestrade concentrated on some of the fringe establishments, ones he thought to be involved in criminal enterprises, but could not prove for sure. He had a carriage take them to Holborn and drop them off outside the Princess Louise. He'd been in the establishment several times, but not in the past year. The pub had been undergoing a total makeover, a costly one, and rumors were that the money for the job was coming from numerous under-the-counter operations.

When he got inside he had to admit it had been money well spent. The island bar gleamed with polished brass, expansive mirrors, high gaslit chandeliers and enough mahogany paneling to build a small boat, and both walls and floor were bedecked in ornate mosaic tiling in brilliant colors. He ordered a pint of bitter for each of them from the barman and they went to sit in a quiet booth at the back from where they could watch without being noticed.

Over the beer and a couple of smokes they talked, not of death, but of better times, old cases that had come with some small comical aspects; Watson talked of some of Holmes' more unusual eccentricities and Lestrade chimed in with details of some drunken misdemeanors in the Commissioner's youth that he wouldn't like being made public now he was 'a man of influence.' All in all it was a most pleasant way to pass half an hour. Lestrade was brought back to the job at hand when he saw a face he knew.

Lestrade turned away, hoping not to be recognized, but Watson was in plain view, and the newcomer knew them both. A few seconds later a big man joined them at their table, carrying three pints of bitter. Shinwell 'Porky' Johnson was a lumbering chap with a bullet head, a chest as wide as a bear's, but remarkably light on his feet, carrying himself like a prize fighter.

"Well met, Doctor," he said to Watson as he put the beers on the table. He only acknowledged Lestrade with a nod; a former criminal's grudging respect for the man who'd put him away, not once but twice. Johnson had gone straight since his last spell inside some three years ago, and Lestrade knew that the big man had helped Holmes out on occasion over that time, but Lestrade retained an old copper's cynicism and couldn't quite bring himself to trust the man. Johnson knew this, of course, but it didn't seem to be affecting his mood any; he'd had a nice win on the ponies and was feeling lavish with his temporary good fortune. He went so far as to offer Watson and Lestrade a slap-up meal at the pie and ale place round the corner, but Watson declined for both of them.

"On a job are we, gents?" Johnson asked. "Well, give me the gen, maybe it's something old Shinwell here can help you with, if you catch my drift." He rubbed his fingers together and Lestrade sighed. He knew from long experience how poor the information given out by narks in pubs tended to be. But Watson was already outlining their case to the big man, only neglecting the bits about the woman being not quite fully dead.

Johnson looked thoughtful.

"I did hear tell this morning about a bit of shiny being on the market," he said. "Do you want me to ask around?"

Lestrade was about to say no, then thought better of it. Johnson left with hopes of a small reward in his head, and Lestrade and Watson visited several of the jewelers in Hatton Garden, the center of the city's diamond trade. They bumped into Sergeant Clarke outside one of them.

"Any joy, Clarkie?"

"Nothing yet, sir. Just rumors and tall stories. Most of the shopkeepers here know there's something on the market, but they don't know who's selling, and I suspect, what with us showing up mob-handed like, it's now too hot for them to handle."

"Keep at it then, lad," Lestrade said. "I'll be back at the Yard trying to figure out what to do about the morgue situation if you need me."

Watson took his leave when their return carriage reached Leicester Square.

"I've got a clinic this evening. Would you mind if I check in later? I'd like to keep an eye on progress, if you don't mind?"

"The more calm heads on this the better," Lestrade answered.

The morgue situation had not changed much in Lestrade's absence, if anything it had deteriorated. He arrived downstairs to find a queue of constables in the hallway before the morgue door; they were taking turns to see 'the show.'

"Maybe I should be charging an admission fee," Lestrade said dryly from behind them and had to stifle a laugh at the scurrying, embarrassed flight of coppers who suddenly had somewhere else to be.

He took a look inside. She was still sitting on the edge of the trestle, legs dangling, hands searching at her neck. The gaslight overhead flickered alarmingly, sending dark shadows dancing in her eye sockets and giving her an even more deathly appearance, but Lestrade saw now there was more to be pitied than to be feared here.

"I'll fetch it back to you, don't you worry," he whispered into the dark.

The gaslight flickered in reply as he closed the door quietly behind him.

He made his way upstairs, and was not surprised to find the Commissioner waiting for him in his office. Lestrade stood in front of his own desk while his superior berated him six ways till Sunday, waving the coroner's report in Lestrade's face.

"What does this mean, 'the corpse still shows signs of life.'? Either it's a corpse or it isn't, so which is it?"

Lestrade wasn't given time to answer, which was something to be thankful for at least, for the truth was likely to send the Commissioner into apoplexy in his current state of mind.

"It's all over the Yard. And if it reaches the papers, we'll be a bloody laughingstock from now until Christmas. Get it sorted. Get it sorted now, or I'll have you back on the beat on permanent night shift."

After the Commissioner left Lestrade drowned his sorrows with sweet tea and smokes, trying to come up with a plan that might placate the brass upstairs. He was getting nowhere fast when Clarke arrived with news from Watson.

"Shinwell's on to something. Meet me at the house in Belgravia as soon as possible. Bring a weapon."

Twenty minutes later a carriage deposited Lestrade and Sergeant Clarke outside the victim's house. Watson, with Shinwell Johnson at his side, stood on the porch steps.

"So why are we here, doctor?" Lestrade asked.

Johnson answered. "A little birdie told me that this was an inside job," he said. "So I asked around about the cook and the manservant. Turns out I've met them before, or him at least, last time I was inside. Geordie Duncan's the name, a mouthy git from Glasgow."

"That proves nowt," Lestrade said.

"Ah, but here's the thing. He was in for safecracking but he'd done time before for GBH. And the cook, his missus, was doing time in Holloway as his accomplice."

"And they're in the house?"

Watson answered this time. "No, they don't stay on

the premises. They've got a flat above the Star Tavern."

Johnson butted in. "My wee birdie also told me they're holed up there, waiting for things to blow over. Your lads asking around about the necklace has got them right rattled."

"Well, let's go and rattle them a bit more, shall we," Lestrade said.

"Do you want me along, Inspector?" Johnson asked. "I can be handy if it comes to fisticuffs."

"Just don't hit anybody unless I say so," Lestrade replied. "You can stand around and look ugly. You're good at that, too."

The Star Tavern was only a short walk from the house and they reached it five minutes later. Johnson pointed to a lit window.

"That's the one. Number three. There's an entrance round the back so we don't have to go through the bar."

"That little birdie of yours was very talkative," Lestrade said.

"I can be very persuasive when I want to be," Johnson replied, and showed Lestrade a fist like a lump of rock.

Lestrade took the lead round the back of the pub and up an iron staircase to a door onto a first-floor landing. The only light was coming from number three.

Lestrade drew out his service revolver and motioned to Johnson that he should take the door. The big man went through it as if it wasn't there, scattering splinters of cheap wood in his wake.

There were two people in the room beyond. A small, wiry man was reaching for a weapon when Lestrade entered.

Lestrade showed him the revolver. "I wouldn't do that, Sonny Jim," he said.

The man had the good sense to draw back his hand and the woman, after an initial shriek on their entry, was now giving Lestrade a sullen stare from under heavy brows.

"What's the meaning of this?" the man said, his Scottish accent coming through strong. Lestrade ignored him.

"Clarkie, I want this place searched, top to bottom. I'll keep an eye on these two. Watson, Porky, watch the door. If they try to do a runner and get past me, you can hit them as hard as you like."

The small man looked like he wanted to complain again, but went quiet when Johnson gave him a long hard stare. Clarke started a search of the room.

The occupants hadn't been very imaginative; Clarke found what they were looking for rolled up in an oilskin cloth tucked up under the mantelpiece. He unrolled it and the big diamond on its heavy silver chain gleamed, almost red in the gaslight. Clarke passed the necklace to Lestrade, who put it in his jacket pocket.

"Right," Lestrade said. "Job done. Clarkie, head off and get a Black Maria down here. Watson and I will keep an eye on things at this end until you get back. Porky, you'd better make yourself scarce; I don't want to have to explain you to the Commissioner."

The big man gave Lestrade a mock salute, and if he lifted something from the sideboard that looked like a wallet as he was leaving Lestrade chose not to notice, seeing it as payment for a job done.

After Johnson left nobody spoke for a while. Watson passed Lestrade a smoke, and the two suspects continued to stare sullenly at them. The fact that they were not pleading their innocence made Lestrade suspect that he had them bang to rights. He was feeling pretty satisfied with the night's work, right up until a scream scratched through the air from the street outside.

The gas lights on the walls flickered as if a stiff breeze had just blown through, and Lestrade knew what was coming as soon as he heard the first step on the iron staircase outside.

The Duncans squealed in terror and hung tightly to each other when Mrs. Courtby walked, unsteadily, into the doorway. Watson stepped aside to let her pass. The lights guttered, almost went out as she came forward, the flaps of skin at the incision in her chest waving as if in a wind, her gaze fixed on the couple.

The man reached for the gun, not caring that Lestrade still had them in his sights, his terror overriding any other fear. Before Lestrade could stop him he'd picked up the weapon and fired. It drilled a hole in the woman's abdomen but that was all it was, just a hole. There was no blood, and she didn't slow.

The Duncans both screamed again.

The undead woman had almost reached them and had stretched out her arms toward them when Lestrade spoke up.

"They don't have it," he said softly. "I do."

Mrs. Courtby turned at the sound of his voice. Lestrade took the necklace from his pocket and dangled it in his fist, the jewel hanging downward. He held it out to her. In the corner of his eye he saw Watson step forward and disarm Duncan but Lestrade didn't dare take his gaze off the woman in front of him. When she reached, slowly, for the necklace he let it fall into her hand.

She moaned from somewhere deep in her ravaged chest, reached up, again painfully slowly, and dropped the necklace over her head, the diamond coming to rest just above the Y shaped incision. She looked down at it, looked up at Lestrade, and smiled, just once.

He saw the light go out of her eyes as she fell and even without Watson checking he knew.

She was dead, fully dead this time, before she hit the floor.

There was hell to pay with the Commissioner, of course, but Lestrade had caught the murderers, the public could sleep easier in their beds, and the story of the walking dead woman, while it would pass into Yard legend, never reached the papers.

A week later Watson accompanied him to Highgate

Cemetery, and they watched the widow Courtby being laid to rest beside her husband.

"And the jewel?" Watson asked as the coffin was let down into the ground.

"It's in there with her. It cost me a few favors, seeing as how it's evidence and all," Lestrade said, "but they've got a bit of glass from Hatton Garden that'll pass for it at the trial. I couldn't let her go without it; she might decide to get up again."

The Black Temple

The last person Lestrade expected to see at his office door that fine Saturday morning was Langdale Pike. "If you've come searching for scurrilous gossip for those rags you get published in, you won't find any here," Lestrade said.

Unfortunately insults were like water off a duck's back to Pike, who daily dealt in so many they had quite lost any power they might otherwise have. He was the kind of chap Lestrade took against at first sight, a supercilious wastrel with an overblown sense of his own self-importance, an inflated ego brought about by publicity in the gutter press, most of which Pike wrote himself. He wore expensive, well-tailored clothing in a manner designed to make everyone notice it, more rings than was natural on a grown man, and he smelled— perfumed like a whore's boudoir. When he smiled, as he did now, there was no humor in it; it was just a movement of his face calculated not to offend. Even his voice grated. Lestrade knew that Pike was an East End lad born and bred, but he affected a Home Counties accent that merely sounded false to Lestrade's ears, but no doubt fooled some of the so-called celebrities in the circles in which he moved.

Pike ostentatiously brushed a lock of hair away from his forehead; then, for the first time in Lestrade's memory of him, looked serious.

"Actually, I have come to pass on some information to you, Inspector," he said. "It is of a rather delicate nature. Scurrilous it may be, but you have my word it is not gossip, for I saw it with my own eyes, just last night."

"And this information, it involves criminal activity?"

"Most definitely," Pike said.

"You'd better come on in then, lad. Park your arse and let's be having it."

Pike made quite a show of brushing the visitor's chair with a handkerchief before sitting and when Lestrade offered him a cigarette he declined, instead lighting up one of his own French imports that smelled even worse than his pomade. Lestrade lit a cigarette to cover the odor and sat back to listen to the man's story.

"As you know, the origins of Lord Collingwood's newfound wealth have been the subject of much speculation in the city."

Lestrade knew no such thing, but to interrupt the man on his first statement was only asking for trouble that he did not need, so he let Pike continue.

"Were I to be the man to discover the source of these newfound funds I could name my price for the articles I could write on it, so I decided to do some discreet investigation. Collingwood himself maintains that he had a windfall from the sale of a diamond mine in Southern Africa, but I did some digging at Companies House, and I asked around among the kind of chaps who know what's what in the diamond business. I can discover not a single piece of evidence to support Collingwood's assertion. The money appears to have fallen in his lap out of nowhere and we both know that the most likely source of that kind of windfall is from something nefarious. I dug further.

112

"I soon discovered that his Lordship was spending Friday nights apart from his wife; I know this because our Ladyship has been less than discreet with her dalliances when left alone, but that is a story for other ears. To return to the matter at hand, Collingwood spends every Friday night with a tight group of friends who have been together since their days at Eton. Knowing the ways of alumni from that school, I expected that they met to relive their youth: sexual high jinks of a less than savoury nature, overindulging in food and strong drink, that kind of thing. I was soon to discover that my expectations had been too mundane.

"I guessed that if anyone knew the source of Collingwood's new wealth it would be one of this group. I followed young Lord Postlethwaite from his club last Friday, having chosen him as being always the most inebriated member of the coterie, and as such least likely to spot me following him. My intention was to waylay him, bribe him with booze and women, and get him to talk.

"We were in the Strand at the time; there were too many people for me to easily make my move, and then I almost lost him in the crowd near the George Tavern, until I spotted him entering the main bar. I thought my luck was in; I could intercept him at the bar, pay for his drink and have an entry point into a conversation. Instead I got into the bar just in time to see the barman open a doorway at the back of the bar, let Postlethwaite through, then close it behind him.

"Of course, I wasn't going to let the small matter of a closed door stop me. The barman wasn't as easily bribed as some, not as difficult as some others and, a florin lighter, I was soon allowed passage through the self-same door.

"I stepped through to find a rough set of stone steps of some antiquity heading down into the dark. There was a shimmer of reddish light somewhere down in the gloom, and a murmur of several distinct voices. I headed down.

"Some two dozen steps down the stairwell opened out into a larger chamber beyond. I stayed back in the opening, ensuring I was hidden in shadow and found a vantage point from where I could watch proceedings. I found myself looking out at what was obviously a temple of some antiquity, but as to what god or gods might have been worshiped there, I do not have the education to say. All I knew was that it was older than anything practiced in the great churches in the city above me, a place of ancient corroded stone and pale lichens that hung from the arched roof like grasping fingers. The chamber was lit by wrought-iron candlesticks as tall as a man, arranged in a wide circle around a central altar, a massive block of what looked to me like a single slab of polished marble, although my view of it was less than perfect.

"A dozen cloaked and hooded men were arranged around the altar. They began to chant. It wasn't Latin; I have just enough education to have recognized that. It was a language I did not recognize, a hoarse, guttural thing that sounded rough in their throats, more akin to barking than singing. It seemed to resonate around the chamber, as if the very walls themselves were vibrating in time, and the candles flickered although there was no apparent breeze.

"One of the cloaked figures stepped forward, and in doing so created an opening such that I got my first proper view of the altar. I almost cried out then, for there was a woman, no more than a girl really, splayed out there on her back, hands and feet bound to iron rings at the altar's corners. She was completely naked, and I do believe she must have been under the influence of some kind of narcotic, for she did not react in the slightest when the man— I saw as the candlelight caught his features that it was Collingwood—stepped forward and raised a silver dagger high above his head.

"The coarse chanting rose to a crescendo, pounding like a drum in my ears and, without warning, Collingwood shouted one word I did not understand, and brought the dagger down hard, piercing the girl through the heart and sending great gouts of blood all over the altar. Collingwood laughed like a maniac as the chanting continued.

"As for me, I took to my heels and fled."

Lestrade waited to see if there was any more to Pike's story, but it seems it was done, having all come out of him in a rush.

"Let me get this straight, lad," he said. "Peers of the realm, rich, powerful men in their own right, are meeting under a pub in the Strand, performing some kind of unholy rituals, and killing young girls. And you just stumbled into it by accident?"

Pike nodded. "I swear to you, Lestrade, it's the God's honest truth."

"Lad, we both know that you and the truth have been strangers for quite some time. How do I know you're not spinning me a line in order to create a story for yourself? I wouldn't want to see myself in the gossip papers under a "Gullible copper chases Satanists" story, now would I?"

"I know I'm not your idea of a reliable witness, Lestrade," Pike said. "All I can do is implore you to go and see for yourself. You can manage that discreetly, can't you? I don't even have to be there. Just go and look. Please?"

Lestrade's first instinct was to dismiss the man out of hand, but he hadn't expected this kind of pleading and when he looked Pike in the eye he saw tears there, and more than a touch of panicked terror. It was so far from the man's usual, somewhat insolent, manner that Lestrade could not help but be intrigued.

"I suppose there's no harm in looking," he said, and saw relief wash over Pike. "You stay here, drink tea, smoke your godawful cigarettes. I'll go and have a butcher's. If you're having me on, you're going to be in trouble."

"I knew that before I came," Pike said. "And yet I came. What does that tell you?"

Lestrade was still pondering that question as he called for Sergeant Clarke.

"Get your trousers on, Clarkie. We've got a pub to visit."

If the barman in the George was expecting a florin from Lestrade he was going to have a long wait.

"I need to see your downstairs room," Lestrade said. "And don't play the innocent with me, son. All I have to do is check the two-bob bit in your pocket. Now, quick as you like, let us through."

The barman opened the door and Lestrade peered down a long flight of old stone steps to what looked like pitch darkness. There was no sound below; the only thing of note was the faint smell of damp.

"There's nowt down there, Guv'nor," the barman said. "Used to be our cellar but it was too damp for the beer to keep well and we had a new one dug on the other side. I say new, that was fifty year ago now and ..."

"Son, do yourself a favor: keep quiet. And fetch a lantern."

Two minutes later Lestrade followed Clarke down the steps, the Sergeant swinging an oil lantern ahead of them. Lestrade counted as he went. After two dozen steps they reached the bottom.

"Just like Pike said," he muttered to himself, then went quiet as the sound seemed to be magnified and echoed around them.

The chamber was much as Pike had described it, with a few exceptions; there were no tall candlesticks, no cloaked men, and most definitely no naked girl spreadeagled on the altar. The whole place had an air of disuse and although Lestrade looked very closely there was no trace of blood on the old marble or on the iron rings at its corners. There was a hint of something else in the air; it might indeed have been the tang from burning candles.

"Or it might just be some old lad smoking a pipe upstairs," Lestrade muttered.

He had Clarke do two full circuits of the chamber, and another close examination of the altar, but there was no evidence that anything untoward had happened here, at least not in the last few centuries.

Pike was still in Lestrade's office when they got back to the Yard, and the reporter's face seemed to fall in on itself when he heard what Lestrade had, or rather had not, found under the pub.

"They've tidied up after themselves," Pike said, almost to himself.

"And they made a bloody better job of it than my housekeeper," Lestrade said. "That is, if there was ever anything there to clean in the first place?"

"You still don't believe me?"

"I believe in evidence, lad, and so do the courts. Bring me some and I'll see what can be done with it. But as of now, there's nowt I can do for you."

Pike was still talking to himself. "I can't let him get away with it. I can't." His hands shook as he lit one of his foul-smelling cigarettes, but his eyes were sharp and clear when he looked up at Lestrade.

"Evidence is it? Well then, I'll get it for you, just you wait and see. And when I do, I'll be expecting you to act on it. If you don't, your name really will feature strongly in the gossip papers, and it will be to your detriment."

"Don't try to threaten me, boy," Lestrade said.

"It wasn't a threat, Inspector. It was a promise."

Pike left, leaving the stink of his cigarettes lingering for most of the day, but once Lestrade opened a window the stench went away and all thoughts of Langdale Pike went with it. Lestrade was kept busy with other cases; in London, crime never sleeps. He was writing up his notes of one such case on a pleasant Saturday morning two weeks later when Clarke arrived with a telegram.

It came from St. Barts Hospital, and it was from Pike.

"Need to see you. Urgent. It concerns his Lordship."

Lestrade looked up.

"Am I at the beck and call of newspaper men now?"

117

"That's just it, sir. He can't come to you. A report came in last night; he was found in the Temple area, all cut up. Someone, or something, had been at him. They say he's lucky to be alive."

It was a much-changed Pike who greeted Lestrade from the hospital bed. He looked smaller, sunk in on himself and had lost much of his air of cockiness, it having been replaced with a nervous tic in his left eye and a general air of terrified panic. His torso, at least that much of it as could be seen under his hospital pajamas, was swaddled in crisp white bandages and when Pike spoke it was with a wince of pain at every word.

"Is this evidence enough for you, Inspector?" he said, in barely more than a hoarse whisper, as if something was torn inside him. He made to bend over toward a small table at his bedside, then had to stop when a fresh wave of pain wracked his body.

"I have been tracking his Lordship these past two weeks. I cannot tell you all that I have discovered since our last meeting. But I made copious notes as I went along. They are in my journal, in the top drawer. You should read it. You must read it. Collingwood must be stopped."

Even that short speech was almost too much for the stricken man. His face had gone gray, all color having leached from it and beads of sweat had risen at his brow.

A fussy matron came into the room and immediately set on Lestrade. "Shame on you, sir, questioning a sick man like that. Get out with you. Quiet and rest is what he needs, not policemen."

Lestrade didn't bother pleading his innocence; he knew from long experience that he would never win an argument with a woman protecting her charges. He went quickly to the bedside table and removed a small leather-bound journal before she could stop him. Pike only said a few more words before the matron ushered Lestrade to the door, but the Inspector could make no sense of their meaning.

"I saw them dance, Lestrade. I saw them, and they saw me. They do not like being seen."

The sight of the stricken journalist stirred something in Lestrade. There was pity for the state the poor man was in, for sure, but there was something else too, a touch of shame, guilt that he had not paid enough attention to the man's story.

Well, I'm paying attention now.

He was going to have to play this close to his chest though; if the Commissioner got wind of any unauthorized investigation of peers of the realm, Lestrade might find himself stripped of rank and shipped off to Bognor Regis on permanent night-shift duty. On return to the Yard he logged Pike's attack with the Desk Sergeant as 'GBH by person or persons unknown' which should give him enough leeway for investigation, for now, given that Pike was a 'celebrity' in his own right, and as such the Yard could be expected not to ignore it.

He called Sergeant Clarke into his office.

"It's a rum do, this one, Clarkie," he said. "And sensitive. We'll need to go by the book, or at least look like we're doing so, so get some lads out to where Pike was found, ask around for witnesses, the usual drill."

Clarke left to make a start, Lestrade brewed a pot of strong tea and retired to his office with a mug, his cigarettes and Pike's journal, hoping that it might offer up some clues, or at least a place from which Lestrade could pin something definite on Collingwood.

It did not start auspiciously. The journal was a new one, started the very day of Pike and Lestrade's first meeting on the subject. Pike had a neat, tidy hand but the script was small, as if he was intent on cramming as much of his 'evidence' as possible onto every page. Lestrade had to drag his chair closer to the window to get enough light to read it by.

Lestrade does not believe me, but he will. By the time I am done everybody will be forced to believe me.

That struck Lestrade as having more than a hint of obsession to it, and the detail that followed only served to underline that theory. Over the course of the week that followed Pike made meticulous notes of Collingwood's movements, all dated and timed, even going as far as to note his bowel movements although Lestrade did not need or want to know how Pike got that particular information. It all made for very dry reading, until the journal reached the following Friday.

They have come back to the George and gone down to the crypt. I cannot bring myself to go down there again. I write this in a corner booth in the bar from where I can watch the comings and goings. Collingwood and Postlethwaite were first to arrive. I also recognized Boothby, Chingford and Willis. Not sure about the others as they were keeping their faces turned but I am willing to bet it's all of the old Eton club, together again in nefarious activity. Seconds ago, when the bar went quiet for a second, I believed I heard their hellish chanting rise up from below. Someone struck up a song in the bar, and thankfully spared me from having to listen to it again. They will be back up from the hell beneath soon enough and I will follow his Lordship closely. If I can find where they dispose of the bodies perhaps that will satisfy Lestrade and spur him into action.

If Pike had found anything that night, he had not logged it in the book. Lestrade flicked forward over some more detailed timings of Collingwood's activities on the Saturday before his eye caught another mention of the

George. The note had been written on Tuesday and was in a more hurried hand.

> *Collingwood is at his club and I know from experience that he and Postlethwaite will take lunch there. I have made time to visit the British Library and have uncovered a snippet of history of the George that may be relevant. In 1719, Philip, first Duke of Wharton, started the first Hellfire club in the premises, having been inspired, it is said, by a visit to the cellar. Wild rumors abound, but the one that has caught my eye, and keeps coming to mind, is of ritual sacrifice of a local virgin, with the intent of 'consorting with imps and demons.'*
>
> *Is Collingwood trying to raise some Hell of his own? Could it be that he has succeeded?*

Lestrade put the journal down to get a cigarette and a fresh mug of tea. It wasn't telling him anything apart from the fact that Pike's obsession was taking him down some strange paths. Indeed, when he got back to it minutes later, he thought he was now detecting more than a hint of paranoia.

> *I am being followed, I am sure of it, but whoever it is is dashed good at the job, for I can never catch sight of him, only hints and shadows in the corner of my eye. Does Collingwood know I am on to him? I must be even more circumspect, for Friday is approaching again, and with nothing to show for my work so far, I must attempt to gather some solid evidence that will convince someone, anyone, that action must be taken.*

Lestrade skipped forward through more boring details of Collingwood's days to the last entry, dated and timed on the Friday night at eight p.m.

121

I am resolved. When they go down into the crypt I shall follow again, and this time I will not be circumspect. My shadow has been following me these past two days now, but if Collingwood means to throw me off the scent he does not know his man. I will confront this new 'Hellfire Club' this very night, and on the morrow I shall expose them for all the world to see. I cannot allow another girl to die. I will not.

Lestrade looked in vain for anything more but there was not a single clue, beyond this possible shadowy follower chap who might be all in Pike's obviously addled mind in any case. If he was going to find Pike's assailant, he was going to have to do it the hard way.

His first port of call, accompanied by Sergeant Clarke, was back to the George, but as before there was no sign that anything at all had happened in the crypt since their last visit. The barman was giving them his see-no-evil,-hear-no-evil routine and would not be budged either with bribery or threats of conviction. If the man did know something, Lestrade guessed that he was being protected by someone with deeper pockets than the Yard possessed.

It appeared they had nothing whatsoever to go on, but caught a glimmer of hope when one of the beat coppers turned up with a witness. Lestrade's good mood lasted only long enough to get back to the Yard and find that the witness was Annie Ross.

Annie was known to every copper in the Yard; alcoholic, beggar and weaver of tall tales if she thought there were a few pennies in it for her. Lestrade had never trusted anything she had to say and wasn't about to begin now. He passed a cigarette across the table to her and lit one for himself, more to disguise the smell that rose from her than any great desire to have one.

"This is all you get, Annie," he said, "so make the most of it."

"But I saw him, Guv'nor," she said, her Scottish accent coming through clear. "Yon toff who's always scribbling away in his wee book. I kent it was him as soon as I saw him running out of the pub."

"Just to be clear, you saw Pike running out of the George?"

"Aye, I said that, didn't I?"

"And when was this?"

"Last night, around midnight."

"And did he seem himself?"

"Well seeing as I'm not sure what hisself is, I wouldna ken, would I? But I'll tell you something for nowt, he wasnae right in the head."

"How do you mean?"

"Well, he was batting and flapping his arms about his heid as if he was getting attacked by something; bloody pigeons I thought at first, then I saw there was nothing there but shadows, flitting around and flickering in the gaslight. Whatever it were, he were bloody terrified. Ran past me as if Auld Nick hisself was on his heels, and away he went, shrieking like a bairn, off doon toward the Embankment. I didnae think owt of it until your mannie asked if anybody saw anything. Is there a penny in it for me?"

He gave her a farthing, and she went away happy enough, but still left Lestrade with more questions than answers. He was fast coming to the conclusion that the only way to the truth of it would be to ask Pike directly.

Matron wasn't going to like it.

It was Thursday morning before the doctors—and Matron—would allow Lestrade in to see Pike, and even then he was only allowed ten minutes and not a second more. He'd spent the intervening days getting nowhere fast, holding off from bearding Collingwood or his known associates directly until he'd spoken to the journalist.

Pike wasn't at all happy with this seeming inaction in the face of his 'evidence.' "What more do I have to do to convince you? Will it take my death?"

The smell of disinfectant in the small room was almost over-powering, and Lestrade felt an urge for another cigarette; Matron would definitely not approve of that, so he pressed on with his questions.

"I need to know exactly what happened to you on Friday night. You were seen leaving the pub in somewhat of a state."

"Bloody right I was in a state. You would be too if you saw what I saw."

"And what did you see, Pike? If I'm to help you, I need to know."

"I fear I am beyond help," Pike said. "But yes, you need to know. Come close. This should not be overheard."

When he spoke it was barely above a whisper, and with some effort, but he seemed determined to have the story out so Lestrade sat in the bedside chair and leaned in close to hear him.

"I waited in the corner of the bar until all of the club members had arrived and gave them ten minutes to get themselves prepared, then I passed the barman some money ... he demanded two florins this time; an exorbitant amount, but one I could not quibble with, and we both knew it. Then I began my descent. I don't apologize for telling you that I was in a state of some funk, but thinking about the columns I might write, and the fame that might accrue, did much to stiffen my resolve.

"I arrived in the crypt just as the coarse chanting was starting and now that I knew what I was looking for I picked out Collingwood immediately. As before they had a young girl spreadeagled on the altar and when Collingwood stepped forward and drew the dagger from the folds of his cloak I made my move.

"I had been worried that they might be expecting me, but I arrived among them screaming blue murder and my appearance seemed to discombobulate them; all that is, save for Collingwood. He showed no sign of even registering my presence. I was still six feet away from him when he raised the dagger, still three feet away as he shouted out that one unknown word, and had only just managed to touch the cowl of his cloak as he brought the dagger down, hard into the girl's heart.

"I tasted fresh blood on my lips, felt hot spatter on my face. It was only then that Collingwood seemed to take note of me. He turned from the girl's body, a grin on his face the likes of which I have never seen before ... and hope never to see again.

"He spoke, and again it was almost a chant, but this time I knew the words, and their source.

"'*Look upon my Works, ye Mighty, and despair!*'

"He stood aside as if to allow me a look at the dead girl, as if I hadn't seen enough already. The dagger was still standing up proud in her chest, but that wasn't what caught my attention. Dark shadows, darker even than those in the darkest corners of the crypt, grew around the wound, shifting, cavorting shapes in a mad dance. I began to discern the shapes among them, a head here, an arm there, small, leathery bat-like wings on another, half a dozen of them, straight from hell, called to the dance.

"'They've been expecting you,' Collingwood said, and as he gave an evil maniacal laugh, so did the shadowy imps leap from the girl's chest and launch themselves directly at me.

"I felt a slash of pain in my ribs and looked down to see a small creature, no more than eight inches long, green and warty like some hideous goblin from a dark fairytale, drag a talon as sharp as any knife through my skin. My shirt seeped red, then more red as it had another cut at me. I tried to grab at the thing and got a deep wound across my palm for the trouble. Another one landed in my hair and proceeded to tear lumps out of it while a third, the winged one, fluttered around my face, another talon searching for my eyes.

"Once again I fled.

"And as I ran they stabbed at me, laughed at me, screamed their joy in my ears and stabbed again. I was aware by this time that I was outside the bar, running in the street. My only thought was of escape but they kept at me, kept cutting, and darkness crept in around me ever closer until finally I let it take me away."

He stopped, his tale done, fresh tears in his eyes.

"I saw them dance, and they saw me dance. They dance still."

Lestrade saw that Pike was looking at a spot in the corner of the room. When Lestrade followed the man's gaze he seemed to see dark shadows, shifting and whirling. It might only have been a trick of the light, but it clearly had Pike terrified. Lestrade's response was the instinctive one of an old copper doing his best to help someone in distress.

"Now you just leave this chap alone," he said, addressing the shadows, but for the benefit of Pike. "If you want to terrorize somebody, why not try me? I've seen most everything a man can see in this city, so have at it. Do your worst."

The matron arrived at that point to shoo Lestrade out. Pike spoke once more, another whisper.

"You don't know what you've just done, Lestrade. I thank you. But you don't know what you've done."

When Lestrade turned to leave, the shifting shadows in the corner moved along the wall and when he reached the doorway they seemed to gather around him. Pike called out from his sick bed.

"Find Collingwood and stop him. It's the only thing that will save you now."

Lestrade kept a close eye out the carriage windows on the way back to the Yard, unable to shake the feeling that he was being watched. The feeling persisted even as he sat in his office with tea and a smoke. The hairs on the nape of his neck seemed to twitch, an itchy, nervous feeling that couldn't be scratched. He was still trying to make sense of what Pike had told him. The man was clearly disturbed, but he hadn't inflicted his wounds on himself; there was a perpetrator to be caught. And the only other clue Lestrade had was in Collingwood and his coterie of friends.

Commissioner be damned, it was time to shake the toff tree and see what fell out.

He set Clarke off to find the man that Pike had identified as the weakest link in the group of friends, Gerald Postlethwaite. While Clarke was about that task, Lestrade attempted to catch up on his paperwork, a job he truly believed was becoming the bane of modern police work and liable to swamp the Yard completely in years to come if they weren't careful. Despite the monotony he couldn't settle; the feeling of being watched persisting, getting stronger if anything.

On his way back to Vauxhall he was convinced he was being followed. He took a longer way home than necessary, up and down side streets he rarely frequented, but he couldn't shake the feeling off. Once he got home he lit all the gas lights in the front parlor and sat with a book, but still couldn't settle; the shadows seemed to dance and caper around him, and he was reminded all too clearly of Pike's story. In the end it took the best part of half a bottle of Scotch to get him to sleep, and even then his dreams were of dancing, cavorting imps awash with the flames of hell.

The itchy feeling was still with him when he got to the Yard the next morning, but his mood was improved by Clarke reporting that he had tracked down the probable whereabouts of Gerald Postlethwaite. It appeared young Postlethwaite was a man of rigid habits and could be found of a Friday morning in his club, Boodles on St. James' Street, in the billiard room and losing money hand over fist more likely than not.

"Time to rattle a few cages, Clarkie," Lestrade said. "Let's see what this lad is made of, shall we?"

Clarke's information proved to be correct. They found Postlethwaite in the club billiard room. Despite it being not yet noon, he was clearly three sheets to the wind and intent on staying that way. He was in the middle of a particularly ribald joke when the officers arrived at the doorway. He turned, saw Lestrade, and went as white as a sheet.

"Stay away from me!" he said in a bellow of fear. "Don't come any closer."

He wielded a billiard cue like a club.

"Threatening a police officer in the course of his duties. Did you hear that, Sergeant Clarke? I do believe we're within our rights to take this lad down to the Yard for a chat."

Lestrade took two steps toward Postlethwaite.

"You've seen them, and they've seen you," the lad wailed. "Don't try to deny it. Stay away from me. Don't let them see me."

"Come on now, lad, let's have no more nonsense. We just want a quiet chat."

"I'm not going with you. I can't go with you," he shouted and swung the cue, hard, aimed directly at Lestrade's head. Luckily Lestrade had been waiting for it, and caught it one-handed, in the same motion pulling Postlethwaite toward him, getting him off balance, and holding him tight in a headlock.

"Assaulting a police officer now, that's a tad more serious. Clarkie, fetch the cuffs. A few hours in the cells should quieten him down a bit."

"Do you know who I am?" Postlethwaite shouted as Clarke dragged him outside.

"Yes, sir, I do believe I do. And you know what? I don't care. You're coming with us."

They left Postlethwaite in the cells to let the drink wear off and the reality of his situation creep in. The duty sergeant reported that he was loud and demanding at first, promising all manner of retribution for his mistreatment, but that had been replaced by intermittent bouts of pleading and weeping. Lestrade gave him another fifteen minutes of that to soften him up further, then had him brought up to the interview room. It was a much-chastened young lord who sat at the table as Lestrade entered.

Postlethwaite took one look at Lestrade and went white again. "Oh, God. I was hoping it had been a trick of the light in the billiard room. But it's true. They've seen you."

"What are you havering about now, lad? We're not here to talk about me. We're here to talk about last Friday night, and your shenanigans in the crypt below the George bar."

"I won't talk about that. I can't talk about that."

"Lad, you attacked a Scotland Yard inspector with a billiard cue in front of witnesses. If you don't cooperate I could have you up in front of a judge this very day and see you in Newgate prison for thirty days or more. How does that sound?"

"You don't understand. It's forbidden."

"Forbidden? By who? Your pal Collingwood? He's not above the law, lad."

"No, but they are."

"*They?* Who in blazes are you talking about now?"

"You know. You've seen them and they've seen you."

"Not this bally nonsense again. We're going around in circles here. Tell me what I need to know, or you're going back downstairs while I contact a judge."

The young lord appeared to come to a decision and spoke more firmly.

"Collingwood calls them," he said. "They come to do his bidding in return for a sacrifice."

Lestrade was about to reply when something seemed to flicker near his left eye, a fast-moving shadow in an otherwise evenly lit room. When he turned toward it there was nothing to see there, but all of a sudden the lad opposite had taken a funk again.

"They've seen me. I've said too much and they've seen me. You've got to help me, Lestrade. They'll be coming for me, then they'll be coming for you."

"You still haven't told me who 'they' are, lad."

"I can't say any more. I mustn't."

Postlethwaite had now stood, knocking over his chair in the process, and was backing away toward the far wall, trying to put as much distance as possible between himself and Lestrade, his gaze fixed over Lestrade's left shoulder.

"They've seen me. Dear Lord save me, they've seen me."

He collapsed to his knees and burst into a fit of most piteous weeping that would not be stopped. Lestrade had him taken back down to the cells until he could figure out what to do with him, and retired to his office for a much-needed smoke.

The strange feeling of being watched would not leave him, nor would the memory of the young lord's reaction in the interview room, but he could not countenance an idea as outlandish as that as he was being expected to believe. London had more than its own share of evil without adding demons into the melting pot. To keep the itch at bay he busied himself in more paperwork and a chain-smoked series of cigarettes. He had almost managed to put both the shifting shadows and Postlethwaite to the back of his mind when he realized that the feeling was gone, as quickly as it had come, as if something had just lifted off his shoulders. He was about to light up a celebratory smoke when a scream echoed up through the corridors from somewhere below.

Lestrade's heart sank; he knew who it must be, even before he went headlong down the stairs to investigate.

The duty sergeant stood at an open cell door, looking like he'd rather be anywhere else in the world at that moment.

"There's been nobody got past me, sir," he said to Lestrade. "I'll swear that on my old ma's life."

Lestrade gently pushed the sergeant aside and looked inside.

Postlethwaite was bunched up tight in the far corner of

the cell, as if he'd been trying to escape from something. He sat in a still-growing pool of his own blood. His chest, what Lestrade could see of it, was punctured by a myriad of tiny wounds that had also torn his shirt to shredded ribbons. But the death blow had been the one at his neck, a neat, almost surgical wound that had severed the jugular.

Shadows fluttered in the air above the body, and when Lestrade went to the corner in a futile attempt to check for a pulse the darkness seemed to shift and dance. Something whispered close by, like a bird heard in the wind, but Lestrade was too intent on the body to take note. His Lordship's dead eyes stared up at him accusingly, and Lestrade heard his words in his mind.

"They'll be coming for me, then they'll be coming for you."

Lestrade turned to the Duty Sergeant.

"The Commissioner will be wanting a full report and somebody to blame," he said. "But don't you go worrying about your pension, Sarge. This one's on me, and I'll be telling him that myself. There's something I have to do first, though, so keep this under your hat for a couple of hours until I come back. Can you do that?"

The older man nodded. "Try to save both our pensions if you can, sir. But catch the bloody bastards who did this first."

"I intend to," Lestrade replied. "But the paperwork is going to be a bugger."

He left the desk sergeant at the cell door and went in search of Clarke, finding him in the canteen.

"Get your revolver, Clarkie; we're going out for a pint."

"What are we going to do, sir?"

"Something I should have done weeks ago," Lestrade replied.

As they left the Yard he turned sharply to look back, earning himself a worried look from his sergeant.

"Anything wrong, sir?"

Lestrade didn't answer. He felt something tickle at his left ear and heard a whisper.

It sounded like laughter.

They took up station in a secluded doorway opposite the George, waiting for the participants in the Friday night ritual to arrive. They were going to be a man short, of course, but somehow Lestrade didn't think that would stop Collingwood; he'd never met the man, but was beginning to get a sense of him through the way he left a trail of broken people behind him.

Several expensive-looking carriages arrived and deposited well-dressed young men on the pavement outside the bar before moving off. The last, a handsome, huge black cab drawn by two strong horses, let a tall aristocratic chap out; Lestrade could make a good guess that this must be the master of ceremonies himself, Lord Collingwood. They were too far away on the other side of the road for him to make out the man's face, but he carried himself like someone who expected deference, someone who knew his place in the world to be above everyone else, and that was the way it should be.

Lestrade waited for fifteen minutes, then motioned for Clarke to follow, heading across the road and into the George bar.

The barman took one look at Lestrade and without saying a word handed him a lit lantern and opened the door at the back of the bar. Coarse chanting echoed up the stairwell, and it seemed to Lestrade as if something much nearer his ear joined in the chorus. He took out his revolver, gripped it tight, steeled his nerves and made his way quickly down the stone steps toward the red, flickering, light below.

The scene that met him at the foot of the stairs was much as Pike had described it. The chant echoed and rang around the crypt, as if the walls themselves were joining in. Something laughed at Lestrade's left ear and he felt a flash of pain. When he put a finger up to check he felt fresh, hot blood there.

"I've had just about enough of this," he muttered.

Out in the chamber a tall figure, Collingwood, had stepped forward from the main circle toward the altar. A naked girl lay there, bound and spreadeagled. Just the sight of her made Lestrade's blood boil with righteous indignation. Without waiting for Clarke he stepped forward into the chamber, raised his revolver, and fired a shot at the ceiling. The whole crypt echoed as if a great drum had just been pounded, the chanting stopped, and the only sound now was the hissing, guttering from the tall candlesticks.

Lestrade stepped inside the circle of cloaked figures and pointed his gun at Collingwood's back. "Don't even think about doing anything stupid, chummy. You're under arrest."

Collingwood turned slowly, and smiled. "I think not, Lestrade. We've been expecting you."

There was a fluttering at Lestrade's ear, a cackling laugh and another burst of pain. Warm blood ran down under his collar. While that distracted him, Collingwood made a move, taking a long silver dagger from the folds of his cloak and stepping forward toward the altar.

"Get away from her," Lestrade shouted. He raised his weapon again, aiming for Collingwood's broad back. Just as he pulled the trigger a darker shadow flitted over his wrist and there was a new lancing pain as a fresh wound opened in the webbing between his thumb and forefinger. He pulled the trigger anyway, the blast pounding and reverberating around him. Collingwood went to the floor; the shot had been off target, but had taken him in the right shoulder, forcing him to drop the dagger which fell on the ground with a clatter before silence fell once again.

Lestrade stepped over and kicked the dagger away, sending it skittering and clattering into a dark corner.

"We must finish it," Collingwood said through teeth gritted in pain. "Quickly, before they see me, before they get both of us."

"I'm pretty sure I know who they'd really like to see,"

Lestrade said, and heard a chorus of laughs in his ear in reply.

A shadow flitted away from his gun hand; Lestrade almost saw it clearly for the first time and had an impression of a hand-sized, bat-winged thing, green and covered in orange-red warts, with a snout like a wolf and eyes like burning coals. It went straight at Collingwood's face.

A scream echoed around the crypt.

More shadows fluttered and capered, descending on the prone man, almost cloaking him in darkness. Blood flew, the shadows danced faster and the screams grew louder, only to be replaced by gurgling, liquid moans.

It was all over in seconds. The shadow things lifted away and fluttered among the candles, setting them flickering. Then everything fell still.

The thing that was left on the ground was hardly recognizable as having been a man at all.

Lestrade looked around to see Clarke holding a gun on the other cloaked men.

"Good lad, Clarkie. I'll keep an eye on this lot. You go and get a doctor for the lass here and some men to help me get these back to the Yard. The judge is going to have a busy night."

It was several days later before Lestrade got a chance to look in on Langdale Pike in the hospital. The journalist was sitting up in the bedside chair and looked much improved, although he had a long hard stare at Lestrade as the inspector entered the room.

"You've done it?" he said. "You got rid of them?"

"Sent them back to where they came from, and Collingwood with them," Lestrade answered.

He closed the door to avoid the matron's attentions, opened a window, pulled up another chair and lit them each a cigarette. While they smoked he gave Pike the whole story.

"Of course, the instinct of the higher-ups is to cover

this up, keep it all hush-hush, public scandals among the gentry being seen as injurious to the health of the nation," Lestrade said when he was finished. "It would be a real shame if someone were to write this all up and get it widely published before they had a chance to do it."

"It would, wouldn't it?" Pike said, and smiled.

Mrs. Hudson's Fancies

Lestrade thought he had seen most moods that Sherlock Holmes' landlady had to offer. He'd seen her amused, seen her angry, seen her irritated, seen her sorrowful, all brought about in one way or another by the consulting detective. What he hadn't seen before, and what he was in no way prepared for, was to see her in tears, wracked with worry.

He was sitting in the kitchen scullery in Baker Street. He was more used to being upstairs talking to Holmes, but if truth be told, sitting here sharing a large mug of tea, a smoke and some of the landlady's renowned fondant fancies was more his style, or rather, it would have been, if the lady had not been in quite so much distress.

"Is it Holmes?" Lestrade asked. "I could have a stern word with him, if you'd like?"

She wiped away tears with a delicate handkerchief before replying.

"No, it's not him. And I don't want you talking to him about this either," she said. "I asked you round because it's not something he can help with. It's a woman's matter."

Lestrade's heart sank, wondering what he'd let

himself in for in answering the telegram. But the lady was obviously sorely vexed about something, so he waved a hand to indicate she should continue.

"It's my friend, Mrs. Humphrey," she said. "She was made a widow last year by an accident in the digging of that new underground railway line down Vauxhall way. She's been quite beside herself ever since. I've tried my best to be a good friend to her, but you know better than most the ways of grief, Inspector. It's a hard road to travel. I was saying to Mrs. Murphy in the butcher's shop just the other day that ..."

Lestrade coughed discreetly, hoping to stop any side travels before they got too far away from the point; he knew from experience that once a woman of a certain age gets going on a story, it could be dashed hard to drag them back on track. His cough earned him a withering look, but at least it had the desired effect.

"The thing is," she continued, "she's taken to consulting a spiritualist. In the past six months she's tried half a dozen different ones, from Hammersmith to Hackney. But recently she's settled on one in Islington. She says she speaks to her George, as clear as if he's there with her. She says he knows things only George would know. And she also says that she's spent almost all she has to live on, and the spiritualist is asking for more. She is going to destitute herself and be put out on the streets, but she does not care, as long as she can talk to her George. I've tried and tried to speak to her about it, to warn her and now I'm at my wits' end. This has to stop, one way or the other. Will you help me?"

It had all come out in a rush and now she was weeping again, her eyes red with it.

"It's not against the law to take money, even for a spiritualist, Mrs. Hudson," he said softly. "If your friend does not want to be helped, she can't be helped."

"Nonsense," she replied. "Stuff and nonsense. It's a parlor trick, and as such is, how would you put it in your words, taking money under false pretenses. That surely is illegal?"

"It is, if it can be proven." Lestrade said. "But with these chaps, that's often the hard part. A good con man is a good con man and knows what he's about. Tricky buggers, the lot of them."

"So how would you go about catching them at it?"

"You've got to expose them in the act. Go to one of their meetings and shine a bright light on all their gimmicks, let your friend see the tricks behind the curtains and under the tables."

"So it's possible?"

"If you know what you're about."

"Good. So you'll come with me, then?" she said, almost causing him to drop his teacup.

"Now, wait a minute! I never said that. I have no grounds to investigate."

"We're not talking about an investigation though, are we? We're talking about helping a friend. You will come with me, won't you? You don't have to be Inspector Lestrade. You can be my gentleman."

So it was that later that night Lestrade, wearing his Sunday best, turned up at Baker Street, staying in the shadows outside, not wanting to be observed by Holmes or Watson, then getting into a carriage with Mrs. Hudson to be introduced to the other occupant, the aforementioned Mrs. Humphreys. She was an imposing lady, being broad across the shoulders, heavy-chested and square-jawed, all contained inside a voluminous mourning coat even blacker than the carriage itself. If she took any note of Lestrade being introduced as Mrs. Hudson's gentleman, Geoffrey, she did not show it, merely nodded, then went back to staring, unfocused, into space.

Mrs. Hudson did her best to try to initiate a conversation all the way to Islington, but it was like drawing blood from a stone and Lestrade was more than pleased when they came to a halt and were let out onto Upper Street before a tall Georgian terraced dwelling.

"I'm in the wrong game," he muttered to himself as they were shown into an expansive, almost palatial, hallway of marbled floors, sweeping staircase and what looked to Lestrade's admittedly non-expert eye to be expensive, gilt-framed artwork. A tightly starched butler showed them through to the front parlor, a room dominated by an antique oak table large enough to seat a dozen should it be used for dinner. There were no places set, the only thing breaking the expanse of well-polished wood being a tall, ornate centerpiece depicting a prancing, pipe-playing depiction of the Greek god Pan. It looked to have been carved from the same wood as the table; indeed it almost appeared to grow organically from the gleaming surface, and Lestrade had to look closely to see the carpenter's join.

Four large gas lamps glowed in sconces on the walls in the corners, making the room as bright as daylight; an ornamental candle-holder hung from the ceiling directly above the sculpture of Pan, but none of the candles were lit. There was a plush Persian-style rug underfoot and the walls were lined in mahogany so dark as to be almost black, punctuated at intervals with floor-to-ceiling mirrors in burnished silver frames that seemed to glow in the gaslight. The whole effect was of luxurious decadence, and it made Lestrade more than a little uncomfortable, as if he did not belong amid such opulence.

There were only two other people in the room. One was an elderly, stooped clergyman who nodded to acknowledge their presence but was otherwise silent; the other a young, well-dressed lady who rose to greet them with a smile that looked warm around the mouth but did not quite reach her eyes. She approached Mrs. Humphreys first, and took the widow's left hand in both of hers, as if holding a small bird.

"Mrs. Humphreys, it is so good to see you again. George has been waiting for you. And I see you have brought company."

She turned, not to Lestrade but to Mrs. Hudson, who

immediately astounded Lestrade with a performance that wouldn't disgrace any of the West End stages. The landlady shook the young woman's hand warmly.

"This is my gentleman, Geoffrey," she said. Lestrade got a side-eyed look from the younger woman then was immediately dismissed as Mrs. Hudson continued. "But I am here to speak to my son, Isaac. He passed away recently, and I miss him most sorely."

Lestrade thought he glimpsed a hint of a tear in the landlady's eye, a touch of verisimilitude that brought a wave of sympathy from the younger woman, although again Lestrade noted that the emotion did not show in her eyes.

"Come and sit down," the younger woman said. "You shall be next to Simon, as it's your first time."

She led Mrs. Hudson and Mrs. Humphreys away, leaving Lestrade standing abandoned in the doorway. The ladies were seated at either side of the head of the table, just in front of a fireplace as big as Lestrade's sitting room in Vauxhall. The aged clergyman motioned that Lestrade should come over and sit by him; the old man was tapping out a pipe in an ashtray, and Lestrade took the opportunity to light up a cigarette of his own, noting that the smoke was drawn in a definite draft toward the great hearth. Just as he took note of it the gas lights dimmed, although no one had gone near any of them.

"A neat trick, wouldn't you say?" the clergyman said in a voice kept low enough so that only Lestrade would hear. Before Lestrade could answer him the mirror to the left of the fireplace swung noiselessly and smoothly open to reveal a smoke-filled passageway beyond. A slim, expensively tailored man stepped forward. To Lestrade's eye he looked more like a stage-magician than anything else, in a well-cut suit, patent shoes shined to a mirror-like sheen and an elaborate waxed mustache turned up in a curl at either end. His hair, suit, shoes, even his shirt and tie were deep black. The only hint of color came from a ruby gleaming red in his tie pin.

141

"Good evening, friends old and new," he said as he took the ornate winged chair at the head of the table. He had a hint of an accent; French, Lestrade thought, and a deep, almost bass in tone voice with a slight rumble to it, as if something in his chest might be broken. His somber clothing only seemed to accentuate the paleness of his face. and in the now-dim light his eyes seemed to be sunk too far back in their sockets, like black stones in white sand. He had brought some of the smoke from the room beyond with him, and it swirled around his head atmospherically before joining Lestrade's cigarette smoke in the draft heading for the fireplace.

Lestrade had the clergyman to his left, with Mrs. Hudson beyond that, then the man, Simon, at the head of the table, with Mrs. Humphreys beside him and the young woman next to her. It seemed the audience for the evening was complete, for Simon nodded once, the gas lights dimmed even more to leave the room in deep gloom, and the performance proper began.

"We are gathered tonight," Simon began, "to explore the mysteries of the afterlife. Be warned, its pathways are dark ones indeed, and I must request your forbearance while I call for our guide on the journey. It may take some time, for the paths are torturous ones."

There was two seconds of silence, then Simon began to sing in a tenor that belied his speaking voice, in a language that Lestrade did not understand. He'd heard an old Highland chap singing Gaelic songs while drunk in the cells one night and this had some of the same lilting, almost ethereal quality to it. The singing took on resonance and depth, echoing around the room until it seemed there were several voices joined in a chorus, coming from far off as if heard in a strong wind. The dimmed lights flickered and a breeze ran through the room; Lestrade felt it at the gap between his socks and his trousers, like a winter chill. The singing rose as if coming to the end of a chorus, the breeze blew one last, stronger blast, then the whole room fell as quiet and still as a tomb. The smoke from Lestrade's cigarette went up toward the chandelier, as straight as a pencil with no wavering.

This time when Simon spoke it was in a tenor voice, with none of the associated rumbling from his chest. If Lestrade hadn't known better he would swear he was listening to a completely different man.

"I have George here with me," the voice said. "Does anyone wish to speak to him?"

Mrs. Humphreys showed the first signs of animation Lestrade had seen from her all evening. Her face lit up in a smile that took years off her. "George?" she said, her voice high and girlish. "It's your Lillibet. I'm here. I'll always be here."

Simon's voice changed again, to a rough and ready London accent, a smoker's voice.

"Ah, lass, it's good to hear you. It brings light to me in this dark place. But I've got someone else here with me tonight too, a young lad looking for his mam. Does anyone here know an Isaac?"

Lestrade looked across the table and saw Mrs. Hudson staring directly at him. She winked then turned toward Simon.

"Isaac? Are you there, lad?"

"I'm here," a child's voice said from Simon's throat. "Are you my mam?"

Mrs. Hudson didn't get time to reply. A voice Lestrade knew only too well spoke at his left.

"I have had just about as much as I can take of this tomfoolery."

It was the aged clergyman who spoke, but when he stood, and stripped off a most convincing false nose, beard and whiskers it was to reveal Sherlock Holmes' disguise. The reveal, however, did not appear to be going as Holmes might have planned.

The man Simon at the head of the table let out a high, childish, shriek of surprise, Mrs. Humphreys bellowed in outrage at losing her connection to her George, and a second later the gas lamps extinguished themselves completely, plunging the room into total darkness.

Silence fell, only to be broken by the scrape of a match head on a box. The tiny flame flared and behind it Lestrade just made out the figure of Holmes as he climbed up onto the table and lit two of the candles high overhead.

The light showed Mrs. Humphreys bent over the slumped figure of Mrs. Hudson, and the young woman bent over Simon where he had fallen forward, face down on the table. The younger woman was livid in anger.

"What in blazes do you think you are doing?" she shouted.

"I might as well ask the same question of you," Holmes said calmly in reply, then turned to Lestrade. "Can you see the ladies home, Lestrade?" he said. "I'll go over this room and uncover its tawdry little secrets. I do not think Simon, if that is even his name, will be showing his face in polite society again."

Simon didn't lift his head, but he began to sing, the same high tenor as before, not Gaelic this time, but some kind of sea-shanty.

He sleeps in the deep, with the fish far below.
He sleeps in the deep and the dark.
He dreams as he sleeps, in the deep, with the fish
And the Dreaming God is singing where he lies.

Simon was still singing to himself as Lestrade got a slowly reviving Mrs. Hudson to her feet and hustled both her and a still-blustering Mrs. Humphreys out the door and into the street to hail a carriage.

Mrs. Hudson came back to herself as the carriage rattled toward Baker Street.

"What did Sherlock think he was going to accomplish?" she said as she puffed on one of Lestrade's cigarettes.

"I do believe he intended to be of some help to you and your friend here," Lestrade replied.

Mrs. Humphreys harrumphed at that. The lady was clearly not in the best of moods and had a lowering brow like a thundercloud just waiting to spark off. Lestrade was glad when the carriage deposited him and Mrs. Hudson in Baker Street. He heard the other lady give an address to the driver, somewhere in Hammersmith, then the carriage clattered away.

He went inside with Mrs. Hudson, intent on ensuring she was none the worse for the night's excitement, and was soon again seated in the scullery as she insisted on preparing a pot of tea.

"I'm not sure that Holmes has achieved much of anything this night," she said.

"He is doing what I would have done myself," Lestrade reminded her, "He was intent on exposing their activities to the light. It is why I was there, remember?"

"I remember little of it," she said, and Lestrade saw she had a distant stare, looking at something over his left shoulder. "There was a child, wasn't there? I made him up, but there was a child there in the room."

"That was just that man, Simon," Lestrade said, "Just one of his tricks."

She didn't reply, and when she turned back to the kettle on the range he heard her singing, the chorus to the sea shanty, although how she might know it he had not the faintest clue.

Where he lies, where he lies, where he lies, where he lies.

The Dreaming God is singing where he lies.

Lestrade had just finished his tea and a smoke and was about to leave when they heard the front door of 221B open and close. Lestrade went up to the hallway to see Holmes there waiting for him.

"Well," Lestrade said, "did you find their apparatus?"

Holmes did not speak at first, then looked Lestrade in the eye and shook his head. "I found nothing untoward. And worse than that, I'm afraid to say that the man and the woman slipped away while I was searching that back room he came from. I found nothing but solid walls and floors. The manner in which tonight's performance was accomplished is beyond my reckoning. For now. But at least we got Mrs. Hudson away and safe."

She spoke from behind Lestrade. "I did not ask for your help, Mr. Holmes."

"And I do not not ask for my breakfast, Mrs. Hudson," he said. "And yet we provide what we can for each other, do we not? Now I must bid you goodnight; I leave for Liverpool in the morning; there is a pressing matter involving a lost item of cargo that Watson and I must investigate."

Holmes went up the stairs without another word.

"I am afraid we have done little to dissuade your Mrs. Humphreys from her path," Lestrade said, then saw that Mrs. Hudson wasn't paying him any heed. She had her head cocked to one side as if listening to something.

"Mrs. Hudson?" he said, louder this time.

She shook her head as if to clear it, then smiled thinly. "Thank you for trying in any case, Inspector. "It was nice to have a gentleman by my side, if only for this evening."

Lestrade took his leave, caught a carriage in the street outside, and made his way back to Vauxhall, a stiff drink, and bed.

Lestrade thought no more on the matter for several days; he was behind on his paperwork, the Commissioner was on his back, and a thousand tiny details of ongoing cases all seemed to demand his attention at once. He looked up in irritation when Sergeant Clarke arrived in his office doorway.

"Sorry to bother you sir, but we've got reports of a disturbance."

"A disturbance? In London? Who would have thought it? Send a beat officer. Why bother me with it?"

"That's just the thing, sir. The disturbance is at 221B Baker Street. I thought you might like to come along."

Lestrade was out of his chair and fetching his coat before Clarke finished the sentence.

They took one of the Yard's carriages and arrived

in Baker Street to find a young copper standing in the doorway as if unsure how to proceed.

"What's going on here, son?" Lestrade asked, then didn't have to ask as the sound of breaking crockery could clearly be heard through the small window of the basement scullery. A high clear, child's voice was singing, or rather bellowing, and Lestrade felt a cold chill at hearing the words.

Where he lies, where he lies, where he lies, where he lies.

The Dreaming God is singing where he lies.

He turned to the young copper.

"You can go now, lad. The sergeant and I will take it from here."

The young constable looked relieved and scurried away before Lestrade could change his mind.

"You stay at the door here, Clarkie," Lestrade said. "If Holmes or Watson show up, don't let them in until I see what's what."

Without waiting for a reply he tried the door, found it was unlocked, and let himself in, heading for the scullery from where the song was echoing through the house.

He sleeps in the deep, with the fish far below.

He sleeps in the deep and the dark.

Mrs. Hudson liked to keep her scullery meticulously clean and tidy. The scene that met Lestrade's gaze when he went down the stairs was neither. It looked like someone had run rampage, emptying the cupboards of crockery, cutlery, eggs, flour, milk and preserves, then proceeded to break, smash and trample it all into a mess on the floor, work-surfaces and tabletops. A thin, wild-eyed, disheveled figure stood amid the carnage, singing. It took him a few seconds to recognize it as Mrs. Hudson, for the voice coming from her was most definitely not her own.

He dreams as he sleeps, in the deep, with the fish
And the Dreaming God is singing where he lies.

She turned in a circle, arms outstretched and

whirling like a dancer, four revolutions before her gaze fell on Lestrade and stopped her in her tracks. She looked Lestrade in the eye, but when she spoke it was still the child.

"Are you my mam? I've lost my mam."

With no warning she collapsed in a heap on the floor amid the worst of the mess.

At first Lestrade feared she was gone entirely, for her eyes had taken on the glassy look of a porcelain doll and she did not appear to be breathing, but when he turned her onto her back she blinked, coughed once, then her eyes focused on him.

"Inspector? What are you doing here? And why am I on the floor?"

He helped her up into one of the kitchen chairs. Her eyes went wide when she saw the carnage.

"Oh, my Lord in heaven," she said. "What has happened here?"

"First things first, Mrs. Hudson. Have you any brandy? For medicinal purposes, you understand?"

"Top shelf above the sink," she said. "You'll find two glasses there too."

He poured a stiff measure for each of them and lit them both a smoke. Mrs. Hudson looked down at herself. Her dress was caked stiff with wet flour and eggs. He saw the question in her eyes before she spoke, so he gave her a prompt, hoping to lead her in slowly.

"What do you remember?" he said softly.

"I was making a cake," she said, pointing at the table, "right there, when I thought I heard something, a child singing. But the strangest thing was, I couldn't pinpoint the sound; it was as if it was coming from inside my head. It was that song Simon was singing, the thing about fish and sleeping. I couldn't make any sense of it. I tried to ignore it, but it got louder. And then I was sure there was somebody in here with me, watching me. I called out. And I got a reply all right. The same thing Simon had that child say."

"Are you my mam?" Lestrade said for her.

"That's right; how did you know?"

"Old copper's intuition," he replied. "And what then?"

"And then, nothing. Not until I woke up on the floor just now. Did he make this mess, that child? There is a child, isn't there?"

"I don't rightly know, Mrs. Hudson. But I know a man who might. Can I ask you to make yourself presentable? I'd like you to take a trip with me."

"What about this mess?"

"That can wait."

"Where are we going?"

"To Islington, to see a man about a boy."

If Clarke was surprised ten minutes later when Lestrade exited 221B with a much more presentable Mrs. Hudson in tow he didn't show it, beyond a raised eyebrow and a question as they got into the carriage.

"Where to, sir?"

"Upper Street, Islington," Lestrade said. "And quick about it."

On the way he brought Clarke up to date with as much of the tale as he thought necessary.

"And you think, what, exactly, sir?" Clarke asked when he was done. "I saw a mesmerist at the Music Hall last year. He made people do all kinds of peculiar things. Do you think this is like that?"

"I don't rightly know what to think, Clarkie."

He looked over to Mrs. Hudson. She was staring out of the carriage window. Her lips were moving, as if singing, although no sound was coming out. He didn't have to hear the words, he knew what it was from the cadence.

The Dreaming God is singing where he lies.

He rapped on the ceiling of the carriage and shouted.

"Faster, man. This is an emergency."

The Upper Street house appeared to have been vacated; Lestrade found the main door locked up, and there was no answer to his ringing of the bell. A boy in the street stopped to watch.

"They've scarpered, sir," he said. "Did a midnight flit one night last week. Ain't nobody knows where they gone to. Left owing three months rent too is what I hear."

Lestrade would not allow himself to be thus thwarted.

"They might not know around here where the bally man has gone," he said. "But I know someone who might. Change of plans, Clarkie. We're off to Hammersmith."

He got back in the carriage. Mrs. Hudson was still gazing out of the window, still mouthing the words of the blasted song. Lestrade shook her by the arm.

"Are you quite all right, Mrs. Hudson?" he asked.

When she turned to face him her gaze was blank; not quite the glassy doll stare, but not that far from it so as to cause Lestrade to shudder at the memory.

"Are you my mam?" she said in the child's voice. Lestrade heard Clarke gasp behind him, but couldn't afford to take his eyes off the woman.

"No, I'm not your mam, Isaac," he said softly. "You be quiet now, there's a good lad. You'll see her soon."

Without another word Mrs. Hudson turned back to gaze out the window, once again mouthing the words to the song.

Where he lies, where he lies, where he lies, where he lies.

The Dreaming God is singing where he lies.

He sat back in the carriage seat and lit a smoke. He saw Clarke look over at him. Lestrade shook his head.

"No questions, Clarkie. Not right now. I don't have any answers for you in any case."

Mrs. Humphreys was at home when they arrived at the address in Hammersmith, but she wasn't happy to see Lestrade. He'd left Clarke and Mrs. Hudson in the carriage, and it was just as well for the woman was in a foul mood indeed.

"After that caper you pulled on me in Islington? You

want my help? Well you can whistle for it, my lad. You'll get nothing from me, and that's exactly what you deserve."

"You know where Simon is, don't you?" Lestrade said. "Of course you do. You can't keep away."

"He lets me speak to my George," she said. "If you'd lost someone, you'd know I can't betray Simon. I need him."

"I do know, Mrs. Humphreys," Lestrade said, feeling the old hurt in his chest. "I know only too well how our bereaved ones can haunt us. But we won't find them through men like that Simon. I know that too."

He saw that she would not be budged but he still had a strong hand to play.

"There is someone I need you to see," he said, and then more forcefully when she hesitated. "Please. This is police business. It's your duty."

That did the trick and he was able to lead her to the carriage. Mrs. Hudson was still looking out the window and, as Lestrade had both hoped and feared, obliged him by looking up at their approach and staring directly at Mrs. Humphreys.

The child spoke from Mrs. Hudson's mouth.

"Are you my mam?"

Two minutes later they were on their way, with Mrs. Humphreys aboard alongside Mrs. Hudson, heading for an address in Chelsea.

The apartment above an apothecary on the Kings Road was nowhere near as opulent as the house in Upper Street, but it was still several steps up the social scale from Lestrade's house in Vauxhall, causing him yet again to wonder just how many well-moneyed clients might be availing themselves of Simon's 'services.'

As with Mrs. Humphreys before him, Simon was not at all pleased to see Lestrade at his door, and would have closed it in the Inspector's face had Mrs. Hudson's plight not been brought to his attention. Once again the child spoke.

... a shimmering aurora in which was contained a myriad of black eggs ...

"Are you my mam?" she asked Simon, and the man went pale.

"Your friend the other night interrupted proceedings while the doorway was still open. Something came through that should not have."

"The boy?"

"I doubt very much if that is a boy," Simon said soberly. "But whatever it is, we need to send it back, and right away, for every minute it is here its strength grows."

"Why couldn't it have been George?" Mrs. Humphreys said softly. "I'd have gladly taken him into me."

"Don't even talk about such matters," Simon said brusquely. "There is much you do not understand here, and I have no time to educate you. Come. We must begin immediately."

Simon led them through a narrow hallway to a parlor that was smaller but identically fashioned to the one in Upper Street, even down to the sculpture of Pan in the center of the smaller six-seater table. Simon had Mrs. Hudson sit on his left and Mrs. Humphreys on his right. Lestrade sat opposite the younger woman; he still didn't know her name and she looked in no mood to enlighten him. Clarke had stayed behind in the carriage and Lestrade was beginning to think his sergeant had got the better end of the deal as Simon began without any preamble.

He launched straight into the singing, the same lilting song that had reminded Lestrade of Gaelic. There was a hint of something in it this time that had not been present in Islington; a rougher, coarse quality that spoke of menace. It took on more depth as before, reverberating in a drone around the room and setting the candelabra above to shaking. The song took on a higher tenor tone and switched to English, the now familiar shanty.

He sleeps in the deep, with the fish far below.

The air above the sculpture of Pan shimmered, like hot oil on a skillet, and a small tear appeared, a black rip in the fabric of space. An oily substance oozed through and pinched off to leave a single, black, iridescent egg hanging impossibly in the space between Pan's head and the candelabra.

He sleeps in the deep and the dark.

The egg calved. Two became four became eight became sixteen.

He dreams as he sleeps, in the deep, with the fish.

Sixteen became thirty-two, then Lestrade lost count as the calving increased, faster and faster, the whole ceiling of the room above them roiling and seething in a shimmering aurora in which was contained a myriad of black eggs, all dancing in time to the song.

And the Dreaming God is singing where he lies.

A spiraling column, as wide as a man's shoulders, spun down from the ceiling to just above the sculpture, the whirling eggs within dancing in rainbow colors.

The song stopped, but the column kept spinning.

"I call for the Opener of the Way," Simon shouted in his normal voice. "Sototh, Sarban, hear me. There is one here who requires passage."

"Are you my mam?" Mrs. Hudson said at Lestrade's side, and rose from her chair. She seemed intent on climbing up onto the table toward the spiraling column. Lestrade rose to pull her back.

"Let her go," Simon said. "It's the only way. The thing cannot stay here. It must go back."

"Not if it means losing her," Lestrade said and pulled Mrs. Hudson back down into her chair.

"Are you my mam?" the child said to him.

The answer came, not from anyone around the table, but from the spiraling column, and it was not addressed to Mrs. Hudson.

"Lilibet?" a voice said. Lestrade recognized it from the night in Islington ... and so did Mrs. Humphreys.

"George? Is that you?"

"Yes, darling. I want you to do something for me."

"Anything."

"Fetch the child to me. Fetch Isaac. He'll come for you."

Before anyone could stop her, the woman clambered up on the table. She reached out a hand toward Mrs. Hudson.

"Come to me, Isaac. I'll take you home," she said.

"Are you my mam?"

"I am now," Mrs. Humphrey's said.

Mrs. Hudson let out a loud sigh, as if expelling all the breath in her body and something, a shimmer of dancing light, passed between her and the reaching Mrs. Humphreys. When the woman up on the table spoke again it was with the child's voice.

"Mam?"

"Right here, Isaac," Mrs Humphreys replied.

"Bring him to me," the voice in the column said. Lestrade was already moving, intending to stop her, but Mrs. Humphreys was not to be denied. She stepped forward. The column of swirling eggs descended and engulfed her.

"George?" they all heard her say.

"Right here, lass. Now and forever."

The sea-shanty song echoed around the room, coming from everywhere and nowhere, a massed chorus singing in a wind.

Where he lies, where he lies, where he lies, where he lies.

The Dreaming God is singing where he lies.

The room was lit by a blinding flash and a crack of thunderous sound. When Lestrade looked up there was only ceiling above, and only the gurning face of Pan looking at him from the sculpture on the table.

There was no sign of Mrs. Humphreys and when he looked over to Mrs. Hudson there were fresh tears in the landlady's eyes.

"Do you think she's with her George?" she asked.

He saw, over her shoulder, that Simon was shaking his head sadly. Lestrade ignored him and took her by the arm.

155

"I think she's exactly where she wanted to be," Lestrade said, and led Mrs. Hudson to the door. "Now let's get you home. You've had quite enough excitement for one day."

A Deadly Stare

"I understand you have been receiving death threats," Lestrade said.

The man across the desk looked as if death had found him already; he was ashen in the face, gray at the lips with eyes sunk deep like black coals in a field of snow.

"Threats, no. A promise? Yes," the other man said, barely a whisper.

If Lestrade had not known that Sir George Barnstable had only just passed his fortieth birthday he might have taken him for seventy, perhaps more.

Lestrade was here at the behest of the Commissioner, who was a friend of the family.

"Could all be smoke and shadow, of course," his superior had said. "He's big in shipping, made his fortune in India. Large houses in London, Surrey and the Scottish Highlands. Chaps like that get letters all the time, begging, threatening, cajoling; you and I both know the lengths people will go to to get money they do not have. So go along and see what's what. If nothing else it'll put his mind at rest. His wife tells me his nerves are shot."

Lestrade had met the wife on arrival at the house in

Bayswater; her nerves had not appeared all too healthy either, her hands fluttering like a caged bird at her throat, her eyes darting hither and thither, never settling too long on Lestrade's face, chest, feet, then back to his face again. Something had this household in a grip of fear, something more than the Commissioner's smoke and shadow.

He'd been shown into the gentleman's study, a hugely imposing circular library with a grand bay window overlooking substantial gardens and an expansive pond. The man looked tiny and frail behind a desk the size of Lestrade's office at the Yard.

"May I see the letter?" Lestrade said.

Barnstable pushed, almost threw, an envelope across the desk. It slid to a halt just out of Lestrade's reach and he was forced to get out of his seat to retrieve it. It was expensive stationery, heavy cream, and addressed in a fine-handed flowing script, in the blackest of ink, to *Sir George,* at this Bayswater address. The single sheet of paper inside was of equal quality and was written in the same hand. There was no signature, no return address, just a single line.

"You are the last. You will die when I next set my eye on you."

Lestrade held the paper up to the light. There was a most distinctive watermark, a five-pointed star inside a pair of concentric circles with script, too tiny to make out, running around the rim.

"This should not be difficult to trace," Lestrade said.

"No need," Barnstable said. "I know only too well who sent it, and why." The businessman sighed deeply as if coming to a decision. "You'll find a bottle of brandy, some glasses and a box of cigars in the cabinet by the door," he said. "Be a good chap and fetch them over, please. I have a story to tell that we promised would never be revealed, and I fear it is going to be thirsty work.

Lestrade did as he was bid, and took a cigar and a large-bowled glass of brandy when offered before sitting back in the chair across the desk from the man who at last had some color in his cheeks now that he had taken a deep gulp from his glass.

"I must take you back almost twenty years, Inspector," he said. "There were four of us, all young officers fresh out of Sandhurst, rutting and drinking our way across Northern India while ostensibly overseeing the building of a new stretch of railroad, but in reality spending most of our time in local fleshpots of which, I may add, there were many.

"I was the first one of us to be commissioned, only by a few days, but in the Army a few days is more than enough, so I was effectively in charge of operations, although I was able to leave most of the actual work to a Scottish engineer in the lower ranks who took a personal interest in the railroad and associated engines.

"We had a rare old time those first few months, and I could not have asked for better companionship. Things changed when our Scots engineer arrived in the mess tent one day to inform us that there was a problem with the local workforce; it appeared that our proposed rail line would go through a pass in the hills that was somehow sacred to them, bad juju to disturb.

"Of course, being Englishmen we held no truck with such stuff and nonsense. Well, except for David Morrison; David was a vicar's son ... second son, that is ... and full of all sorts of exotic knowledge garnered from his father's extensive library. David was the only one of us to urge caution, but we other three were in the mood for a jolly jape, so we took ourselves off for an adventure, with David coming along only reluctantly. With a score of riflemen at our backs we headed up the pass to see what the fuss was about.

"We found a temple on a high bluff overlooking the pass, and a strange-looking thing it was too, all angles and sharp edges, fighting with the rock it sat on rather than making any attempt to blend in with the landscape, tall, towering turrets like fingers of jet black stone and scarcely a curve in sight. It hurt the eyes to even look at the thing, and David went white at the sight, saying it reminded him of something he'd seen in a book, a place only ever mentioned in hushed tones. I do believe he would have turned and fled had he not been with us, his brother officers. I took a deep breath and marched the men inside; after all, we were on the Queen's business, and this was her country now.

"We'd been in temples before; you can't throw a stick in India without hitting a place of worship of one bally thing or other, but none of us had ever seen anything like this. The interior courtyard was as black as the towers above. The walls seemed to swallow the sunlight and I felt a sudden chill despite the heat of the day. We were in an open space, an interior courtyard, as I said, and there was no sign of life, no sign there had been anyone in residence for a long passage of years. Again young David was keen to turn and leave, suggesting that the place was empty and of no merit. But my curiosity had been piqued. We left our horses in the yard and went to explore, choosing the largest of four possible entrances as being the most likely to yield a result.

"The interior of the place was darker still, as if it had been devoid of light for eons, but we had tunneled in dark places and knew how to illuminate them; it was not too long before every third man carried a firebrand and we were able to continue."

Barnstable stopped there to partake of more brandy and puff on his cigar.

"We are arriving at the meat of it now. It may not seem pertinent to you just yet, and what follows does not paint me in the best possible light, but remember, I was young, and a gentleman in search of a fortune can become somewhat giddy when one drops into his lap."

He took another puff on the cigar to convince himself it was still lit, then continued.

"We quickly discovered that the place was a regular warren of chambers, tunnels and stairwells with no seeming rhyme or reason in their construction. I split the riflemen up into teams and had them search the lower areas while we, the four musketeers, went upward, intuiting that anything of value that might be here would be in more salubrious quarters where sunlight might be found.

"Our path took us up a long stairwell. Rather than warming the chill in me it got worse, eating at my very bones. I was very happy to see daylight ahead of us. We hurried up toward it, and came out into a balconied room with a view down the full length of the pass. That wasn't what caught our eye, though. The room was lushly decorated in fine rugs, hanging tapestries and the furs of great beasts; wolf and bear in the main. That still wasn't what caught our eye. What got our full attention were the tall pottery jars spaced at intervals around the walls, jars filled with jewels and trinkets, gold and silver coins, and precious stones without number.

"Young David once again counseled caution.

"'These are some kind of votive offerings to their gods,' he said. 'We should not disturb them.'

"'Are you daft?' John Fitzpatrick said. 'We're rich men, the lot of us. Look at this stuff, just here for the taking.'

"He stepped forward and took a fistful of rubies in his hand, letting them slip through his fingers. As if on cue a tall robed and hooded figure stepped forward out of the shadows. The robe was a deep yellow in color, covering the figure entirely, and the hood was pulled forward such that his features were hidden. He raised an arm and a hand that looked so thin to be almost skeletal, pointed at us then at the stairwell; the intent was clear, we were being asked to leave.

"I, for one, was in no mood to obey. I unholstered my service pistol and aimed it at the robed man.

"'Step aside, sir. This is the Queen's country now, and by rights this belongs to her.'

"Of course, we had no intention of sharing this treasure with the crown, but I hoped I might intimidate the man into backing down. Instead he drew a long scimitar from the folds of his robe, obviously intent on trying to stop us. David must have seen my intent in my eyes as my finger tightened on the trigger, for he stepped between myself and the robed man.

"'No,' he said. 'This is wrong.'

"I implored him to step aside. He would not. The man behind him raised the scimitar high and came forward.

"I did what I had to do. I shot David, than shot the robed man. Both fell as if hit by a hammer blow.

"To cut a long story short, the remaining three, myself, John Fitzpatrick, and William Longton-Smythe, filled our bags with all that we could carry out of that room, then, fearing reprisal, fled the scene. We left David and the robed man lying there, not knowing if they were dead or alive, not caring, our only thoughts being for the value of the loot we escaped with.

"We swore each other to secrecy, stashed our treasure in a safe place, built our railway; it went a different route than originally intended, bypassing the temple entirely. We finished our tour of duty and arrived back in England a year later as wealthy men."

Barnstable stopped talking and Lestrade looked up to see tears in the man's eyes.

"I told you I know who sent the letter, Inspector. And I do. John Fitzpatrick got one last week, and died soon after. I don't know about Longton-Smythe; he is somewhere in New York the last I heard. But I would not be at all surprised if he too has died, having had a letter. In fact, reading that one you have in your hand, I am sure of it.

"The letter is from David Morrison, the man I believed I killed twenty years ago."

Lestrade looked from the letter in his lap to the man across the desk.

"You are sure?"

Barnstable nodded. "He always had the most exquisite penmanship; I'd know it anywhere."

"And you believe he has already killed your friends; that's what's gotten you worried?"

Barnstable nodded again, finished off his brandy, and poured himself a stiff one that went down as quickly as the last.

"Could you investigate Fitzpatrick's death?" Barnstable asked. "If there's anything you can tie to Morrison...."

"Then I can get him off your back. Yes, we can do that; I think that's what the Commissioner would have me do now in any case."

"Then I won't take up any more of your time, Inspector. I wish you luck. Catch Morrison. Before he catches me."

On the way back to the Yard Lestrade was wondering, not about the legality, but about the morality of what he'd been asked to do. Barnstable had admitted to cold-blooded murder and theft. And yet, it had been twenty years ago and far away, a case long gone cold and probably impossible to prosecute. If this Fitzpatrick chap had indeed been killed in the past week, Lestrade had a more pressing matter at hand.

Once back at the Yard he set Sergeant Clarke tracking down the details of Fitzpatrick's death; it wasn't an event Lestrade had taken any note of, but then again, he wasn't much of a man for the society pages of the newspapers in any case. Satisfied that Clarke was on the case, Lestrade then sent a telegraph to the police department in New York, inquiring after anything pertaining to an English gentleman, William Longton-Smythe.

He got a reply as he was finishing up a mug of tea and a smoke. Longton-Smythe was, as Barnstable feared, dead, although there did not appear to be any suspicious circumstances; the cause of death was listed as heart failure, and it had happened in the previous month.

Clarke had better luck with Fitzpatrick, although it was late in the day and almost time for Lestrade to make his way home when the sergeant returned.

"I talked to the widow," Clarke said. "They had a letter, just like Barnstable. Then, one morning last week, they had a visitor who bold as brass introduced himself to the butler as David Morrison. The lady saw what happened. The butler showed the visitor into the man's library. The door was open so she had a clear view. She said the two men just looked at each other, never a word spoken, and the next thing she knew Fitzpatrick fell as if poleaxed to the floor. By the time she reached him he was a dead man, staring at the ceiling. She said he looked like he'd taken the fright of his life. When she thought to look for him, Morrison had taken his leave."

"Perhaps the man did die of fright," Lestrade replied, "for if Barnstable spoke true, Fitzpatrick had just seen a man he'd thought dead for twenty years. Anything about a letter?"

Clarke nodded, and produced a letter from his pocket; it was to a different address but was almost the double of the one Barnstable had received, save for a slight difference in the text.

"You are the second. You will die when I next set my eye on you."

The watermark was the same five-pointed star inside concentric circles with script around the rim.

"I think it's about time we had a word with David Morrison," Lestrade said. "Put a couple of lads on it, see if we can find out where he's gone to ground. I'll check in on you in the morning."

Lestrade had expected that Morrison would be lying low and keeping his head down, but Clarke surprised him as soon as he got to his office the next day.

"Found him, sir," the sergeant said. "He's working a nightly show in the upstairs room of the Market Porter in Borough Market and has taken a room at the back to sleep in. Some kind of magic routine I gather; going by the name The Great Suprendo. My snout tells me he usually drinks too much afterward, and spends the morning sleeping it off so we should catch him off guard."

"Just what I need to start the day," Lestrade muttered, "A murderer with a hangover."

As it turned out, Clarke's informer had got it wrong, on that morning at least.

Lestrade knew the Market Porter well; sitting as it did in one of the busiest markets in the city, it was a hub for many and various activities, most of them criminal. Today it had its best face on; two bar staff were washing mugs from the night before, the floor had fresh straw on it, and the bar itself, all mahogany and copper fittings, gleamed as if freshly polished. The barman pointed them to a man sitting alone in the far corner of the bar eating breakfast.

"There's your lad, guv'nor," he said. "Strange cove. Keeps hisself to hisself for the main part. Likes a drink too, although he goes for sweet liqueurs in the main. Hardly a drink for a man, is it?"

If Morrison was indeed a murderer he was the most cheerful one Lestrade had ever met. The man looked up from his breakfast, saw the policemen, and waved them over to his table.

"Tea and toast for these gentlemen, Bob, if you please. And some more of your wife's marvelous marmalade. On my tab," he shouted.

He rose to greet them and pumped Lestrade's hand heartily. He wore a black waistcoat and trousers and a plain white shirt open at the collar. The starkness of the white showed off his tan, for his face was dark-hued and leathery, a sure sign of someone who has spent too long in the sun over the course of some years. Lestrade knew him to be a year younger than Barnstable but the difference in their demeanor, should they be seen together, would make them appear more like father and son, with Barnstable looking much the elder.

"Inspector Lestrade of the Yard," Morrison said as if amused. "I expected you sooner."

"You know what this is about then?" Lestrade said, taking a seat opposite Morrison. Clarke sat to his left, effectively boxing the man into the corner, but if he was at all concerned he certainly didn't show it.

165

"Oh yes. Longton-Smythe, Fitzpatrick and Barnstable. Do you know what they did to me, Inspector?"

"I've had Barnstable's side of the story," Lestrade answered, lighting up a smoke. "How about telling me yours?"

"Where shall I start? Did he tell you he shot me and left me for dead like a dog?"

Lestrade nodded.

Morrison smiled. "Then I need not bother with the preamble. The three of them ran off with their ill-gotten gains while I lay there, my life ebbing away. The high priest of the temple, Ahmed, lay beside me, and I believe it was his acolytes saving of him that also saved me, for I got the same treatment as he did, a suffusion of certain herbs and spices that kept me alive, if not well, for the long months of recuperation that were required. I became somewhat of an acolyte myself thereafter, and learned a great many things."

He took a monocle from his waistcoat pocket and made it dance, like a coin across his fingers, made it vanish in his left palm only to reappear in his right, and made it appear to glisten, a golden orb like a miniature sun in his hand before he tucked it away again in his pocket.

"Some of the things I learned were mere parlor tricks, which have come in handy to keep me from penury. Others are, how would you say it, more esoteric. I have traveled far, Inspector, and learned much that was hidden."

"And now you're back for revenge? Why wait twenty years?"

Morrison shrugged and smiled. "It took me that long to learn the particular trick that would be required."

"It is revenge we are talking about, though? You did kill the other two?"

That got Lestrade another smile. "I did not touch either one of them," he said. 'Both deaths were witnessed, as you will know from your investigations. I had no weapon with me. I was merely a bystander, in the eyes of the law at least."

"At two murders? That's surely no coincidence?"

That only got another smile.

"And the letters? How do you explain the fact that you foretold these men's deaths?" Lestrade asked.

"How do you explain it, Inspector? Surely that is the question any court would be asking?"

The barman arrived with tea and toast. Clarke helped himself but Lestrade ignored it pointedly.

"You think you're smart, don't you, Mr. Morrison?"

"I'm better than smart, Inspector. I'm careful. Are you going to arrest me? For I assure you, I can well afford a good lawyer, or even a bad one, for even the most incompetent would be able to persuade a judge that I could not possibly have killed those men. All he would have to do would be to drag in the witnesses and I'd be a free man minutes later. You know that as well as I do."

"I know a guilty man when I see one," Lestrade replied. "I don't yet know how you do it, but I'll find out, I can promise you that."

Morrison smiled again. "Shall I make it easier for you? I intend to pay a visit to my old friend Barnstable this afternoon. Would you like to meet me there and witness for yourself what happens?"

"You shall not go anywhere near him."

"How will you stop me? I repeat, am I under arrest?"

The man had Lestrade over a barrel, and they both knew it. And Lestrade's temper was in danger of getting the better of him. Rather than bandy words with the man, he chose to leave. As he was getting up from the table Morrison spoke, almost conversationally.

"Shall we say two o'clock, then, in Bayswater? I expect I shall see you there."

"Too smug by half," Lestrsade muttered to himself as they left, but he already knew that he'd be keeping the appointment. He had a feeling that Barnstable's life depended on it.

He had Clarke direct the carriage directly to Bayswater, where he spent a fruitless hour attempting to persuade Barnstable not to take any meeting with Morrison.

"I will not cower like a coward, Inspector," Barnstable said. "I was an army officer once, and by Jove, if this is to be my end, I will see it like the man I once was. I did wrong by David Morrison, and I have regretted it ever since. The spoils of that day have been bitter to tell the truth. So yes, I will face him if he comes, if only for a chance to tell him I am sorry."

There was no time after that to get back to the Yard. Lestrade and Clarke had lunch in a quiet inn to the north of Bayswater itself, then returned to park outside Barnstable's home, smoking cigarettes in silence as they watched for Morrison's arrival.

The man was as good as his word, arriving at five before the hour in a carriage that parked behind the police carriage in the road. Morrison tugged at his forelock and smiled at Lestrade as he headed for the driveway up to the main door. Lestrade and Clarke disembarked and followed some five yards behind.

The butler showed Morrison in. Morrison waited in the doorway to ensure Lestrade was with him as they were led across the hallway to Barnstable's library. As they walked Lestrade saw Morrison take his monocle from his waistcoat pocket and fix it in his left eye.

The library door opened. Barnstable was at his desk, with a brandy bottle and two glasses in front of him as if he intended to have a drink and make peace with his visitor. He did not get a chance.

It all happened in a second. Barnstable stood, put out a hand to be shaken.

"David. I ..."

Lestrade saw Morrison reach up and tighten the monocle in his left eye socket. At the same moment Barnstable clutched at his chest, his mouth wide in a scream that would never come. He was dead before he hit the ground.

Lestrade moved fast. He turned to Clarke.

"Hold Morrison," he said. "Back to the carriage with him, right now."

"Are you arresting me, Inspector?" Morrison said, still smiling. "On what charge?"

"I'll think of something," Lestrade said, and watched as Clarke marched a still smiling Morrison away. Lestrade saw the man take out the monocle and put it away again in his waistcoat pocket.

Then it was all business for a time, getting the butler to get the household in order and see to the freshly widowed wife, arranging for a coroner, making notes for his report, all the small sad routines that always surrounded the scene of a murder. And murder it was, Lestrade was sure of that fact, even though he could not as yet understand the manner in which it had been done.

But he intended to find out, and to find out that very afternoon. Morrison was about to discover just how far Lestrade's tenacity could take him.

It was almost five o'clock before Lestrade got back to the Yard. Clarke had put Morrison in one of the cells. Before seeing the man, Lestrade paid a visit to the men's washrooms. Then, when Lestrade had Morrison brought up to the interview room, he ensured that they collided in the narrow corridor outside, bringing them chest to chest together. Lestrade apologized, then showed the man in and had him sit at the table. Lestrade sat opposite and lit a smoke.

"Are you going to tell me how you did it?" Lestrade asked.

"Did what, exactly, Inspector?"

"You've killed three men this month. You know it and I know it."

"So arrest me or release me. I have a show to do in the Porter tonight."

"Then I'll start, shall I?" Lestrade said, with a smile of his own. "Magicians are not the only ones who know tricks. Old coppers like myself need to know the ways of criminals before they can catch them. Like pickpockets, for example. It's amazing how easy it is to pick up the technique. A seemingly chance meeting in a hallway, a little nudge, and Bob's your uncle."

Lestrade opened his palm and showed Morrison the monocle lying there in the center. He was pleased to see Morrison's smile switch off to be replaced by a frown.

"Having seen you in action now, so to speak, I'm guessing this is part of your method. How does it work, exactly?"

Lestrade lifted the monocle and went to place it in his left eye socket. Morrison reacted as if scalded, throwing himself back in his seat, almost tipping it over.

"No, you mustn't!" he shouted.

Lestrade sat back, his smile widening. He kept playing with the monocle in his left hand. Morrison's eyes never left it.

"So this just isn't part of your trick. This is your trick, in entirety? How does it work?"

Lestrade again moved to put the monocle in his left eye and again Morrison looked terrified.

"I beg you, put it down," the man said. "You don't know what you're playing with."

"So tell me," Lestrade said softly. "Just between the two of us. You said yourself, a good lawyer is guaranteed to get you off. Just tell me. Tell me, or I'll put this thing in my eye and have a look for myself."

Morrison must have seen and heard that Lestrade spoke the simple truth for he smiled thinly in reply. "I am not the magic. All I have are stage magician's tricks, no matter how much time I spent in that temple as an acolyte. It was a hard lesson to learn and one that took me years to finally come to terms with; the monks there had no secrets to impart, no hidden wisdom I could become privy to. They were in thrall to the High Priest, and so was I. Once I had that epiphany my course of action was clear to me. Five years ago now I took advantage of a dark night, killed the old man and high-tailed it for parts west with as much of the loot as I could carry."

"You were no better than the others then?"

"Never said I was, did I, old boy? But back to the story. I knew there was no magic to be learned. But I wondered if it could be bought instead. So began a quest that has taken me these last five years and cost a good part of the fortune I came away with. I visited Lisbon and Leipzig, Morocco and Cairo, Prague and Constantinople, greasing palms with jewels in exchange for the ultimate trick. I was coming to the conclusion that, as at the temple, there was nothing but charlatanry involved everywhere when someone discovered me."

He pointed at the monocle.

"I had this from a very old man in Leningrad and he said he had it from an alchemist who claimed to be four hundred years old, and had made it himself, in the fifteenth century. It's a tall story, certainly, but the proof of the pudding is in the eating. He killed a dog to show me, and I killed another to be sure. It cost me a full third of what I had left. But it was worth every penny, as my three dead former friends will attest."

He sat back, his tale told.

"You expect me to believe that poppycock?" Lestrade said, still playing with the monocle.

Morrison smiled. "If you do not believe in it, may I have it back? It has great sentimental value for me."

"Certainly," Lestrade said. He leaned over the table to pass over the monocle, at the same time putting a hand on the thing in the inside pocket of his jacket, the thing he'd brought out of the men's washroom. When Morrison took the monocle and screwed it into his left eye socket Lestrade was already lifting up the shaving mirror in front of his face, with the reflective side toward Morrison.

"I don't believe your story," he said. "But you do, you all did, and I think that's the important thing here."

A look of pure terror crossed Morrison's face as realization hit. He screamed silently, clutched at his chest and fell sideways off the chair, already dead. The monocle rolled off his face to the floor where Lestrade ground it to fragments of glass under his heel.

"Never try to teach an old dog a new trick," Lestrade said, standing over the corpse. "That's something they should at least have taught you somewhere along the line."

The Faithful Custodian

Lestrade had often considered the weather in London to be somewhat bleak at times, but Balmoral had it beat into a cocked hat when it came to sheer, miserable grayness. *Dreich* the Scots called it; bloody miserable was Lestrade's most polite word for his current situation.

When the Commissioner had informed him he was being put on special assignment for the Crown he expected it to be protection duty at Buckingham Palace; a cushy number he could walk to in the mornings and be home for supper in the evenings, feet up by the fire. The head of the Queen's Guard soon put paid to that idea.

"Balmoral, two weeks at least. Pack something waterproof," the old soldier, Colonel Green, had said. Lestrade had brought his woolen winter coat, but that only served to soak up the dampness such that it felt like a sodden heavy blanket across his shoulders. Sergeant Clarke had shown more sense, having an oilskin cape and hood that were much more efficient against the steady drizzle, but even he was complaining bitterly after the second day of trudging around the large estate.

"Tell me again what we're looking for?" the sergeant asked as they topped a small hill and looked over more of the same bleak, gray emptiness.

"Anarchists, that's what I was told. Russians bent on disrupting their Royal Family by killing off the Queen. But I'm damned sure even Russian anarchists have sense enough to stay away from here."

He slapped at his cheek as another Highland midge took a lump out of him. The insects, even more than the rain, were the bane of his life. Smoking helped to keep them at bay for a while, but even Lestrade couldn't handle chain-smoking throughout the whole course of the day. His face was mottled with their tiny bites, as were the backs of his hands. He stepped in a puddle and another swarm of them rose up in angry protest. He gave in to the inevitable and lit another cigarette, having to use three matches before he got one to light in the damp air.

"Remind me to never again complain about a pea-souper on the Embankment, Clarkie," he said as they headed for the next hill.

They finished their rounds of the estate just as darkness was starting to fall, having disturbed nothing more than a few startled deer and a fox that had strolled imperiously passed them as if they were of no import to its business.

Colonel Green took one look at them as they arrived at the East-side building that was serving as their barracks for the duration and laughed.

"Ah, the drowned hounds return. Anything to report?"

"It's wet," Lestrade said, and Green laughed again.

"Aye, well summer was last week," he said. "Just be thankful it's not snowing.'

"In September?"

"It happens."

"Not to me it doesn't," Lestrade replied, and got another laugh.

"If you need cheering up," Greene said, "I can recommend the Black Bull along the road. Out the main gates, half a mile on the right past the kirk, you can't miss it. Good soup, strong ale and fine Highland hospitality. And they'll have a good fire going, warmer there than the barracks here, that's for sure. A few of the lads pop down there when their shifts are done."

The Black Bull didn't look like much at first glance; a squat thatched roadside building of dark stone and a simple hand-painted sign outside. It was gloomy inside, lit only by candles and oil lamps. Half a dozen locals sat huddled around a roaring fire on stools and the bar, such as it was, was a table placed in front of three barrels at the far end of the single room.

The barman was more affable than the surroundings though, and the two policemen were soon ensconced at a small table in the corner with a pint of dark ale and a steaming bowl of mutton stew for each of them. The stew did much to improve Lestrade's mood and the ale, although stronger and sweeter than his usual tastes, went down very nicely in accompaniment. He was about to light up a cigarette he thought he might actually enjoy when one of the locals got up from in front of the fire and came over to their table.

"Queen's men, is it, sirs?" the newcomer asked. He was an older man, well past sixty at a guess, weather-beaten and racked with arthritis, with several days of gray stubble on his chin. But his eyes were blue and piercing as he met Lestrade's gaze. "Aye, Queen's Men you must be, for you're in a Queen's Man's seat."

The barman shouted over. "Come away and don't bother these gentlemen, Alisdair. They've no time to be listening to your prattle."

The old man ignored that and sat himself down at the table. "Do you ken the tale of John Brown?" he asked.

"I've heard of the man," Lestrade said. "Of course we have. Everybody has."

"Aye. But did you ken he came from around here? Did you ken I went to school wi' the lad? Did you ken he did his drinking in this very pub? Did you ken you're sitting in his seat? Aye, there's a lot you don't ken. And it's thirsty work in the telling, if you catch my drift."

Lestrade yielded to the inevitable and ordered in another round; a pint each for him and Clarke, and a large glass of peaty Scotch for the old man, who smacked his lips eagerly before throwing a full half of it down in one gulp.

"Aye, John and I were great pals as lads," the old man said. "We covered every inch of the hills around here, fishing and hunting, chased a few lassies too. And did a lot of drinking at this very table; he liked a dram, did John, but he never let the drink take hold of him. Never let much of anything take hold of him back then. Then John got the big job and was spending most of his time down your way in your castles and posh houses. But he never forgot us wee folk back home.

"Christmas of '53 it was when things changed for John. He came home from Windsor bearing gifts; hampers full of fine wines, hams and Belgian chocolates for his pals and posh wooden and tin toys for the bairns. He was here to oversee the laying of the foundations for the new big hoose, under strict instruction from Albert as to what was and wasn't allowed. He came in here, sat where you are now, and we had a few drams for auld times' sake, then another few drams just to be sociable, then I went along with him to have a look at the building works.

"They were well along with it by that time; some of the local lads had gotten plenty of work but they were kept hard at it. Albert always was a man for looking after every penny. They had half of the side of the hill looking over the river dug up but when we rolled up for a look they had come to a halt at the west end of the workings and half a dozen men were standing around looking down into a hole where something had caved in.

"Of course John being John, and with a few drams in him, had to have a look, so down he goes into the hole with me; not looking to disappoint him, right at his back.

It was a day much like today, but later in the year, so it was getting dark down there, and getting even darker fast. We clambered over what I saw was old stone; I thought it must have been an auld dry-stane dyke at first then we saw it was what was left of four walls, strong in their day, but that day was long past. We were about to climb back out when something caught John's eye, a glint of metal. He bent and started digging with his hands, urging me to join him. It was wet, heavy and dark earth, but after a couple of minutes we got the thing free, a wee wooden box with what looked like a silver lock and bars, about a foot long and half that wide. John claimed it for himself, of course, said it was on the Queen's ground so rightfully belonged to her, and he brought it up with him out of the hole and into the light.

"We brought it back here and set it down on this very table. It took John a wee bit of effort to get it open; he had to force the lock with a knife in the end, but open it did. There was a finely carved clay plaque inside, a figure of the Virgin Mary and the child Jesus, and alongside it a wee packet wrapped in oilskin. Inside that there were three sheets of thick paper, all inscribed in a fine flowing hand. It was Latin, which neither of us knew, but that wasn't going to stop our John. He sent for the minister and had him take a look.

"I canna quite remember all of it now, and most of it in truth was too dull to tell. But the gist of it was it was from a certain Johann Brune, custodian of the King's Hunting Lodge, the King being Robert the Second, the Bruce's son. Brune had the plaque buried under the lodge, to ward off evil and keep the King safe.

"Now seeing that long dead man's name, John was already smitten with the idea that this was something that had been meant for him to see, for him and him alone. The minister sealed it when he got to the end and read out the date of the thing's burial; Christmas Eve, thirteen hundred and fifty-three, exactly five hundred years to the day from when we found it and fetched it up."

"Neither John nor I were believers in coincidences, but he, as I said, took this as a personal message. And he was right adamant that the thing had to go back where we found it, under the old hunting lodge and eventually into the foundations of the new hoose. He said it was his duty, as the Custodian.

"So there was nothing else for it. We had another dram and headed back out to the building works, although it was nearly full dark by this time and all we had with us was a wee oil lamp that was nearly useless in the gloom. But we knew our way around well enough to find the hole quite quickly; we were the only ones there, the other lads all having given up for the night.

"We went back down into the dark. It was cold down there, winter cold. Although there was no snow on the ground that year, the day's dampness had turned into a hard frost, so that getting the box back in the ground was harder work than getting it up in the first place. But we got it down. It was as we were climbing out again we heard it, chanting, like a chorus of monks, far-off and on the wind. I knew it was Latin but to this day don't know what it meant.

"*Somnia Deus cantat ubi iacet.*"

"The same phrase, repeated three times. John and I looked at each other, his face white as a sheet even in the yellowish glow from the oil lamp. He beat me up out of the hole, but I beat him back here to the bar.

"We had a dram. We had a few drams, but it was hours before the cold of that hole left us. The chanting has been with me ever since and sometimes, especially on cold nights, I hear it carrying across the hills.

"John was a changed man after that, and ..."

The old man's story was interrupted. The barman had come across to their table and was leaning in close so that only Lestrade could hear.

"Begging your pardon, sir, but we've got strangers in the village. Auld Graham was out after rabbits and coming back doon the burn when he saw a coach pull up behind the kirk. He says he saw three men, shifty-looking boogers, he said, getting out and heading along the riverside in the direction of the big hoose. Two minutes ago at most."

Lestrade and Clarke left the bar at a run.

When they got back to Balmoral several minutes later Lestrade sent Clarke off to rouse the barracks while he headed directly for the main building. He found Colonel Greene by the main door and, out of breath, related what the barman had told him.

Greene immediately took charge as a dozen slightly disheveled men arrived with Clarke. He dispatched men to all corners of the grounds and had Sergeant Clarke stand with another of his men in the doorway before turning to Lestrade.

"You're with me, Inspector," he said.

"Where are we going?"

"To the Queen. If anyone gets past my men, we shall be the last line of defense. Are you armed?"

Lestrade patted at his chest where his service revolver was holstered and Greene nodded.

"With me, then," the Colonel said, and led Lestrade into the house, down a long corridor festooned with artwork, stuffed animal heads, suits of armor and tapestries, to the far west end and a hallway outside a stout oak door to the Queen's bedchambers. Lestrade realized with a start that the spot in the auld lad's story, the hole in the ground where they'd found the box, was probably somewhere underneath his feet at that very moment.

Greene took the left side of the door, Lestrade the right. The corridor stretched away in front of them, a dark lane lit by irregular flickering gas lights on the left hand side, only darkness on the right where tall windows looked out over the river to the south. The house fell silent around them. Lestrade got his pistol out of its holster and held it hanging down at his side, reassured by the weight and heft of it.

They stood there for what must only have been a minute but felt to Lestrade like an hour, his every nerve tingling. He was looking back down the corridor when he saw it, a pale glow below the nearest window to him, only six feet away. As if from a great distance he heard, or thought he heard, voices raised in a chant. There was little thought in his next action; he stepped toward the window, raised his weapon, and found that he was looking into the face of a dark-haired, bearded man who, having been startled, was now on the point of raising a gun. Lestrade didn't hesitate. He shot the man twice in the face, the noise of a window shattering, the pistol going off and, a second later a high scream from the bedroom behind him all mingled as one in his head.

He saw Greene burst through the door into the chamber beyond, but all Lestrade could do was stand at the window and look out at the ruin that was left of the man he'd just shot. As the gunshots rang in his ear he thought he could hear music in it, the chanting again, fading along with the ringing.

"*Somnia Deus cantat ubi iacet.*"

Greene came back out of the bedchamber a minute later.

"All's well,' he said. "The chambermaid had a bit of a fright but Her Majesty is more concerned with you, Lestrade. How did you know the blighter was there? I heard nothing."

Lestrade didn't reply, for he had no answer to give, only questions to ask, questions that would have to wait for morning for soon the house was in uproar, the staff all roused, Greene's men searching all the rooms and then patrolling the grounds, Lestrade standing at the main doorway, still shaken, sharing a mug of scalding hot tea and a succession of smokes with Sergeant Clarke. He'd told Clarke what he thought happened in the corridor.

"I let that old rascal's story get to me," Lestrade said. "I should know better, a man of my age."

"And yet," Clarke said in reply, "if you hadn't acted

180

like you did it might be you laid out dead instead of him."

"What's this, Clarkie, your old Irish grandmother speaking again, is it?"

"I'm just saying, sir, sometimes stories are just stories, but sometimes there's a hint of truth somewhere in them."

"I should keep an open mind, is that what you're saying?"

Clarke looked Lestrade in the eye. "I think you know that already, sir. You're just telling me because you want it confirmed."

"You after my job, Clarkie?"

The sergeant smiled. "Not yet, sir. Not yet."

Their conversation was interrupted by Colonel Greene leading a party of four men each holding the corner of a stretcher. A white sheet had been thrown over the body, but that only served to accentuate the red of the blood that seeped through it.

"Not much left of his face for identification purposes," Greene said bluntly, "but his clothing's East European; his dental work, what little there is of it, is atrociously bad, and there's a tattoo on his left arm that might be worth investigating. He's Russian. I'd stake my pension on it."

"Any sign of the other two?"

"Nothing yet. I've sent some men down to the village to the kirk, just in case we get a store of luck and the carriage is still there, but my gut tells me they've scarpered, for tonight at least."

"Will they be back?"

"Either them or somebody else," Greene said. "They're fanatics. They don't get stopped easily."

"No, they don't," Lestrade said to himself as Greene led the stretcher bearers away toward the barracks.

None of them got any sleep that night, the whole contingent of the barracks maintaining alert status for the duration. Dawn came, bringing with it more mist and drizzle. Lestrade sent Clarke off to get some breakfast, but as for himself he had no appetite; he was still seeing the dead man's face in the split second before his shots were fired, an image he couldn't shift. He took a walk to clear his head, out of the main grounds, across the bridge and right toward the village. He diverted into the churchyard, intending to have a look for any tracks a carriage might have made there. Instead he found old Alisdair, crouched down, tending flowers at a grave. Lestrade intended to creep quietly past, not wishing to disturb him, but the man looked up, saw the inspector, and waved him over.

Lestrade saw, with no surprise at all, that the gravestone was that of John Brown. The inscription was clear and sharp, as if it had been put there just yesterday.

Alisdair pointed at the last line at the bottom.

"I will make thee ruler over many things. Enter thou into the joy of the Lord."

"The Queen herself insisted on that line being there. What do you think she meant by that … ruler over many things?"

Lestrade deflected the question.

"You said last night that he changed, after finding the box?"

"Aye, last night. And I heard you had a spot of bother at the big hoose? It might be a wee village, Inspector, but it has big ears."

Lestrade deflected that as well, pretending to study the gravestone.

"Have you a smoke, Inspector?" the old man said. "Two, one for me, one for John here?"

Lestrade handed over two cigarettes, the old man lit them both with a lucifer and laid one to smolder on top of the gravestone. Lestrade lit one for himself then tried to guide the conversation back to where he wanted it to go.

"In what way did he change?"

The old man took so long over his answer that at first Lestrade didn't think he was going to get one, but finally, in a low voice, he started to speak, the tale starting again.

"You must understand, John was a man of duty, born to it you might say. Though before that night he always made some time for himself, for his fishing, for a wee dram. But that all changed. He devoted himself to service, not just of the Queen herself but to the place, to the big hoose. He was convinced that a torch had been passed, from the Bruce's time to now, a handing-over of responsibility if you like. And he was more than willing to take it on, more than willing to become the Custodian, as he now called himself.

"I saw him often over the next thirty years, here and there on the estate and about the village. He was always polite and cordial, but I sensed a certain reticence in him, and we never did share another dram in the Black Bull, more to my disappointment than his, I would guess.

"We grew aulder, John and I. Last time I saw him was in the autumn of eighty-two. I was on the other side of the river, trying to hook a salmon. I could see the big hoose clearly enough though, and there was oor John, standing at the edge of the west wing, just stood there, stiff like a pole, staring straight ahead. A guard, I thought, then checked myself and gave him his proper name.

"The Custodian.

"I never saw him again. Word came in March the following year that he'd taken ill in Windsor Castle and passed away. I heard the Queen cried for a fortnight.

"The whole village, and some folks from towns far and wide, turned out for the funeral. The minister said fine words, we had a wee wake for him in the pub, and that night fell with me three sheets to the wind, out here with a dram in each hand, one for me, one for my auld pal John.

"As I said, I was a wee bit stocious, but not that far gone that I didn't hear yon chanting when it started up. My legs wanted to take me back to the safety of the pub, but my heart wanted to say goodbye to my friend, so I came round that corner there, looked up at the grave; and there was John, stood there large as life, staring the

... looked up at the grave; and there was John, stood there large as life ...

same way I'd last seen him. Yon chanting came up again, louder now, and he started to turn toward me.

"I couldnae take it, God forgive me. If he had any last words for me, I was too feert to hear them. I turned tail and fled. Even dropped the two full drams on the grass, that'll tell you how bad it was.

"I only come here in the daytime now, to leave a wee flower, and sometimes have a dram and a smoke with him.

"He has his duties, and I hae mine."

Alisdair finished his smoke and stubbed it out alongside the other one on top of the gravestone. He only said one more thing as he turned away, tears glistening in his eyes. "If you see anything of him up at the hoose, tell him Alisdair says hello."

Lestrade arrived back at 'the big hoose' to find Colonel Greene and Clarke at the main doorway.

"I was just telling your man here," Greene said, "We've had a report of more of these Russians coming in via Stonehaven Harbor last night."

"How many more?"

"Half a dozen at least. And our witness said they brought a long box ashore with them. About rifle length."

"We've got to get the Queen out of here," Lestrade said.

"And risk an attack in Glenshee on the road south? No, thank you. She's as safe inside these walls as anywhere, and even with six more of them we still outnumber them. Besides, after last night they might be more cautious about attempting anything."

"Or it might only have got their dander up," Lestrade said. "It's hard to tell with anarchists."

"I take your point, Lestrade," Greene said. "But we'll be on full alert until this is done, one way or another. Try to get some rest. You look all-in, and I've got a feeling we'll be needing you come sunset."

Lestrade had a perfunctory breakfast; thin porridge, dry toast and weak tea, then tried to get some sleep on the hard bunks provided in the makeshift barracks. What little rest he got was fitful at best, punctuated by ringing in his ears and the faintest hint of chanting coming with it, so low in volume he could not tell if it was real or all in his head.

He rose in the mid-afternoon, scarcely refreshed, although a cold wash and a change of clothing helped. He found Clarke in the main building in the scullery, brewing one of his special pots of tea, so strong you could almost stand a spoon in it and that, with a smoke out on the terrace overlooking the river, almost had Lestrade feeling his old self for the first time since their arrival.

"Do you think they'll come, sir?" Clarke asked.

Lestrade nodded. "That's the thing about anarchists; they think they're free thinkers, but once they get an idea into their heads they hardly ever change their minds, even when circumstances go against them. They'll come."

"And yourself, sir. How are you doing?"

Lestrade knew what was being asked. Killing, even in the line of duty, was never anything to be taken lightly, and good men had left the force because of it, unable to live with the thought they might be asked to do it again.

"I'll be fine," he replied. "Just let me get home to my chair in front of the fire with a drink and a smoke. I might stay there all winter."

The steady drizzle turned heavy, driven by a sudden cold wind that sent them scurrying inside for cover, where they stayed as darkness slowly fell, watching the rain run in rivulets down the windows.

"They won't come in this, surely?" Clarke said.

"I wonder if Napoleon thought the same. They're Russians, Clarkie. They'll come."

Night fell and the rain slackened off, although the wind got up, howling and whistling around the grounds. Greene deployed his team around the estate, putting Clarke on main-door duty, which the sergeant accepted grudgingly, for it was at least on the side of the house getting most shelter from the wind. Lestrade and Greene took up duty again in the long corridor outside the Queen's bedchamber. He saw that the window he'd shot through the previous night had been boarded up, none too carefully. The wind whistled loudly through the gaps and set the gaslights flickering wildly in the gusts.

'You can smoke if you like," Greene said. "She doesn't mind. Reminds her of better times, she says."

In the three days he had been here, Lestrade hadn't even caught a glimpse of the Queen; he had even wondered if she was here at all. Putting out the news she was in residence to try to draw out the anarchists while she was actually squirreled away safely in Windsor was the kind of idea he could see Mycroft Holmes approving with a thin smile on his lips. It didn't matter either way, though; his duty was clear, so here he would stand, and face what came. Queen and country for him, Queen and Balmoral for John Brown. They weren't all that different from each other when push came to shove.

The evening crept on. At one point they heard music from the room behind them, a piano playing and a high female voice singing an old Scots song about love found and lost.

"She likes the chambermaid to sing for her," Greene explained. "Sad, sad songs in the main, songs about dead men, dead babies. Too much death in this house if you ask me, but then again, nobody asks me."

After a while the music stopped. An air of anticipation seemed to fall over the corridor, as if it had breathed in, waiting for something to happen.

The first shots rang out minutes later.

Lestrade moved to go toward the sound.

"Steady, man," Greene said. "The lads are trained to handle it. Our job is here."

More shots could be heard, clusters of three or four at a time, then silence for a few seconds before they started up again. Lestrade took out his revolver, his knuckles white from gripping it. He peered along the corridor, wondering whether he might see a repeat of the glow or hear the chant. What he heard was the crash of another window breaking, but his heart was in his mouth when he realized that the sound had come from behind him, inside the Queen's bedchamber. A woman screamed, a young voice, obviously the chambermaid.

Greene was through the door first, his shoulder charge almost taking it off its hinges despite its obvious weight. The Queen was abed, sitting up, an expression of, not fear, but outrage on her face. The chambermaid lay on the floor, whether in a dead faint or as a result of some blow was impossible to tell at that moment, for Lestrade's attention was totally on the two bearded men currently climbing in through the broken spars and shattered glass of the bay window overlooking the river.

There was a frozen moment when the men at the window registered Greene and Lestrade's presence, then there was no time to think. All four men raised their weapons at the same time, and Lestrade's life contracted to fractions of a second, moments when either his finger on the trigger was faster, or it was not. He got lucky. The Russian's bullet whistled past Lestrade's ear; he found it later embedded in the plaster of the rear wall. Lestrade's own aim was better; his target fell away clutching his belly, slumping, weapon forgotten and fallen from his hand, to sit amid the broken glass under the busted window.

Greene was not so fortunate. Lestrade saw him spin around as a bullet took him high on the right shoulder, the pistol falling from a hand that had lost its gripping power. The Russian was already tuning his aim toward where the Queen was still sitting up in bed, and Lestrade knew that this time the Russian was going to get a shot off before anything could be done to stop him.

Then he saw it, hanging in the air between the window and the bed, a blue-gray figure, growing more solid all the time; pale eyes flaring like cold flame, lips raised in a snarl, a sporran swinging as it lunged forward toward the Russian. The man fired, twice, not at the Queen but at this impossible thing that seemed intent on attacking him. Luckily both shots went well wide of the monarch, kicking splinters out of the bed frame well above her head.

Lestrade heard the Latin chant rise up, almost a howl, filling the room with noise, then the pale figure was on top of the Russian, spectral arms taking the anarchist around the waist and squeezing, a bear hug that no living man could break.

The sound of the Russian's spine snapping was loud even above the hubbub. The Latin chant rose to a crescendo as the specter turned, a worried look on the wrinkled face. He looked toward the bed, gave a stiff bow, then faded, along with the sound of the chant. The last thing to go were the flaring, pale eyes. Lestrade thought they contained the hint of a smile.

He turned to check on the Queen. She had a hand at her mouth and tears in her eyes. She whispered, one word, and Lestrade would never be sure, but he thought it was a single word, a name.

"John?"

There was a noise at the window. Lestrade turned quickly, raising his weapon, only to see Clarke standing there, a bleeding cut above his brow and a grim smile on his face.

"We got them, sir," the sergeant said. "We got the bastards."

The clean-up ... and cover-up ... took several days and Lestrade knew the full story would never come out. Colonel Greene had been face down on the carpet and the chambermaid in a dead faint when the ... apparition, for want of a better word ... saved the Queen. Only Lestrade and the monarch had seen it, and he was pretty sure she wasn't going to talk. As for Lestrade, he had already resolved not to tell a soul, save for one man.

The night before they were due to depart for London he returned to the Black Bull and sought out old Alisdair.

Over a few glasses of excellent whisky Lestrade told the tale while soft, warm tears filled the older man's eyes, and when it was done they raised their glasses in a toast.

"To John Brown, the faithful custodian."

The Hallowe'en

"Have you heard about the *Hallowe'en,* sir?" Sergeant Clarke said, poking his head round the door of Lestrade's office.

"What are you havering about, man?" Lestrade answered, not looking up from his paperwork. "It's July. Months away yet."

"No, Sir. *The Hallowe'en.* The boat."

"What, the big tea clipper that was wrecked off Devon a few years back?"

"That's the one, sir. Although I don't know about wrecked."

"Why's that, Clarkie?"

"Well, she's moored at Westminster Pier. Came in with the fog last night, they say. The Commissioner wants us down there to have a butcher's."

"It's a boat. I've already seen one."

"Not like this, sir, begging your pardon. There's no crew aboard."

"So search the pubs in the area."

"You're not getting it, sir. It came in without one."

Lestrade finally looked up.

"An empty two-hundred-foot boat that was supposedly wrecked years ago came in with the tide and parked itself up nice and neat at Westminster Pier? That's what you're telling me?"

"Came in, tied up tight to the wharf, and not a crewman in sight."

Lestrade looked down at the pile of paperwork and sighed, but in truth his interest was piqued, and he'd been looking for an excuse to get out of the office all morning. This sounded like a wild-goose chase, a pier master who'd had one gin too many, probably, but it was a chance to stretch his legs and get away from his inkwell and pen for a few hours, so he jumped at it.

"Get your jacket, then, Clarkie; let's go and see how a shipwreck found its own way home from all the way around to Devon."

Lestrade was still treating it flippantly as they walked along the Embankment to the pier. Then he saw the three broken masts festooned in strands of kelp hanging like ribbons from frayed rigging, from which sails hung like tattered and torn handkerchiefs. As they got closer he saw there was a substantial crowd gathered on the Embankment overlooking the vessel.

The tide was out, so the deck was out of sight until he pushed his way through the throng and looked over the wall. The vessel, like the masts, was covered in strands of rapidly drying kelp; the deck, fo'c'sle and wheel all liberally encrusted with limpets and barnacles. The ropes with which the boat was tied up to the pier were green with algal slime, and there was a smell wafting up off the deck; iodine from the seaweed, and rot and decay from the timbers.

"Somebody's pulling our leg here. This hulk didn't come round the coast on its own accord." Lestrade said. "Get these people cleared away, Clarkie. Let the dog see the rabbit. Who reported her coming in?"

"Pier master, sir. He'll be down at the quayside in the

hut; there's a constable with him making sure he doesn't do a runner."

Lestrade made his way down the steps to the pier. The river was sluggish today, muddy brown even in the sunlight, hiding a multitude of sins under its surface. If there had been fog in the night, it was all gone now, and the heat of the day was only serving to raise noxious odors off the moored boat. Lestrade lit a cigarette and made for the pier master's shed.

The master was a small barrel of a man, almost as wide as he was tall, of an indeterminate age due to having skin like old leather, but in his fifties at a guess, with a bald head, a pure white beard hanging halfway down his chest, a plain gold hoop earring in his left ear, and bare arms covered from fingertips to shoulders in a mass of fading tattoos.

"She's the *Hallowe'en* all right," the man said as Lestrade entered a hut that was filled wall to wall with scrimshaw carved whale bone. "I remember the celebrations when she broke the Shanghai-to-London record back in seventy-five. Saw her come in that day, all sails billowing, flags flying, and a crowd lining the Embankment cheering. It's her all right, come home now in her last days."

"I'm more concerned about how she got here, rather than her name," Lestrade said. "Did you see her come in?"

The man shook his head. "I was sitting here, quiet-like, having a smoke and a gin. Weren't nobody due in after midnight, and the fog was rolling right thick, so I doubted there'd be anybody on the water. First I knew of it was when the ship's bell tolled right outside my bloody door. Just after one it were. Gave me a proper shake-up I can tell you. I came out with my lamp, could hardly see my hand in front of my face at first, then the fog shifted, and there she were, all dripping with weed and smelling like the devil, tied up alongside as neat as you like and not a living soul in sight."

"And the crew?"

"What crew?" the man said. "I telt ye, not a living soul in sight."

"Nobody below decks?"

"How in blazes do I know? Do I look daft enough to be wandering around in a ghost ship on my own wi' nowt but a lantern?"

"So there could still be men aboard?"

"Let me put it this way, sir. There could still be something aboard. Whether it be men, or something of a more peculiar nature, I can't say, and I ain't willing to investigate. I'd leave her well alone if I were you. I sent word to the owner that she'd come back; he'll be along soon I guess, and by rights anything salvageable is his anyway. He'll get her taken away, and I can get back to my gin and a good night's sleep."

"Unfortunately, investigation is my job," Lestrade said. "I'll need to borrow your lantern."

He met Sergeant Clarke back out on the quayside and handed the sergeant an oil lantern.

"I've got three men keeping the crowd away up top, sir," Clarke said. "But the newspaper lads have got wind of a story, and you know what they're like. Any chance of getting this wrapped up fast?"

"Just as soon as I know what 'this' is, Clarkie. Just as soon as I know."

The tide was at its lowest ebb and they were able to step off the pier directly onto the boat's deck. There was no sign of a gangway having been lowered; another puzzle to add to the growing list, for when the boat docked, the tide would have been almost full, the deck ten feet or more above the level of the pier. Lestrade put that away to be considered later; there was more than enough to be going on with in front of his nose.

They had to pick their way through clumps of rotting kelp on the deck. Apart from the limpets and barnacles, the seaweed was the only sign of life; even the normally voracious river gulls were giving this hulk a wide berth, whether due to the smell or some innate sense of danger was yet to be determined. The policemen stepped carefully up toward the fo'c'sle where a door lay open, leading inside. The pier master had given them a general layout of the boat.

"Crew quarters and galley to the rear, cargo hold below that and up the front end, captain's quarters above the stern, and that's all you need to know from me," the man had said, and had pointedly gone back to his shed, as if the very sight of the boat at his pier was a personal affront.

Lestrade had Clarke light the lantern, and he took the opportunity to have another cigarette; the smell inside was likely to be worse than out here in the open air, and anything he could do to mask it was going to be welcome.

"Crew quarters first, Clarkie," he said. "And prepare yourself; there was a crew of at least thirty on this boat. If they drowned in the wreck, their bodies might yet be inside, what's left of the poor buggers anyway."

The door led immediately to a short flight of steps, six of them, down into a galley that ran the width of the boat. Tables, kettles, pots, pans and kitchen utensils lay strewn around as if tossed by a giant's hand. Everything was covered in a sheen of green algal scum, even the portholes, which let in green-tinged sunlight to give the scene a sickly hue.

"Does this mean what I think it means, sir?" Clarke said.

"Yes, I think so, Clarkie. It looks like the whole bally thing has been underwater. And for some time at that."

They found more evidence to support that theory in the crew quarters; personal belongings were scattered hither and thither around the cramped, dark area. Empty hammocks swayed in the Thames' swell, green and damp, and the tang of saltwater hung heavy in the air. There was no sign of a crew, alive or dead.

The captain's quarters was also in a state of disarray,

the big oak desk having been tumbled against the far wall, sodden books, torn charts, a bent sextant, pillows and bedding all lying against it in a sodden, slime-covered heap. A long, heavy chest sat snug against the opposite wall; Lestrade guessed it might be the Captain's traveling trunk. Of the Captain himself, there was no sign.

They had just gotten back up onto deck, heading for the forward cargo hold, when they met two men coming aboard.

"I'd ask you to leave, sirs," the taller of the two said. "You are trespassing on private property." He wore a stovepipe hat, a black coat and had a most impressive set of muttonchops, thick, black and oiled to a sheen. His voice had the tone of someone used to getting their own way.

"And who in blazes are you, sir?" Lestrade said.

"Wilson, John Wilson. Rightful owner of this vessel. This here is my quartermaster, Evans. Who the blazes are you?" the man said, echoing Lestrade's belligerent tone.

"Lestrade. Scotland Yard. This is my sergeant, Clarke."

"Scotland Yard? Has there been a crime committed here?"

"That's what I'm trying to ascertain, sir."

"Well kindly ascertain elsewhere," Wilson said. Lestrade had only met the man seconds ago, and already he didn't like him, but he bit his tongue; the Commissioner didn't like his officers antagonizing wealthy businessmen, and from the cut of this man's clothes and the heft of the gold fob chain at his waistcoat, he didn't look like he was short of a few bob.

"Just doing my job, sir," he said.

"And I'm just doing mine. We have a cargo to unload, if you'll let us get on with it."

"I doubt there's much to salvage," Lestrade said. "It's obvious that this wreck's been underwater for a good long time. Any cargo is long since ruined."

"And you're an expert in the transportation of tea, are you?"

Lestrade bit his tongue again, for his reply was not going to be diplomatic if he let it emerge. He chose discretion, and with Clarke at his side stepped off the boat and onto the pier. His discretion, however, did not stretch so far as leaving the site entirely. He and Clarke stood by the pier master's shed, smoking a succession of cigarettes and drinking strong tea brewed by the barrel-chested man, watching while Wilson and his quartermaster had a succession of smaller boats sail up to take away a seemingly endless chain of tea chests that were brought up by winch out of the cargo hold.

"If them's tea chests I'll eat my beard," the pier master said after watching this for almost an hour.

"What do you mean?" Lestrade asked.

"See how careful they's being with them? As if they're fragile? One thing tea ain't is fragile. Any other deckhands would be flinging them around, getting the job done faster, like."

Now that it had been pointed out to him Lestrade saw what the older man meant. The workers were indeed wary with the crates, and Lestrade was getting increasingly curious as to what they might contain.

The cargo hold was eventually emptied. Two squat tugboats came up the river from the East and, after a lot of palaver with ropes and chains, were soon secured to the *Hallowe'en.*

"Where will they take her?" Lestrade asked as the boat was pulled away from the pier.

"Down Wapping way at a guess, guv'nor," the Pier Master said. "Wilson's got a big wharf down there, and a couple of warehouses. Big man in the tea trade, like his father before him."

Lestrade watched the boat being taken off downriver. He wasn't sure whether it was the shimmer of spilled oil, or a trick of the sun on the water, but it seemed to have an aurora dancing in the ruined rigging, a shifting rainbow of color keeping pace as the boat was finally taken away out of site by the bends of the river.

Once back at the Yard, the mysteries of the *Hallowe'en* were all but forgotten; after all, there appeared to be no crime involved. Lestrade's afternoon was subsumed in paperwork. He was looking forward to the evening, a leisurely walk home, maybe a pint in the Old Queen's Head in Vauxhall before bed. Those hopes were dashed when Sergeant Clarke once again popped his head round the office door just after five o'clock.

"Begging your pardon, sir, but there's a chap just walked in downstairs saying that he needs to see you, right urgent-like."

"Can't you deal with it, Clarkie? I've got this lot to finish."

"I think you'll want to see him, sir. Says he was on the *Hallowe'en* coming over from Shanghai. Says he knows what happened to the crew."

The man Clarke showed into the interview room could have passed for the pier master's younger brother; he looked to be in his late thirties, barrel-chested, heavily tanned and weathered, balding with a beard already going salt-and-pepper, and brightly colored, elaborate tattoos of mermaids, anchors, whales and octopuses up and down both arms.

"Tom Norton's me name, out of Hull originally. Saw you down at the pier this mornin', so I did," he said. "Ordering the other coppers about. I knew you'd be the man I'd need to talk to. Took me a while to find you. Asked around the pubs, see, and finally found a man as knows you. Didn't even ought to have been at the pier this morning. I had a shift to do at St. Catherine's Dock, and I'll lose a day's wages, but as soon as I heard the *Hallowe'en* had come in I had to see her, just to make sure."

"Make sure of what?"

"Make sure I ain't been dreaming. Make sure that nightmare trip actually happened. And that what we saw off Devon really happened the way I think it happened."

"You'd better start at the beginning and go slow,"

Lestrade said.

"Aye. Happen I'd better."

"A man can get anything he wants in Shanghai," Norton began. "And Elijah Wilson wanted it all. I saw you talking to the brother down on the deck today; he was always the better-mannered of the two. Elijah was a bear of a man in both size and temperament, quick to anger and fierce with it. He got the captaincy of the *Hallowe'en* from his old man for the first time on that trip, and he worked us like dogs all the way; he was determined to break records, see, get the old girl back in the history books. Had a few men beaten, too, for daring to question him. We were all right glad to make port in Shanghai and the prospect of a few days in the bars with the ladies. But we'd missed the record in that direction by a day, and that vexed Elijah right sorely.

"I believe he did what he did to make up for that, somehow, something he could show his brother on our return as recompense.

"It had been a bad year for the tea crop; not enough rain meant not enough tea, and we found precious little cargo waiting to be loaded for our return trip. Elijah could not face coming back to London with a loss-maker, so he went out into the city, looking to make a deal, any deal as long as it was something that could be converted to cold hard cash back in Blighty. Being as I'm a big lad and can handle myself, me and three others like me were tasked to go with him, for parts of that city are as rough, rougher even than the old girl here."

Lestrade interrupted him.

"Opium? He brought in opium?"

Norton laughed bitterly.

"He was stupid, but not that stupid. No, something not that bad. But also something infinitely worse. I'll get there if you give me another smoke. Just let me take my time; it's a thing that haunts my dreams, and talking about it makes it worse, somehow.

There was a pause as they lit cigarettes before Norton continued.

"To cut a long night short, palms were greased, favors were agreed upon, and eventually we were shown into what I took to be some kind of a palace, into the presence of a man introduced to us as Shunyuan. He styled himself as a descendant of the old Khan warlords, and whether that is true or not he was a most imposing chap. Not that I got to spend much time in his presence, mind you, for Elijah and the warlord went away to a quiet place to discuss business for a while, leaving us to make the most of a table of food and some sweet, strong wine.

"It was almost dawn by the time Elijah returned, and he had a smile as wide as the Thames. He spent the morning back at the *Hallowe'en* writing a long letter to his brother in London, and he was jolly pleased with himself as he had it sent off in a dispatch.

"Later that day, we took delivery of a hold-load of crates; not tea, but porcelain. Ming Dynasty, Elijah says, and worth a king's ransom back home. I asked him how he could have afforded to make a deal for such a thing, and where such a thing could have come from, if it was legally sourced. Elijah tapped the side of his nose, and said he was doing the Khan a personal favor, one that could not be talked about, and that was the last I heard about that for a while. I was told that night in the galley that one last crate had been loaded, not into the hold but directly into the Captain's quarters, but I was too tired by that point and made my way to my hammock, for Elijah had declared that we would sail with the next tide."

"The trip home started well enough, although we were sorely troubled by marine animals who took to shoaling all around us, some whales even going as far as ramming us head-on, although our iron hull meant that they always came off second best in those exchanges. The beasts' attention did, however, ensure that we would have no possible chance of beating the speed record back to London. Elijah, to our astonishment, showed no sign of being concerned and had developed a casual, languorous approach to the voyage.

"Things were almost pleasant for a time. Our troubles really began as we were approaching the Cape of Good Hope. Our sailing master brought to our attention that there appeared to be no rats at all on board the boat. Now I don't know as you know owt about seafaring, Inspector, but rats are ubiquitous, a veritable plague in some cases. To have none at all could in some ways be seen as a blessing, but the crew chose to see it as a foreboding of worse to come. As it turned out, they were right to do so.

"As we came up the west coast of Africa a great sickness fell over us. Stumpy Jack, our cook, cleaner and makeshift doctor, declared it a previously unknown insect-borne tropical disease, one that brought lassitude and weakness to almost all of us and manifested itself only via the presence of bite marks, pairs of them, either at neck or wrist. The only man unaffected was the captain, although even he had taken to keeping himself to himself in his cabin, and when he infrequently emerged he looked to be a troubled man, much changed from the one who had been so happy on making the deal in Shanghai."

"The first man died as we were passing between Africa and the Canaries. Jimmy Kerr would never see Glasgow again. We found him on deck, white as ivory and cold as ice despite the beating sun. Soon after that rumors spread, of a tall, dark man being seen prowling the decks under moonlight, and when a second man, then a third, were found in the same condition as Kerr we were ready to mutiny in search of answers.

"We must have made a sorry sight when we converged on the Captain's cabin one morning as we were off the coast of Portugal, for not a one of us had been spared the sickness and we were bone-weary, almost ready to drop. Our plan was to force the captain to make for Lisbon and seek proper medical attention, but he would have none of it, and he had two advantages over us: he still had his strength, and he had the only firearm on board, a short-barreled shotgun that would cut any one of us in half if fired.

"The gun, our sickness, his sheer force of will, and promise of a large payday for us all in London, all conspired to quell our revolt, and we continued our weary way toward home.

"Three more men died but by then we had hove past the Scilly Isles and were heading up the Channel, so close to home we could almost taste it. Fate had another card to play yet, though, and as chance would have it the discovery of the Captain's secret fell to me to uncover.

"I was too tired to sleep. I got up and went up top to have a smoke, and that's when I saw him, a man I'd last seen in Shanghai, a man I'd been introduced to as Shunyuan. Only it wasn't a man at all, at least none I recognized. He had Stumpy Jack in a clutch hold, almost an embrace, and was sucking the cook's blood from his neck in great gulps. The attacker's eyes flared, red like hot coals in the moonlight, when he saw me. He dropped poor Stumpy in a cold white heap on the deck and came for me. I just had enough time to throw myself backward, tumbling arse over tit into the galley where the noise I made roused the crew. I looked up the steps to see a dark figure outlined with the night sky behind him, those red eyes piercing into my soul. He snarled, more like a dog than a man, then was gone.

"We roused every man and searched the boat but found no trace of Stumpy's attacker, until the only place left to search was the Captain's cabin. This time our dander was up, and even the shotgun didn't stop us, although Big Bill Greenard had his left arm almost blown off at the shoulder and died of blood loss before he could be helped. Elijah had to give way and we poured into his cabin.

"We did not find Shunyuan. But we found a long crate there, much like a coffin for indeed it was lined inside with velvet as black as night, thick and plush and showing a definite indentation in the material where a body might have lain there.

"Elijah was full of bluster and rage, but as I say, we had our dander up. We were off the coast of Devon, waves crashing on rocks way off to our port side. We took control of her, turned the *Hallowe'en* around, set her on a course for the rocks, and took to the lifeboat.

"The captain refused to come. The last I saw of him he was wrestling with the wheel. A tall figure stood beside him, lending his strength, those red eyes clearly visible even in the teeth of lashing rain and wind.

"The *Hallowe'en* was still making straight for the rocks when we last saw her."

It had all come out of the man in a rush, and the ending had come rather abruptly, leaving Lestrade with too many questions. It all sounded too far-fetched.

"You've been reading *Varney the Vampyre* and drinking too much cheap liquor, haven't you, lad?"

"I swear to you, Inspector, every word of it is true. Why would I come to you with such a story if it were not?"

"That's what I've been asking myself," Lestrade replied. "Why would you?"

"Don't you see? If she's still afloat, still intact, then he might still be on board, that Shunyuan. And if a fiend such as he gets loose in London there would be no end of mayhem and death. Who knows where it might end? He styled himself as a Khan, an emperor. What if he has designs on a new Empire?"

"That is a touch grandiose for my liking, lad."

"But I have given you enough doubt that you'll be paying the Wilson yard a visit?"

Lestrade thought long and hard about that, then sighed. "I suppose you have, at that, lad, if only to satisfy my curiosity. You could come along if you'd like?"

"Not me, sir. As soon as I'm out of here I'm off north, as far as I can get as fast as I can get. London? You can keep it."

Lestrade knew he had no evidence to allow him to go in mob-handed on a raid. All he had were suspicions, and pretty tenuous ones at that. The most he could investigate was the possibility that Wilson was involved in the illegal import of antique porcelain. Hardly the crime of the century, but probably enough to get him a foot in the door. He ordered up two carriages, himself and Clarke in the front one and four constables in the second, and headed for Wapping. The last he saw of Norton was as they were leaving the Yard, the sailor heading off, north as he'd promised.

He took Sergeant Clarke into his confidence in the carriage over a smoke, relating Norton's tale. Clarke took it all in and sat quiet for a minute before answering.

"A vampyre, sir? Really?"

"That's what the lad said," Lestrade answered. "But we're going in after dodgy porcelain imports, so we'll start with that, and if anything else comes up we'll deal with it as and when."

Dusk was falling as they approached Wapping. Lestrade was hoping to catch Wilson and his men in the act of transporting the porcelain, betting on the late hour giving them a sense of safety that he hoped to disrupt. But on arrival at Wilson's wharf they found the site lying quiet. The crates they'd seen being unloaded at Westminster lined the dock, intermingled with a dozen large barrels of pitch that stank nearly as badly as the rotting kelp had earlier that day, and the warehouses sat dark and looming on the far side of the wharf. The ruined hulk of the *Hallowe'en* herself was moored up alongside the quay. Light flickered near the prow, coming up from the cargo hold below. Lestrade led his party of six toward it.

He left the four constables on the main deck near the fo'c'sle doorway.

"If anybody comes out this way, take them into custody," he said. All four were just young lads and looked almost relieved not to have anything more onerous to do as Lestrade and Clarke crept forward toward the open hatchway to the cargo hold. Even before they reached it they heard what appeared to be an argument; heated on one side, calm and measured on the other. Lestrade crept closer and peered downward.

The heated party in the conversation was Wilson, the man he'd met earlier on the boat. The other voice, the calmer one, came from a tall figure dressed all in black who stood inside a pentagram that had been painted in red on the hold floor. An oil lantern sat at each point of the star, and the twin concentric circles that ran around it appeared to glow, as if lit from below. There was a great coffin-length chest inside the diagram; Lestrade had last seen it in the Captain's quarters that morning. The black-clad man stood beside it where it lay closed.

Wilson stood six feet outside the diagram and when he spoke again Lestrade heard the anger in it. "I want to know what you did with my brother," Wilson said, almost shouting.

"No, you don't," the calmer voice replied. There was an accent there, but only a hint of one. The dark-clad man sounded almost urbane, and most definitely nonchalant and totally at ease with the current situation.

"If you have drained him I shall ..."

"You shall what, exactly?" the dark man replied. "We had an agreement; you, your brother and I. This mummery we have here was no part of it. Of course I expected you to have prepared defenses against me; it is ever thus. But I have brought you your porcelain. I was to have passage into your city, if you remember? You were to invite me ashore?"

"That agreement was made years ago, when my brother was ..."

"Alive? Yes. But you have your own crew to blame for his misfortune, not me. And as for the delay; it took me time, after the unfortunate wreck, to recover my powers enough to conclude my end of the bargain. But see, it is done. I have brought you your ship, you have your cargo. Let me go, or it will go badly for you. Breaking an agreement with such as me comes with consequences."

"What happened to my brother?" Wilson shouted.

"Let me go," the dark man replied softly.

Lestrade saw that it was a standoff. He also had a pretty good idea who might turn out the winner. As he inched closer he smelled something more than the rotted kelp underfoot; the distinctive tang of pitch. He saw the reason when he looked beyond Wilson, farther into the hold. There was an overturned barrel there, oozing a spreading pool of black tar across the cargo hold deck, almost lapping at Wilson's heels.

Wilson took a matchbox from his waistcoat pocket, took out a match and held the head against the sandpaper. He motioned toward the spreading pool of pitch.

"Tell me what happened to my brother, or you burn."

The man in the pentacle shrugged. "As I said, you really did not need to know. But if you insist ... come close. You will need to be close to see this."

Wilson stepped tentatively closer. Lestrade had the best view of anyone, directly down into the crate, as the dark-clad man opened the lid. A shrunken thing like a piece of old leather lay in the bottom. Lestrade saw with horror that it had once worn a matching pair of mutton-chops like his brother.

"I had to have sustenance if I was to fulfill my end of the bargain, you do see that?" the dark-clad man said. "And your crew had fled, so I had no other choice. In any case, it still does not nullify our bargain. You still owe me passage ashore."

"You'll get exactly what you deserve," Wilson said. He struck the match and tossed it into the pitch which immediately caught flame. What he hadn't noted was that he had stood too close to the edge of the pentagram.

"As you refuse to acknowledge our agreement, I have no other choice but to terminate it with immediate effect," the dark-clad man said. As swift as a striking snake his hand reached out, caught Wilson by the throat, and tossed him, single-handedly, a full twelve feet across the hold to land squarely in the deepest part of the oozing pitch, a part that was already well alight. Wilson's screams were terrible, but thankfully short-lived, for his rolling in the pitch only served to let it cover him more fully, and in seconds he was no more than a burning pool of flame.

The old wood of the hold started to pop and crack as fire took firm hold. A blast of heat came up out of the hatchway, forcing Lestrade and Clarke to back away quickly.

"Quickly, Clarkie, back onto the dock. This old girl is going to go up fast."

"What about that other chap?" Clarke said as Lestrade pushed him toward the dock.

"I don't think he's going anywhere."

The younger officers, on seeing the situation, had already gone ashore and, showing initiative, were busy releasing the boat's moorings. Clarke stepped ashore and Lestrade followed. Just as he put both feet on the quay an urbane, cultured voice spoke at his back.

"Would it be too much trouble if I asked you to welcome me ashore?"

Lestrade turned, and looked into a pair of blood-red eyes. Later, it was almost all he could remember of the man, apart from a vague sense of foreignness and a small, tight, beard, braided Eastern style. A sheet of flame had risen up from the cargo hold, outlining the figure before him in fire that matched his eyes.

"You can come ashore if you can come ashore," Lestrade said.

Out of the corner of his eye he saw Clarke organize the younger officers in using long poles to push the old boat away from the quayside toward the open river. It had started to move, but only slowly, and Lestrade felt heat grow at his face as the fire raged ever more ferociously.

"There is much I can offer you," the dark-man said.

"I've seen exactly what you can offer," Lestrade replied. "I saw what you offered to this boat's captain. So if it's all right by you, I won't be offering you anything, let alone a welcome."

The boat started to drift faster, being caught by the tide, but they hadn't moved quickly enough; flames had spread to the quayside, and were already lapping at the stacked barrels of pitch.

The policemen were forced to flee, making safe ground in the nick of time just before the first of the pitch barrels went up like a firework. Soon the whole quayside was alight.

The last Lestrade saw of the *Hallowe'en*, she was out in the center of the river, burning like a flare. Just before the river took her he saw the dark man, high in the rigging, still trying to avoid the flames. They caught him at last, and a final scream echoed across the water as he burned. The *Hallowe'en* sank slowly, almost gracefully, until the Thames flowed silently over the top of what was left, leaving no trace.

It took all night for the Thames' fire services to get the fire under control and in the morning there was nothing left of Wilson's wharf but burnt timber, rubble and ash; his fine porcelain cargo had also been consumed by the flames.

"How are you going to write this one up, sir?" Clarke asked him as they took the carriage back to the Yard.

"There was no crime committed, at least none that I'm willing to acknowledge," Lestrade replied. "It'll be written up as a tragic accident."

And if truth be told, Lestrade thought that was as close to the truth as anything.

A Thing of Shreds
and Patches

Lestrade stood looking up into the arms of a large oak tree to where a body was wedged tight between two of the larger branches. Blood had run down the trunk and frozen there at some point in the chill December night, looking like wet paint on the old bark.

"How in blazes did they get him up there, sir?" Sergeant Clarke asked at his side. "It's got to be twenty feet or more."

Lestrade had already studied the ground around the base of the tree; there was no sign that a ladder had been used, no apparent prints of any kind, and while that might be explained by the heavy frost, he'd have expected to see some scuff marks or indentations.

"Maybe we'll know more when we are able to identify the body," Lestrade said.

He looked up again. The victim was a portly chap, that much was clear, but hidden too much by shadows and branches for any detail to be made out. He had sent two constables off to fetch a long ladder, and there was little they could do now but wait.

A dog-walker in Green Park had found the body just after dawn that morning, and by the time Lestrade and Clarke arrived on the scene three constables were keeping a crowd of gawkers away. Most of them had dispersed now, an hour later, the cold, crisp air moving them along better than the officers could manage. A hard core of half a dozen remained, and Lestrade wasn't at all surprised to see the reporter Langdale Pike among them.

"Wouldn't have thought this was your thing, Pike?" he said, going over to the man. "Not exactly a society function, is it?"

"That depends on who it is up the tree," Pike said, and smiled as if he had a secret.

"Come on, out with it, lad," Lestrade replied.

"Not yet. Call it a hunch, that's all. If it's who I think it is, I'll have something for you. But I'll expect first dibs on the story."

"You can expect all you like. You can also come down the Yard and explain yourself there if you'd prefer; I'm sure you remember what that's like?"

Pike didn't flinch, just smiled again, that same knowing smile. The constables turned up with a ladder before Lestrade could ask any more, then it was an exercise in logistics to get the ladder in the right position to allow a man to get up and at the body. After much huffing and puffing Lestrade realized that there wasn't going to be any easy way to get the man down, but the decision was made for him when the constable up there gave one strong tug too many, dislodged the corpse and sent it crashing through the branches to land with a sickening thud on the ground.

"Well, if he wasn't dead before, he is now," Lestrade muttered, then walked over and turned the body face up. He realized with a start that he knew the victim.

"Bloody Nora. It's Teddy Horsham," he said.

"King Ted of Wapping?" Clarke said and came over for a look. "So it is. What's he doing out of his home turf and away over here?"

"More to the point," Lestrade said, "if he's way over here, what the hell's going on in Wapping?"

The self-styled 'King' Ted lorded it over most of the East End docklands. He'd started small, running a protection racket on smaller boats and local businesses. Over the past fifteen years his own business had flourished and grown, and now almost every boat that went down or up the river paid a tithe into his coffers in exchange for his 'protection,' such as it was. There were more than a few burned-out hulks under the Thames that Lestrade had hoped, one day, to pin on the man. That wasn't going to happen now, but his death would leave a vacuum that would be filled soon enough, and likely not before more blood was shed.

Lestrade tried to concentrate on the matter at hand. Whoever had killed Teddy had done a thorough job of it. His eyes were black holes, burned out by a hot poker at a guess, and his tongue was gone. The death blow, however, looked to be the wound that ran down and across his more than ample belly, a cut from left nipple to right hip, done by something big and heavy if Lestrade judged right; sword or maybe even an ax. Teddy's guts poked through the slit, thankfully frozen enough not to have escaped in the fall from the tree. There was enough of a mess here already without causing any more.

Lestrade left Clarke to organize getting the body to the morgue and walked back over to where Pike still stood among the gawkers.

The reporter didn't say anything, just took a sheet of paper from his pocket and handed it to the Inspector. It was a short note in a firm, confident hand.

"*I do this today because you do not,*" it read.

Below that was a list of five names, all known big-time criminals on whom the Yard had never been able to pin anything firm. The first two were struck out in a hard line where the writer had pressed down so hard he'd almost gone right through the paper.

Hon-Shu Lin
Edward Horsham
Abel Silverstein
Irene Adler
John Fredrick Glass

Pike smiled grimly.

"I have it on good authority that Lin was found just after midnight last night, hanging, almost disemboweled, in the rafters of his opium delivery warehouse in Rotherhithe ... thirty feet up in the rafters."

Lestrade waved the paper in Pike's face.

"And how did you come by this, lad?"

"It came by me, Inspector. When I arrived in my office this morning it was there on my desk, a plain envelope, no name on it, with only this single sheet inside."

"It's obviously meant for us," Lestrade said to himself.

"Obviously," Pike replied. "So what's to be done?"

"Normally I'm not averse to criminals thinning the herd for themselves," Lestrade replied. "But taking out big names just means that ambitious little names start to get ideas above their station. I won't be a bit surprised if both Wapping and Rotherhithe are not already in an uproar."

"I meant, what's to be done about the other three names?"

"I can find Silverstein any time I want," Lestrade said. "He's the only one of the three that hides in plain sight. As for the other two? I've no sodding idea whatsoever. Does anybody?"

Pike tapped the side of his nose. "Leave it with me, Inspector," he said. "I know a man who knows a man."

"I just bet you do, lad. I just bet you do."

Clarke had organized a hearse from the morgue; the body was getting wheeled away, the gawkers dispersed, but Lestrade stood there for a few more minutes, looking high up into the branches of the tree and wondering again how the killer had managed to cart a twenty-stone man, a dead weight, way up there. The Commissioner was going to want to know. And Lestrade, as yet, had no answer for him.

He arrived back at the Yard to news that his hunch was proving correct; a bloody, running gang war was being waged on the docks and quays of Wapping, and three separate warehouses were alight in Rotherhithe, all three suspected of being hubs in the opium trade. Lestrade waved Pike's sheet of papers at Sergeant Clarke.

"This joker thinks he's done us a favor, Clarkie," he said. "All he's done is overturned a barrel and upset the delicate balance that was holding this city together. Get your trousers on, we're going to see a man about some diamonds, before he too ends up with his guts on the outside."

They took a carriage to Hatton Garden.

Ostensibly, Abel Silverstein was the most well-off of a whole coterie of very well-off diamond merchants concentrated in this small area to the north of the City, catering to a high-class clientele all over the country. Lords, ladies, even royalty, were known to avail themselves of his services. What was also known, but never able to be proven, was that every year a vast quantity of illicit uncut diamonds made their way through the man's hands from Holland and, once cut, out onto the streets at a huge profit to himself. Lestrade knew that Silverstein was bent, Silverstein knew that Lestrade knew ... and didn't care a jot, for he had his own kind of protection, the kind that comes from knowing the secrets of people with a great deal of money and, even more importantly, influence.

His smile when Lestrade and Clarke were shown into his presence in the back room of his grand store told Lestrade that he thought he was untouchable. The smile slipped a notch when Lestrade told him about the day's deaths, the sheet of paper, and the fact that his name was next on the list.

"We can offer you protection," Lestrade said, and Silverstein laughed long and hard.

"Oh, no, you can't. Not the kind I need anyway. But I assure you, Inspector, my security is very well looked after here. I'm better protected than the Bank of England."

"Possibly," Lestrade answered. "But the Bank of England isn't about to get its belly opened up by a sharp instrument."

"I have no intention of falling prey to a vigilante killer," the jeweler said. "And I will not have my name associated with the deaths of common criminals. If anything concerning my part in this little charade appears in the papers, I shall hold you responsible."

"You can do whatever the blazes you like," Lestrade said. "I came here out of concern for your safety. But we will not stay where we are not wanted. Good day to you, sir."

They left Silverstein in his office. As they walked through the store Lestrade spoke to Clarke in hushed tones.

"I want three good men on him at all times, round the clock surveillance. I'm pretty sure many of his clients have the ear of our top brass; I don't want them saying we didn't do our job."

Once back at the Yard his first stop was to the morgue. Carruthers already had Teddy Horsham laid out on the slab.

"Any number of things could have killed him," the coroner said. "The trauma to the eyes, the wound in the belly, or the beating he obviously took before either." He pointed at purple bruising around the chin, at the neck and at the genitals.

"If I were to put my pension on it, I'd say his heart gave out over the stress of it, for the belly wound hasn't bled near as much as it would were he still alive."

"And the wound itself? Sword?"

"Possible, although it would be a big weighty blade at

that; something like a medieval longsword in heft."

"Something that would take a strong man to wield?"

"Definitely. Although, given where you found the body, you're looking for someone almost preternaturally strong."

"Or more than one man?"

"That's more in your realm than mine, Lestrade."

"I take it Hon-Shu Lin's body didn't come through here?"

Carruthers shook his head. "Gathered into the bosom of his community never to be seen again. Same as it ever was."

Lestrade nodded, had one last look at Hersham's body, then headed upstairs, intending to make a preliminary report to the Commissioner. He only got as far as his office and was surprised to see John Watson standing in the doorway.

"She came looking for protection, looking to employ the services of Holmes. Alas, he is out of the country at present. I have taken her under my wing, so to speak, Inspector, and I would be grateful if you go easy on her. To my eyes she has recently endured a most terrible fright."

Irene Adler looked up at Lestrade from the visitor's seat as he walked into his office. "Just to be clear, Inspector, I am not here to confess to anything, not here to admit to having committed any crime whatsoever."

"Then what are you here for, Miss Adler?"

"Protection, Inspector. Although who, or what I need protection from, I am not entirely sure. All I know is that it nearly got me this morning."

Lestrade saw that the woman's hands were shaking, and there was a tremble in her voice he did not associate with such a renowned thief, said to have nerves of ice and steel.

He had Clarke fetch a pot of strong tea, sent Watson down to the morgue to have a look at Teddy Horsham, and lit a cigarette for both himself and the woman before

... in a black cloak that gave him the appearance of some great corvid.

asking for her story. It came haltingly at first, then more assuredly as the tea and smoke did much to settle her.

"I was ... let's just say somewhere I should not have been ... in the early hours of this morning, making my way across a rooftop in Belgravia. The city that lay before was laid out like a sparkling carpet, and I stopped at a high point to admire the view. I thought myself quite alone, so you can imagine my shock when I heard someone at my back, no more than an arm's length away it seemed, singing. I recognized it straight away, from *The Mikado*.

"As someday it may happen that a victim must be found
I've got a little list—I've got a little list
Of society offenders who might well be underground
And who never would be missed—who never would be missed!"

"The voice carried a distinct air of menace, and I suddenly felt quite exposed there in that high place. I turned slowly ... and looked into the face of The Lord High Executioner."

She stopped there to request another smoke which she lit from the butt of the previous one, then took a long gulp of Clarke's strong tea, as if she needed fortification before continuing.

"I had to look up, a long way up, to look into his eyes, for he loomed high over me. You must believe me when I say the figure was somewhere over eight feet tall, and dressed head to toe in a black cloak that gave him the appearance of some great corvid. His face was hidden behind a mask of bone, or rather, ivory, and again had an almost bird-like appearance to it. When he moved, something clanked below his waist, like steel plates clashing together. He stretched out his arms wide, as if to engulf me in the folds of the cloak. All I could see inside its depths was blackness. Fortunately I have found from experience that it is best to travel prepared for such unexpected encounters."

At that she reached inside her bodice and drew out a

217

slim switchblade which, when pressed, revealed a lethal six-inch length of steel.

"I let him have it, six times in the chest with all my force. He fell away from me, tumbling over the edge. I thought I had sent him to his doom. But when I stepped over to look down there was nothing on the pavement. I heard a rustle in the air, and a hideous laugh echoed around me, followed by a repeat of the last line of Gilbert and Sullivan.

"*And who never would be missed—who never would be missed!*"

"I stabbed him six times, Inspector, with this very blade. And yet, you can see for yourself, there is not a drop of blood on it, nor was there any on the rooftop as I turned and fled.

"I do not know what I met last night. But it is not done with me.

"And it is not human."

Lestrade had no idea what the lady might have seen, or whether he believed her story. But he'd been looking into her eyes, and was certain that she believed it. He told her about the note that Pike had received and she went pale on hearing of the injuries inflicted on Teddy Horsham.

"Do you think it's the same thing? The thing I saw on the roof?"

Lestrade had no answer for that, although it was surely more than a coincidence that she should have mentioned an executioner's list before being prompted. He was denied any more conversation with the lady by the arrival of Sergeant Clarke, and Lestrade knew from the look on his face that it was not good news.

"It's Silverstein, sir," Clarke said. "I'm afraid he's been murdered."

Lestrade turned to Watson.

"She stays here until we return," he said, "if that's okay by you, old chap?"

"Certainly. I am pledged by my promise to protect her," Watson replied, and showed Lestrade that he wore his service revolver in a shoulder holster. Lestrade led them to an internal, windowless room, ensured they had smokes and plenty of tea at hand, then left alongside Clarke, heading back to Hatton Garden.

They found two constables guarding the doorway of Silverstein's store. Their other man was in Silverstein's office, standing over two burly lads who looked like they'd been terrified half to death. The floor was littered with broken glass.

"The body's up there, sir," the constable said, pointing upward to a ruined skylight window. "You'll find stairs up to the roof out back. It's not a pretty sight."

That was an understatement.

Silverstein's body lay on a flat area of the rooftop, but his internal organs had been bloodily torn out and displayed like trophies; guts draped over chimney pots, his heart sitting between his legs, his ribcage splayed open to show where his lungs had once been, organs that were now impaled on a weather vane at the highest point.

Lestrade didn't waste any time on the examination of the body; just long enough to note that the eyes were burned out, the tongue was removed and the main wound looked to have been done by a heavy sword.

"Same man," he said to Clarke. "Little doubt about it. We're looking for a ruddy maniac here, Clarkie."

"Another Ripper, sir? Or maybe even the same one?"

"No, he did street women, and he did them slow. But like Jack, this lad's trying to tell us something. I only hope I can find out what, and dashed soon at that."

They made their way back down to Silverstein's office. Lestrade sent Clarke to organize the removal of the body ... and its parts, while he attempted to get some sense out of Silverstein's guards.

"We weren't expecting nothing to happen," the larger, more coherent of the two said. "Not in broad daylight, what with there being coppers out front and back and all. Jackie here and me, we was in here with the boss for instructions for the night when there was an almighty crash. Didn't know what in blazes had happened at first; just that the window had come down. Some bloody big black bird ... begging your pardon, but that's what it looked like ... a big black bird came down, lifted the boss up sweet as a nut and ... whoosh ... away back up and out with him. It were over before we had time to move."

"And then we heard the screams," the other one, Jackie, said. "Horrible they were."

"Did you go up to try to help him?" Lestrade asked.

The big one answered for them both. "No, we bleedin' didn't. And I'm damned glad we didn't, otherwise we'd have got the same treatment. Only went up afterward, after it had been quiet a good while. And we were back down sharpish as soon as we saw what that bird had done, weren't we, Jackie boy?"

"We were at that. But it weren't no bird, no sir. I heard tell of it on my granddad's knee and have always thought it were just one of his stories. But it weren't no bird. It were Springheel Jack, that's who it were."

"Springheel Jack, sir?" Clarke asked once they were back in the carriage, following the hearse bearing Silverstein's remains back to the Yard.

"Before your time, Clarkie," Lestrade said. "Before my time too if it comes to that. Bit of a sensation back in the middle of the century; I always thought it was just posh lads dressed up and having a lark, jumping about and scaring folks. Nobody got killed that I know of, just a lot of young lasses getting a scare. He popped up several times over the years after the first flurry of appearances; it's said he was ten feet tall and could leap over buildings. But then, a lot of things get said, don't they?"

"Not a murderer then?"

"As I said, no. But maybe we have somebody employing similar scare tactics to try to cover his murders, to blind us with theatricality. It's been working pretty well for him so far; we're still no nearer to getting a clue as to who he is or why he's doing it."

"Or how, sir," Clarke said quietly.

"That's the bit that's got me particularly puzzled," Lestrade said.

They traveled the rest of the way back in silence. Once at the Yard Clarke went to ensure the remains got to the morgue and Lestrade went back up to his office.

He walked in on a scene of chaos. His window was smashed ... inward, not outward, his desk was overturned and his paperwork and filing boxes were strewn far and wide to all corners. It was going to take him months to get it reorganized, and the Commissioner was going to have a fit. He was still surveying the disaster when Watson spoke at his back.

"We had a spot of bother in your absence, Lestrade," he said. The doctor looked disheveled, his hair awry and his eyes showing the look of a man who has just seen action and is unsure what to make of it. "I don't suppose you've got any whisky squirreled away in here anywhere, old boy? A snifter or two and I'll be ready to tell you all about it."

Given the day he was having, Lestrade thought whisky might be just what the doctor ordered. He produced a bottle and three glasses, all thankfully unbroken, from his desk drawer and followed Watson back to the internal room where he'd left them. Irene Adler was seated at the table; she too was looking out of sorts and somewhat ruffled, although she managed a wan smile as Lestrade showed them the bottle. He poured a stiff one for each of them, then they all lit up cigarettes.

"So what in blazes have you done to my office, Watson?" he said.

The doctor smiled. "Reorganized your filing system using Holmes' methods, old chap," he said. "I would have made a start on it earlier but we were rather rudely disturbed."

Lestrade sat back as Watson told the story of it.

"It was about an hour back now," Watson said. "We were sitting here having a smoke when we both heard it, singing in the distance, more Gilbert and Sullivan. Not the little list song, but another, as if he was announcing his arrival.

"Behold the Lord High Executioner
A personage of noble rank and title—
A dignified and potent officer
Whose functions are particularly vital!

"We were still coming to terms with the singing when there was an almighty crash, that was your office window coming in."

"It's almost fifty feet off the bally ground," Lestrade exclaimed. "How did the blighter manage such a thing?"

"I had no idea, and no time to consider it right then," Watson said. "At the sound of the window breaking I was off and moving, the old soldier's instinct kicking in; I had my pistol in my hand without realizing I had drawn it from its holster as I ran along the corridor there.

"By the time I reached the office doorway the thing ... I hesitate to call it a man ... had already climbed through the window and stood behind your desk. Its head touched the ceiling and even then it had to bend to accommodate itself in the space. It was as Ms. Adler said, like a great blackbird, topped by a face of ivory, a grinning skull. It saw me there, and spoke, or rather sang.

"'Defer, defer to the Lord High Executioner.'

"It began to open up the folds of the great black cloak, revealing a thing that at first appeared to be only shifting darkness and shadows. Then I discerned there was some form and shape to it, at least from the waist down. Now, I know you won't believe me, Lestrade, but the bally thing looked almost mechanical and both legs ended at the knees, replaced below that with what appeared to be huge coiled springs. When that cloak opened out like huge wings stretching across the whole width of the room my nerves could take no more of it. I emptied the revolver into its center; I distinctly remember one bullet ricocheting off something with a very metallic clang. The pale bone face stared down at me, and blow me if that ivory didn't move, setting the lips into a smile.

"'The day is not yet done,' it said, again almost singing, and then it bally well threw your desk at me! I had to dodge sharpish out of the way, and when I looked up again it had gone back out the way it came in and the only thing fluttering was your files, settling like white birds amid the ruin of your office, for which I am most sorry."

"The day is not yet done? What do you think he meant by that?" Lestrade asked.

"It was in that note of Pike's too," Watson said, "something about him doing what he must do today? Perhaps he has set a time limit on his activities."

"Or had one set for him," Lestrade added. "It still doesn't answer how the bugger got access to the window from outside though."

"Or how he took six bullets in the body and laughed. Not to mention Ms. Adler's stabbings."

Irene Adler spoke up for the first time. "As I said before, I sincerely doubt we are facing a human adversary."

"I am not allowed the luxury of that way of thinking, ma'am," Lestrade said, "however much I may agree with you. It is where we go from here that concerns me now."

There was a discreet cough in the doorway and Lestrade turned to see Langdale Pike standing there. "Bleeding hell, it's like Piccadilly Circus in here today," Lestrade said.

"Then I suggest we go somewhere less busy," Pike said. "I have located Glass, and have him secreted away in a safe place, but he dearly wants to talk to you, Inspector; he says he knows what is happening, and he is a man in great terror."

"I'm heading that way myself, lad. Take me to him, fast as you like. It's time we got to the bottom of this once and for all."

It was a busy carriage that headed away from the Yard; Lestrade and Clarke facing forward, Watson, Irene Adler and Langdale Pike rather uncomfortably squeezed together opposite them, although Lestrade thought with a wry grin to himself that Watson did not look the least bit put out to be so nicely snuggled up to Miss Adler.

"How, may I ask, did you find Glass when all the powers of the Yard have failed to do so this past year?" Lestrade asked.

"He gambles," Pike said, "And he plays for big money. He also likes a drink, and has a fondness for a certain variety of peach schnapps that only comes in via one particular retailer. There weren't that many places to look, really."

John Fredrick Glass had become last year's society sensation when it was discovered that the well-known rake and lad about town was also responsible for the theft of tens of thousands of pounds worth of jewels from the more mature ladies on whom he fixed his fancy. He had gone to ground just after Christmas, rumored to have taken the Duchess of Norfolk's prize necklace with him, and had been seen no more from that day to this.

Lestrade was only slightly surprised to find that the "safe place" chosen by Pike to hide the gentleman was the thick-walled stone cellars of Ye Olde Cheshire Cheese pub in Fleet Street. On the rare occasions that Lestrade actually needed to talk to a journalist, this was where he came to find them. Lestrade had always found it to be a rather basically appointed establishment in comparison to the West End's dazzling gin palaces, but the newspaper men seemed to revel in the place's rough-and-ready nature and always had, from Dickens all the way back to Pepys if the innkeeper was to be believed. And Lestrade had to admit that a cellar, encased within many feet of ancient stone, was not the worst spot to hide from an enemy more inclined to be dancing on rooftops.

Glass did not look happy with his situation. He wore an evening suit of obvious quality but his collar was open.

He'd lost the top three buttons of his shirt and an egg-sized purpling bruise hung over his left eye. He nursed a flagon of ale in one hand and a rather foul-smelling cheroot in the other while sitting, feet swinging, atop an empty beer barrel.

"How the mighty have fallen, eh, Irene?" he said, addressing Miss Adler.

"Speak for yourself, John," the woman answered. "I take it I have you to blame for our current predicament?"

Glass waved the now empty flagon in their direction.

"Fetch me some more ale and park your posteriors down. I have a tale of stupidity to relate, and forgiveness to ask."

He would say no more until ale was fetched; Sergeant Clarke did the honors and Lestrade could hardly rebuke him for returning with a full complement of flagons for all present. It was getting late in the day, a long day, and ale was a welcome distraction from its problems.

Glass lit another of his cheroots before beginning.

"You see before you the dissolute husk of the gentleman I once was. I have been brought low by time and circumstance, and I fear my ladies of old would turn up their noses at me in my current state. I have been reduced to using what little skills I possess in service of some rather unsavory types. It was one such type, Teddy the so-called King of Wapping, who employed my services just yesterday for a job in one of the most well-to-do houses in Belgravia. As you see, I went dressed for the part, for I have found that if you are discovered wandering a rich man's house while wearing a good suit, you are more likely to be taken for a guest than a common thief.

"So it was that at five minutes to twelve or thereabouts, I entered from the garden via a rear-facing set of French doors to find myself in the strangest room I have ever had the displeasure to frequent, and believe me when I say I have found myself in many strange places these past twelve months.

225

"It was not so much the set of the room itself as the feel of the place that discomfited me. There were grotesque statues, lurid artwork and mirrors that seemed to give off smoke rather than reflections. Heavy tapestries likewise vied for what little wall space books were not taking up, but there were no carpets or rugs, just an expanse of wooden flooring cunningly inlaid with a large mosaic of a huge red serpent eating its own tail. I had been told that the thing I was after was in a glass cabinet to the left of the large fireplace that dominated the far end of the room. I had just made my way over there, skirting the serpent for I did not wish to put a foot on any part of it, and opened the cabinet door when I heard someone singing; Gilbert and Sullivan, of all things.

"The object I was after, a rather ordinary glass bottle, a mere six inches tall, blue and sealed with a crude stopper, sat on a velvet pillow. I lifted it up, was about to turn and leave, when a door opened to the hallway beyond and a stern voice spoke in the darkness.

"'There is a price to pay if you wish to take that off these premises,' he said. He was an older man in an ankle-length silk dressing gown in gaudy colors and smoking a cigarette in a long, ostentatious holder. I decided to brazen it out.

"'Any price is a price I am willing to pay to honor my duty in this matter,' I said.

"The man laughed. 'Then this will be simple indeed. Name me the five worst criminals in London tonight, and you may take it ... if you can take it.'

"Of course I thought he was jesting ... any sane person would have thought the same. I reeled off the first five names that came to mind ... for which, my dear Irene, I am most sorry ... but not as sorry as for the fit of pique that made me append my own name as fifth on the sorry list.

"As soon as the naming was done I heard more Gilbert and Sullivan; to my frayed nerves it sounded like it was coming from the mouth of the damned red serpent on the floor. A tall clock in the corner began to chime for twelve.

"The man in the doorway waved a hand toward the French windows, as if indicating I was free to leave. Not wanting to look a gift horse in the mouth I took the glass bottle in hand and set off across the floor. In my haste I quite forgot my earlier reticence about stepping on the serpent. That was my undoing, for as soon as my foot touched that portion of the mosaic the floor bucked as if alive; you must believe me when I say that I tripped, not over my own feet, but over the rising head of a great red snake."

Glass stopped in his tale, head cocked as if listening to something, then, seemingly content that there was nothing to be heard, continued.

"Of course I dropped the blasted bottle, smashed it to pieces on the bloody floor and damned near smashed my head along with it. I heard Gilbert and Sullivan again as I rose to my feet groggily. At first I put what I was seeing down to the blow on the head, for the red serpent seemed to writhe and squirm, the head rising up out of the floor, darkening as it rose into a black pillar that loomed high over me. There was a face up there, pale as ivory. When it grinned at me, I ran.

"The man in the dressing gown laughed long and loud, the sound of it counterpointed with more of the blasted operetta as I fled, out through the French windows, across the garden and over the back wall, the song following me all the way.

"*Behold the Lord High Executioner.*"

Lestrade thought the man was done, but after a pause to take some more ale and light another cheroot he continued.

"I kept hearing that blasted song in my head all night, and no end of drinking could dispel it. I kept worrying about my fate now that I had failed the King of Wapping, so you can imagine my relief when young Pike here found me and told me that Teddy was dead. That relief lasted only long enough for him to tell me of the fate of the Chinaman. Then, this afternoon, when the news came filtering through about Hatton Garden I knew the kind of trouble I was in. I sought out Pike again, he led me here, and now you have the story. I don't know if I can be saved; I don't know if Irene here can be saved. I only know that it's my fault that it is after us. And I need your help."

Lestrade thought that the man might weep, so abject did he appear. He was about to speak when Glass cocked his head to one side again, listening. And this time Lestrade heard something: a scraping, rasping sound, getting louder by the second. It sounded like it was coming from the other side of the wall directly to Lestrade's left.

"It's him," Glass said. "He's coming."

"Calm yourself, lad," Lestrade said. "That wall's at least three feet thick. And I'm guessing there's just dirt beyond that. It's nothing at all."

"It doesn't sound like it's nothing at all," Irene Adler said. "In fact, it sounds like something heavy and metallic scraping ... digging. You haven't seen the thing, Inspector. I have. I believe it to be capable of almost anything."

The noise continued to get louder and perhaps closer. Lestrade felt the stone floor of the cellar vibrate in sympathy underfoot, and fine dust fell from the ceiling as the noise got faster, more frantic. It was no longer possible to deny; something was intent on making its way into the cellar. And he didn't think it was a social call.

"Right, everybody out, right now," he said. "Make for the carriage. We'll head for the Yard."

The next minute was one of barely concealed panic as they all made for the stairs. Lestrade was the last to leave. The noise was almost deafening now and just as he turned he saw the wall give way in a puff of dry dust and, behind that, two gleaming silver springs, whirling as if driven by some unseen engine.

Lestrade took the stairs two at a time as a voice rose in song behind him.

"Bow down, bow down, for the Lord High Executioner."

The others had already piled into the carriage when Lestrade climbed up behind them, an even tighter squeeze now that Glass had joined them. Night had fallen while they were down in the cellar and a persistent cold rain was keeping people indoors, the normally busy street now fallen silent and empty of pedestrians.

"The Yard, as fast as you can!" Lestrade shouted to the driver, and the carriage rattled along heading west on Fleet Street.

"Are you sure the Yard's the safest place?" Irene Adler asked. "It got into your office easily enough, did it not?"

Lestrade didn't get a chance to answer for just then they all heard a high tenor voice singing, loud even above the rattle of wheels on cobbles.

"Behold the Lord High Executioner."

A second later the carriage juddered as if hit by something heavy landing atop it and a silver blade as long as Lestrade's arm came down through the roof, just missing taking off Glass's left ear.

As the blade retracted Lestrade, Clarke and Watson were already in movement, weapons drawn and aimed upward. At the first sight of the blade's next descent they fired as one, a volley of deafening shots that almost blew the roof of the carriage away. The carriage juddered and swayed and there was a rustle, as of wings taking flight. When Lestrade peered out the window he saw only a darker shadow against the night sky, a shadow that was, impossibly, gaining height even as the sound of the singing echoed along Fleet Street.

"A dignified and potent officer whose functions are particularly vital."

"The Yard isn't going to be secure enough, is it?" Watson said.

Lestrade was forced to agree.

"How do we fight such a thing as this?"

Glass spoke up in a voice carrying a distinct tremor.

"I think we need to go back to the source: to the house in Belgravia. If anyone knows how to stop it, surely it must be the man who demanded the list from me in the first place?"

Lestrade slapped his forehead and damned himself for a fool. It had been a strange, busy, day right enough but that was no excuse for sloppy police work.

"I should have thought of that in the first place. Belgravia it is, then," he said, and had Glass give the address to the carriage driver while they sat, ears still ringing from the gunfire and getting wet now from where the rain came in through the tattered remains of the roof.

Belgrave Square provided upper-class homes for dukes, minor royalty, high-ranked military officers and foreign dignitaries. If the man who answered the door of number two to them that night belonged to any of those classes, Lestrade would eat his hat.

The earlier description they'd had from Glass still applied. His silk dressing gown was colorful to the point of being garish, and he carried the long cigarette holder as if the cigarette itself offended him. He was a slender chap, in his fifties at a rough guess, with skin as soft as any baby and a bouffant haircut that looked to have been soaked in oil and smelled like a tart's boudoir. He looked the six new arrivals on his doorstep up and down and sniffed, as if ensuring they wouldn't be bringing any unwelcome odors into the house, before allowing them entry.

"I thought Mr. Glass might be back, given the events of the day," he said as they stepped out of the rain into a long marble-festooned hallway. "But I had no idea he had so many friends."

"He's no friend of mine," Lestrade said, and introduced himself. The man gave a little bow, all the way from the waist.

"Your reputation precedes you, Inspector, of course," he said. "I am Sullivan Manners, and I am at your service, although for the life of me I cannot see why you have turned up at my door."

"If we can have ten minutes of your time, sir, we may be able to get to the bottom of this business."

A large ornate clock on the wall to Lestrade's left began chiming the hour and Lestrade was surprised to find it was already eight o'clock. Manners smiled.

"We have four hours, Inspector, not a minute more or less, those are the rules."

He left that cryptic remark hanging.

Lestrade turned to Clarke.

"You stay here, Clarkie. At least it's out of the rain. Any funny business, I'll shout and you come running."

While Clarke stood by the front door, Manners showed the rest of them along the hall and into a large room overlooking the back garden. It was dimly lit by two gas lanterns high on opposite walls, both turned down low. The red serpent mosaic on the floor seemed to grin at them. Glass held back, unwilling to step inside, until Lestrade took his elbow.

"Come on, lad. This was your idea in the first place, remember?"

Manners insisted on providing them all with a glass of sherry before he would take any questions, and Glass was becoming increasingly agitated.

"It could be here any second," he said, almost shouting. "Do something!"

Manners put a hand to his chest in mock surprise.

"Me? My dear boy, what do you think I can do? I am a mere collector and distributor of admittedly rare and curious antiquities. But I am no expert in the kind of thing you unleashed last night."

"But surely ..." Lestrade started.

"Surely nothing," Manners replied. "I bought the bottle that Mr. Glass handled so unwisely in Baghdad ten years ago. It came with rules, rules which I have followed meticulously, rules that I intend to follow again in ..." he looked at the tall clock in the corner, "... three hours and fifty-seven minutes' time. I'm afraid you're on your own until then."

"You must know something about it," Irene Adler said.

"Only the rules, and what I have read in books. Books any of you could read for yourselves in any decent library. Have you heard of the djinn?"

Watson spoke first. "I came across stories in the Afghan, of desert devils."

"Of deserts now, but of cities in the past," Manners replied. "The djinn were made, or rather called up from the beyond, in antiquity, to do the things that mere men were too squeamish to do for themselves, for as soulless things, they can never carry the burden of guilt. From what I can gather most of the great cities had one; a dark knight, if you will. And who knows; some cities might have them still, don't you think?"

Lestrade interrupted him. "But how do we stop it?"

"By evading it for another ..." he looked at the clock again, "three hours and fifty-five minutes. That is all I know. It has but a day to do its duty once released, those were the rules of its entrapment."

"Duty?" Lestrade asked.

"The names I gave it last night. Those too were part of the rules I was told had to be followed to the letter."

"And then what?"

"Then, as I said, I will continue to follow the rules. But rather than bandy words like this for the rest of the evening, I suggest we step inside my protections. I believe I have another visitor on the way."

They heard it before they saw it, *The Mikado* again, but a different song this time.

"A wand'ring minstrel, I. A thing of shreds and patches. Of ballads, songs and snatches, and a dreamy lullaby."

Something dark fluttered in the garden outside the French doors.

Manners stepped nimbly past Lestrade to stand within the circle made by the red serpent mosaic on the floor.

"I most strongly suggest you step in here," he said, "especially those of you on his list. I cannot guarantee it will hold for the time needed, but I can guarantee it is better than the alternative before you."

The French doors blew in and black wings rushed into the room. All of them quickly stepped over the serpent to stand beside Manners. Glass was too slow and had only one foot inside when there was a flash of silver and a spatter of blood on the floor. By the time he'd finished his step to stand beside the others he'd taken a long wound in his left shoulder. Watson moved immediately to take charge of the man, whose pained wails were now counterpointed by more singing.

"Bow down, bow down, for the Lord High Executioner."

A tall dark figure, its head almost touching the high ceiling, drifted anti-clockwise around the mosaic serpent, a black cape draped over its form so that it almost looked like it was flying. A pale ivory skull-mask looked down at them.

"I'm frightfully sorry about the Gilbert and Sullivan," Manners said almost casually, as if this was a mere front-parlor conversation. "It appears to pick up things from its surroundings ... shreds and patches, ballads, songs and snatches, as the song goes. It conforms to our expectations of it, or so I believe."

"A personage of noble rank and title," it sang as if in response.

Lestrade looked down. Watson had Glass sitting on the floor. He'd made a makeshift tourniquet with the man's belt and was tightening it up at the top of the arm.

"We need to get him to a hospital," Watson said. "And quickly, else he'll lose the arm."

"Good luck with that," Glass said through gritted teeth.

At the same moment the door out to the hallway opened and Lestrade saw Clarke framed in the doorway, the sergeant having come to investigate the commotion.

"Stay back, Clarkie. I don't think it's after us."

The caped figure continued to circle the mosaic, paying no attention to the sergeant.

"What can I do, sir?" Clarke called out.

"Just watch the hallway," Lestrade replied. "Don't let anyone else in … we're in enough trouble already here. We've been told the show stops at midnight, so give it till then, and we'll see what's what."

Clarke nodded, and went back out into the hall, closing the door behind him.

"Now what?" Irene Adler said.

Manners replied first. "Now we wait. I don't suppose any of you has a deck of cards?"

The tall clock in the corner ticked down the minutes. The caped figure kept circling, and kept singing so that after only a short time Lestrade was sure he would never wish to hear a single more second of Gilbert and bloody Sullivan.

Watson stood at Lestrade's side. He touched his revolver in its holster. "A few rounds sent it packing the last time, Lestrade. I'm up for trying again if you're game?"

"There will be no gunfire in this room, gentlemen," Manners said. "Not unless you wish to be sued within an inch of your lives for the damage incurred. My collection is the most valuable in the land, perhaps in the world. Besides, you must trust me, and trust my protection here. I will have the matter in hand when the clock turns round to the appropriate time. Just follow the rules."

"But this man here needs to get to a hospital," Watson said.

"You're welcome to try to take him, if you feel that strongly about it," Manners replied.

Glass answered from the floor below them. His voice was low and his face pale, but there was determination when he spoke.

"I'm going nowhere until midnight," he said. "We've all seen this bloody thing in action now. We know what it can do. Why are we even talking about it?"

The singing continued, indeed it appeared to be getting louder as the hour approached midnight.

"My catalog is long, thro' ev'ry passion ranging

And to your humors changing, I tune my supple song."

Lestrade found it hard to keep his gaze from returning to the hands of the tall clock. They seemed to be creeping ever more slowly, no matter how much he willed them to pace. On the floor, Glass was drifting in and out of consciousness and Watson was getting ever more concerned for his well-being, but in his lucid moments Glass insisted that he not be moved until the matter was concluded … one way or the other.

Irene Adler and Manners were deep in conversation on the matter of current fashions in hosiery of all things, and Lestrade was rolling himself a cigarette when he noted that the circling figure had started encroaching closer to the mosaic circle, as if testing the defenses. As he watched the caped figure slowed and began to move closer to a certain area of the mosaic. Lestrade saw that it was the spot where Glass' blood had spattered on taking the shoulder wound. The droplets showed as darker patches against the serpent's red scales. He interrupted Manners' conversation and pointed out this new behavior.

Manners pursed his lips.

"Will it hold?" Adler asked him.

"Either it will or it will not. Worrying about it avails us naught," Manners replied, but Lestrade saw the man throw a nervous glance at the clock. Manners took a small blue bottle from the pocket of his robe and began turning it over in his hands. Lestrade saw that it had but recently been roughly mended with thick glue, it having been broken in several places.

It was twenty to midnight. They had almost made it, but the dark thing was drawing ever closer to the serpent.

Glass came back to his senses after another fainting bout as the clock hands reached two minutes to the hour. The black-caped figure loomed high over him, standing right up tight to the outer edge of the serpent, and Glass let out an almost girlish shriek of fright at the sight of it. He looked down to avoid looking at its face, and Lestrade saw him take note of the stains on the scales of the serpent. Before anyone could stop him he'd leaned forward and, with the sleeve of the right arm of his jacket, started trying to wipe the serpent's scales clear.

The singing rose to a crescendo.

"Behold the Lord High Executioner."

The black cloak opened and a scaly arm, black as ebony, thick as a man's thigh and wielding a gleaming blade, came out and struck down, pinning Glass' right hand against the scales of the mosaic. Blood spurted and flowed, a pool of it, totally covering a section of the serpent. The caped thing screamed.

"Defer! Defer!"

And stepped forward into the serpent to stand over Glass.

One minute to twelve.

Lestrade and Watson were already drawing their pistols but Lestrade knew he was going to be too late; the sword, having been pulled from the ruin of Glass' hand had been raised and was descending again, heading for the man's head.

Out of the corner of his eye Lestrade saw Manners step out of the side of the circle and place his blue bottle by the serpent's head.

The caped thing screamed again. *"Defer! Defer!"*

Two things happened almost at the same time.

Something silver flashed by Lestrade's head and he saw it hit the pale face dead center. Irene Adler's knife had found its target. At the same time Glass rolled away, putting his weight on his wounded shoulder and letting out a scream that echoed even louder than the djinn's singing. It seemed to give the thing pause; the sword

236

stroke faltered, and that was all the time Lestrade and Watson needed.

Lestrade, with Watson at his side, stepped over to where Langdale Pike was already dragging Glass backward away from the action. The two of them raised their pistols at the same time and emptied their cylinders into the body of the thing.

Great wings fluttered and the air was rent with a scream like a gull in a seaside wind.

The tall clock chimed the first stroke of midnight.

The room fell quiet as the first chime echoed away.

"It's time," Manners said.

The robed figure drifted away to hover above the blue bottle; Lestrade saw that the stopper had been removed. The thing sang sadly as the clock continued to chime the hours.

"A wand'ring minstrel, I. A thing of shreds and patches."

It seemed to fade and become diffuse, less solid with each chime, soon little more than wisps of dark smoke being drawn down and away into the bottle. The song was the last thing to go, plaintive and mournful to the last syllable which coincided with the final chime of the clock.

"Of ballads, songs and snatches, and dreamy lullaby.

"And dreamy lullaby."

Manners bent and put the stopper in the bottle.

"Well, now, that wasn't so bad, was it?"

Things moved quickly for a time before slowing again.

Clarke and Watson bundled an unconscious Glass into the Yard's carriage and made for the hospital with all speed. Pike went with them, following the story as always. Irene Adler took the opportunity to slip off quietly into the night; Lestrade had no doubt he'd be hearing of her again before too long.

Lestrade was left in the doorway with Manners, who was still holding the blue bottle.

"By rights, you know," Lestrade said, "I should be confiscating that as evidence."

"Really, Inspector? And how would you write that up in a way that your superiors might believe?"

"Blowed if I know, sir, so I'll be leaving it in your care … you do promise to take more care of it from now on?"

"You have my word on it."

"Good. Because I need to get back to the office. We've caught John Fredrick Glass in the act of committing a crime, and unfortunately he was injured while evading arrest; the Commissioner will like that story."

The blue bottle went away into Manner's pocket, then Lestrade shook his hand and walked out into the rain, remembering that he would be going back to the ruin of his office.

He had more than enough bally paperwork to do already.

About the Author

William Meikle is a Scottish writer, now living in Canada, with over thirty novels published in the genre press and more than 300 short-story credits in thirteen countries. He has books available from a variety of publishers including Dark Regions Press and Severed Press, and his work has appeared in many professional anthologies and magazines. He lives in Newfoundland with whales, bald eagles and icebergs for company. When he's not writing he drinks beer, plays guitar, and dreams of fortune and glory. More at **williammeikle.com**

About the Artist

ENnie Award-winning illustrator **M. Wayne Miller** still continues his quest to synthesize the perfect blend of science fiction, fantasy, and horror with his work. Primarily focusing on science-fiction and horror imagery for limited-edition book covers, lavish interiors, and numerous role-playing games, Wayne strives for constant improvement as an artist and illustrator through continuous education, training, and pushing the boundaries of his skill set.

A primary goal is to gain work for Magic: The Gathering, a client that has proven as elusive as it is prestigious. His list of clients include Weird House Press, Chaosium, Thunderstorm Books, Modiphius Entertainment, and Pinnacle Entertainment Group.